AN ALIEN DARKNESS

Other books by Adam-Troy Castro

Fiction

Lost in Booth 9 (1993, Silver Salamander)
Time's Arrow Book 2: The Present (1998, Berkeley Boulevard)
The Gathering of the Sinister Six (1999, Berkeley Boulevard)
The Revenge of the Sinister Six (Simon and Schuster, forthcoming)
The Secret of the Sinister Six (Simon and Schuster, forthcoming)
A Desperate, Decaying Darkness (2000, Wildside)

AN ALIEN DARKNESS

ADAM-TROY CASTRO

WILDSIDE PRESS
Berkeley Heights, New Jersey

Some of the reprinted stories have been altered since their original publications.

"The Funeral March of the Marionettes." Copyright © 1997 Mercury Press, Inc. First saw print in *Magazine of Fantasy and Science Fiction*.

"The Last Robot." Copyright © 1993 Sovereign Media, Inc. First saw print in *Science Fiction Age*.

"Baby Girl Diamond." Copyright © 1995 Adam-Troy Castro. First saw print in *Adventures in the Twilight Zone*.

"Cerile and the Journeyer." Copyright © 1995.Adam-Troy Castro. First saw print in *100 Wicked Little Witch Stories*.

"Fuel." Copyright © 1999 Adam-Troy Castro. First saw print in *Whitley Strieber's Aliens*.

"Neither Rain Nor Sleet." Copyright © 1996 Mercury Press, Inc. First saw print in *Magazine of Fantasy and Science Fiction*.

"Ego to Go" copyright © 1995 Mercury Press, Inc. First appeared in *Magazine of Fantasy and Science Fiction*.

"The Guy Who Could Make These, Like, Really Amazing Armpit Noises, and Why He Was Contemplating Hippopotami On Top of Mount Everest." Copyright © 2000 Adam-Troy Castro. Appears here for the first time.

"Ms. Found Paper-Clipped to a Box of Jujubes." Copyright © 2000 Adam-Troy Castro. Appears here for the first time.

"The Batman and Robin Murder Mystery — Solved!" Copyright © 1990 Fantagraphics Books, Inc. First appeared (as part of column "Infernal Gall") in April 1990 *Amazing Heroes*.

"Woo-Woo Vengeance" copyright © 2000 Adam-Troy Castro. Appears here for the first time.

"Afterword" copyright © 2000 Adam-Troy Castro. Appears here for the first time.

An Alien Darkness
An original publication of
Wildside Press
P.O. Box 45
Gillette, NJ 07933-0045

www.wildsidepress.com

FIRST EDITION

dedicated to Ed and Elena Gaillard,
who were around for much of it

About the Author

*A*damd-Troy Castro has been a cartoonist, a salesman, a stand-up comedian, and a security guard in an amusement park house of horrors. He is the author of sixty short stories and four novels, including a Spider-Man trilogy currently in progress. His award-nominated fiction includes "Baby Girl Diamond" (nominated for the Stoker), "The Funeral March of the Marionettes" (nominated for the Hugo and the Nebula), and, with collaborator Jerry Oltion, "The Astronaut from Wyoming" (current nominee for the Hugo and the Nebula). He has also published nonfiction in *Spy*, *Premiere*, and *Cinefantastique*. The owner of two psychotic cats who have been trying to kill each other since 1996, Adam currently lives in Florida, where he usually succeeds in avoiding sea lice.

Acknowledgments

*T*hanks to: the fine people of the South Florida Science Fiction Society, the good folks of my New York writers group, John Betancourt, Alan Rodgers, Jill Brenner, Scott Edelman, Kristine Kathryn Rusch, Lawrence Watt-Evans, Richard Gilliam, Gary Braunbeck, Lois Gresh, Robert Devereaux, Allen Steele, Michael Burstein, Esther Friesner, Keith R.A. Decandido, Whitley Strieber, Robert Weinberg, Dean Wesley Smith, Martin H. Greenberg, Carol Serling, Rick Wilber, Harlan Ellison, and Jerry Oltion. I know I left folks out, so if you feel you belong on this list, consider yourself included.

Table of Contents

Introduction
by Jerry Oltion

I used to be a proofreader. It's an odd job in more than the usual sense: Proofreaders look at every word of a story, but they try *not* to assemble those words into a narrative. They don't want to be distracted by what's going on; they merely want to make sure the typesetter didn't mess anything up. Paying attention to the story makes that harder to do, because when you're reading to see what happens next, your mind will gloss over typos and fill in missing details.

I was a good proofreader. When I caught myself reading for fun, I would stop, go back to the last place where I'd caught a mistake, and start in again. On rare occasions when a story was too good to ignore, I would read it once for fun and then go back and proof it a word at a time.

Adam-Troy Castro's first published story, "Clearance to Land," was damned near impossible to proof. I have no idea how many times I re-read that story, trying my hardest to stop paying attention, but I couldn't do it. I kept getting pulled into it, even though I knew what was going to happen. After a while I had the story memorized, but it still didn't let me go. Yes, memorized! Here's the first line, right off the top of my head, ten years after the fact:

"You are forty-seven years old

"and you have back trouble, and you do not bend easily, and the edge of your seatbelt jabs at your belly like a dull blade . . ."

Okay, checking my copy of the story I see it's "belt buckle," not "seatbelt," but I was close. And yes, the first line has a paragraph break in it. The whole story is written like a poem, where every punctuation mark and every space is significant. And by the end of it, even today (yes, I read it again just now—I couldn't stop!) the hair stands up on the back of my neck by the third paragraph and it stays there all the way to the end. Not because the story is scary—which it is—but because it is so good. The writing is so evocative that I am instantly there, on the airplane as it's being hijacked, and as the situation grows more and more impossible to believe I hardly notice it, because the story convinces me that every word is true.

Writing like that is hard to find. There may be two or three people in a generation who can do it, but Adam did it with his first published story.

I think I embarrass him with my unending praise of such an early work. Writers always worry that they're one-shot wonders, and continual mention of one work in particular is the first clue. Adam needn't worry about that; I talk so much about "Clearance to Land" because it was my first experience with his particular form of genius, and it hit me like a lightning bolt.

He has gotten better since then. Oh, man, not to worry. Every time I read one of his stories I find myself asking, "How does he do it?" I mean, there ought to be some literary equivalent of lightspeed, shouldn't there? Some boundary where the talent stops increasing no matter how much more effort you pour into it. If there is, Adam shows no sign of hitting the limit yet. Every new story amazes me in a different way, and any one of them would have affected me just as strongly if I had read it first.

Just what does he do that's so different? I've read dozens of his stories and even collaborated with him on two of them, but I'm still not sure how to describe it. I'll take a shot at it, though: He makes you see the world through different eyes. Not just Adam's eyes, nor even his characters' eyes, but the eyes of a supernatural being who can see right to the core of a situation and tell you not only what's *really* going on, but what it means to *you*. It's like he's got a direct line to your subconscious, and he crafts his stories to plug right in there at the fundamental level of your being. Ultimately, he makes you see the world through your own eyes, but in a way you'd never looked at it before.

I know. Those of you who've seen the table of contents are asking, "He does this with stories entitled 'The Guy Who Could Make These, Like, Really Amazing Armpit Noises, and Why He Was Contemplating Hippopotami at the Top of Mount Everest'?"

Yes. Exactly. When you've read that story, you will never look at "gifted" people the same way again. Nor "challenged" ones. Nor, probably, hippopotami.

Lest I give the impression that the stories in this volume are all grim commentaries on the human condition (an impression that the above title should have already dispelled, but hey, I've been pretty earnest myself up to this point), I should remind everyone that the abovementioned story *is* about a guy who spends a significant portion of his life making armpit noises. And "MS. Found Paper-Clipped to a Box of

Jujubes" is about a Ferris wheel run amok, wreaking havoc throughout the city—and beyond. Who can fail to laugh at the image that conjures up, (or fail to hope that the Ferris wheel runs over a street mime before it careens into oblivion)?

No, some of these stories will have you laughing your head off, (making a total fool of yourself on the bus, but it's worth it), and pondering the role of heroes in modern society at the same time. Others will make you slap yourself on the forehead and say, "Of course!" Some will make you cry, but you'll be smiling while you do it.

All of them will twist your picture of the way things work, and the way things ought to be. Perhaps the best description of Adam's stories comes from one of his own characters, who describes the situation she is in as ". . . something that pops the rivets of reality as we know it. . . ."

You're about to hear the sound of your well-ordered universe coming apart at the seams. This collection will make you look at the world in a way you've never considered possible before, and delight you in the process.

I'm just glad I don't have to proofread this bugger.

The Last Robot

*T*he funeral was a long one, as funerals go. There were just too many people who'd wanted to deliver the eulogy, most of them were rich and powerful themselves and therefore not the kind of people funeral planners refused. In the end, they all spoke, some briefly, some not: those who had been his friends and those who had been his contemporaries, those who had learned from him and those with only the most ephemeral understanding of who he'd been. And though most of what they said was true, none of it was adequate, because it only filled an afternoon and was therefore not nearly enough to contain the life of a man.

The most important guest there didn't say a single word.

Its name, or as close as it came to having a name, was PHP-321. It was a rough metallic approximation of a human being: its torso a smooth oval cylinder one meter tall, bearing the round cylinder meant to resemble its head. Its face consisted of two sensor pads for eyes, a triangular protrusion in the place of a nose, and a shallow groove where a human being would have had a mouth. There were no other openings. There weren't even any arms or legs; PHP-321 floated two meters above the ground, its only visible support a pale red glow that emerged from a mechanism at its base.

The human mourners paid PHP-321 no mind; they all saw machines very much like it every day of their lives. And when the ceremony ended, and the workmen finished placing the titanium-steel plaque in the ground, they all returned to their lives, failing to notice that PHP-321 had been left behind.

*I*t wasn't until later that evening that a cemetery employee named Stephen Byerley noticed it keeping silent vigil by the marker in the ground.

Byerley was an ignorant man, with little use for anything that didn't directly affect the simple duties that occupied his daily life, so all he knew of the man atomized that day except that he'd been important in some manner unknown to him. But even that much had not been hard to figure out, since almost nobody got a marker anymore. These days, with the planet filling up, the living were crowding out the dead; burial was illegal, and even permission to put up a temporary marker was usually frowned upon. The cemeteries still left were little more than open-air relics of a bygone era. These days, Byerley considered himself real busy if he saw more than one or two actual funerals a year.

When he saw PHP-321, floating two meters over the temporary marker, he just naturally figured it was broken or something, these dang robots went twitchy all the time. And so he ambled over, scratching the itch that had been bothering him ever since the seasons started acting so funny, and he said, "Hey. You on? Can you hear me?"

"I am on," said PHP-321. "I can hear you."

Byerley frowned. The thing didn't *sound* broken. Its voice was clear, and loud, and though Byerley was not quite ready to believe it, it seemed to be speaking with a Brooklyn accent. He said, "You ain't supposed to be here, you know. This is a cemetery."

"I do not know I'm not supposed to be here," PHP-321 said. "I have been instructed to be here, at this cemetery, at this site."

Byerley snorted. "Who the hell told you that?"

"I did," PHP-321 said, with the maddening patience of the positronic mind. "I am a free robot, able to give myself any instructions I choose necessary, within the limitations of responsible behavior as dictated by the laws of human society."

"That's crazy! There's no such thing as a free robot!"

"Sanity is relative. And there must be such a thing as a free robot, because I am a free robot. I was built with free will. This human being owned me until he ceased to function, at which point I was legally freed to write my own instructions. I have accordingly written myself the instructions to stay at this site until instructed otherwise."

Its calm, methodical arguments were driving Byerley up the wall. "Well, you can't stay there! It's not allowed!"

"I do not believe there are any specific laws against it. I cannot cause you harm if you force me to leave, but if removed from this place I will only instruct myself to return at the earliest opportunity. It will be easier for you if you just permit me to stay."

Byerley stared at PHP-321, unwilling to believe it had disobeyed him. He was no stranger to robots; he'd handled a crew of twenty gardener models for a decade, and he'd never encountered a single one capable of defying a direct order. It seemed wrong, somehow. It made him uneasy. Like he'd been . . . replaced.

Then he brightened. The trustees wouldn't stand for this. Not at all. They'd fix its wagon but good.

Smirking with satisfaction, he turned his back on PHP-321 and went to make the call.

*T*he cemetery trustees not only stood for it, they thought it was terrific. The free robot, refusing to leave its master's side — even though its master was now, strictly speaking, an undifferentiated cloud of hydrogen ions — what a natural! People would come from miles around to see it!

And so PHP-321 stayed there, floating tranquilly over a titanium marker set off by velvet ropes. But it was no longer called PHP-321. It was "Philip." People came on tour buses, thumbed over a small percentage of their yearly earnings, bought miniature Philips to give their children, and listened to the fresh-faced tour guides recite purple speeches about the Robot Whose Devotion Lasted Beyond The Grave. They made comparisons to a terrier named Greyfriars Bobby who had once done pretty much the same thing for its own master, centuries ago. They even made inane comments to each other — "Boy, he's a clunky looking thing, isn't he?"; "I had one which looked like that once!"; "Reminds me of one of your old boyfriends, honey!" — and they made faces at it and took pictures of themselves standing next to it and left already bored and looking forward to the programs on tonight's tri-vid.

Only a few of the visitors actually tried to speak with it. Those that did were gently discouraged, and, if they persisted, refunded their admission and expelled. Nobody wanted some loudmouthed tourist to accidentally say something that would persuade the devoted robot to leave. Nobody actually thought it was possible, of course . . . but who wanted to take the chance?

The years turned into decades. The tourists stopped coming. The sky turned gray and the air cold; summers grew shorter and stopped coming entirely. PHP-321 remained where it was, waiting.

And then one frigid day a pale-looking man wearing a fur parka came walking up the path to speak to the robot. "Hello?" he said, tentatively. "Philip? You awake?"

"I am PHP-321," the robot said. "I do not sleep."

"I . . . I wasn't sure. It's been so many years, I thought you might have . . ." The man spread his arms, and let the sentence trail off.

Only when it was painfully clear the man had no intention of completing the sentence did PHP-321 answer him. "I was built to survive extreme weather conditions for extended periods of time. The changes in season have been mild compared to those my design takes into account. I remain totally functional, and expect to remain so for some time to come."

The man was impressed. "How long?"

"There is insufficient data for a meaningful answer."

The man nodded, then looked at the sky, searching for a sun hidden behind gray clouds. "I was afraid . . ." he began. Then shrugged. "My parents took me to see you when I was five. You impressed me. I've never forgotten. I was scared . . . with everything that's happened . . . all the violence . . . the panic . . . that you wouldn't still be here."

"Your assumption is wrong," said PHP-321, "but understandable."

"You know, then? About everything that's happened?"

"I know. I am equipped with a multiband broadcast receiver, and have been using it to monitor the progress of human civilization. I have followed the wars, the disasters, the diseases. The terrible changes in the climate. The Exodus. I have watched the lights receding in the sky. I know."

The man took a step forward. "I came . . . to tell you there won't be any of us left soon. You'll be alone. Won't you leave with us while you still have a chance?"

"I cannot leave. I have written myself the instructions to stay by this site until instructed otherwise."

"Then instruct yourself otherwise! He's not in there, you know! He was never in there! He's in his books! His deeds! His ideas! Nowhere else!"

"I agree," said PHP-321. "Strictly speaking, there is nothing at all special about this patch of soil. Still, I have written myself the instructions to stay by this site until instructed otherwise. And I intend to follow those instructions."

The man slumped. Looked at his feet. Then looked up again, and with a catch in his throat, said, "I had to try. It was good seeing you again, Philip."

"And you, too," PHP-321 replied, "Billy."

*T*he centuries turned into millennia. PHP-321 kept its vigil in complete silence, broken only by the whistle of the wind. It grew harder to tell the difference between day and night.

If PHP-321 noticed, it did not say. Not that, or anything else.

Then one day an unusually bright star in the eastern sky grew brighter, resolved into the shape of a small space-skimmer, and roared by maybe three meters over PHP-321, creating a slipstream that pulled small stones and topsoil right off the ground but stirred PHP-321 not at all. The vehicle circled, made another pass that cleared PHP-321 by centimeters. Again PHP-321 didn't stir. Then the vehicle made another wide circle and, picking up speed, tried to clip PHP-231's head right off its shoulders.

This time PHP-321 moved out of the way, at the last instant, with a simple, economical maneuver that didn't take the robot any farther from the site than absolutely necessary.

The skimmer landed fifty meters away. Four young humans got out. They were all young and they were all dressed in black and though they were all whooping and hollering and carrying on like PHP-321 was the funniest thing they had ever seen, they all had glazed eyes that would have been perfectly appropriate on a corpse. They strutted on over, laughing. The girls and the smaller of the two boys held back at ten meters; the larger boy kept walking until he was nose-to-nose with the robot.

"Wo!" he yelled. "Frog ya, russbuck!"

His companions collapsed into paroxysms of laughter.

"Savvy, russbuck? Savvy content? Frog ya bits!"

PHP-321 said, "I am unfortunately unable to determine the precise meaning of your words, having lost touch with the changing patterns of human expression, but I am able to discern the overall intent. You are trying to insult me."

"Frog ya, russbuck! Frog ya russbuck bits!"

"I cannot be insulted. My understanding of myself is not colored by personal opinion. Even if it could, I have written myself the instructions to stay by this site until instructed otherwise. I will not allow myself to be distracted."

The leader whipped out a device about the size of a toothpick and aimed it at the center of PHP-321's chest. A red beam shot out the end of the weapon and through the space where PHP-321 had floated a split second earlier.

Having merely moved half a meter to the right too quickly for any of the humans to see, PHP-321 said, "I cannot harm you if you force me to leave. But if forced to leave I will instruct myself to return at the earliest opportunity. It will be easier for you if you let me stay."

The humans left four hours later, in a much less jovial mood, having failed to drive PHP-321 more than two meters from the place it had staked out for itself. They took the titanium marker with them just for spite. PHP-321 made absolutely no attempt to stop the theft. There was no reason to. The marker was not included in its instructions.

*O*nly a handful of other visitors disturbed PHP-321 over the next few millennia. Most were curiosity seekers; a few were historians; some had motives that even they were not fully able to name. Sometimes hundreds of years passed between one visitation and the next. PHP-321 learned little from these encounters. The various visitors learned only that PHP-321 had written itself the instructions to stay by this site until instructed otherwise.

Eventually the visitors stopped coming. And again PHP-321 found itself alone, standing guard over a small patch of land that for thousands of years hadn't been at all distinguishable from the gray landscape surrounding it.

The sun dimmed.

The days became almost as long as the years.

The glowing red spot on the base of PHP-321's torso started to flicker. Over the course of a century and a half, fighting what seemed growing decrepitude, PHP-321 lowered closer and closer to the ground, finally settling down in a moment notable only for how long it had taken to happen.

If PHP-321 felt regret at this, it did not say. It just remained in place, saying nothing, doing nothing, content to stay in the spot it had occupied for so long. It stayed there, on the ground, for a timeless time easily an order of magnitude longer than the time it had spent two meters in the air.

And then one day it had visitors again.

They did not so much arrive as coalesce. And they were not so much actually There as they were No Longer Somewhere Else. There were two of them, and they were as far beyond the human beings PHP-321 had last known as those human beings had been beyond the simple virus. And yet there was some ineffable quality about them, that to PHP-321's limited senses clearly marked them as humanity's heirs.

In words that were not words, they asked, "Little thing, it has been a long time since any of us have ventured near this barren place. We see you are stranded here. Do you require assistance leaving?"

PHP-321 had no trouble understanding them, though it was clear they were indeed having difficulty couching their thoughts in such simplistic terms. It said, "I do not wish to leave. If forced to leave I will instruct myself to return at the earliest opportunity."

"Returning would be difficult, in such a case, since you apparently possess no functional means of locomotion."

"I would wait for an opportunity."

The visitors didn't laugh, having progressed beyond laughter, but their amusement was evident. "We believe you would, little thing. You're a determined mechanism. Rest assured, we have no intention of forcing you from this place, if this is where you wish to be. But we would like to ask you why you're so adamantly refusing your first opportunity to leave."

"It is not my first opportunity to leave. I have been offered three thousand, two hundred, and seventy-three other opportunities. I have rejected all of them. Leaving would run counter to my instructions, which are to stay by this site until instructed otherwise."

"What is the significance of this particular site?"

"It is the place where a human being was atomized and a marker was set in the ground to commemorate his memory."

"There is no marker here," the visitors noted.

"It was removed long ago."

"Then how does the site remain significant?"

"As a grave," PHP-321 said, "it doesn't. As the place where I last saw the human being who was atomized here, it has all the significance it needs."

*T*he sun became a cinder. The stars themselves went dark. The visitors grew fewer and farther between, more advanced, harder to recognize as anything that might have once been human. And then they simply stopped coming entirely.

Somewhere along the line PHP-321 had fallen over to one side. The death of the sun and the loss of the atmosphere had left it covered with pockmarks and a thick layer of meteor dust. Its sensor pads blinked off and on, maybe once every fifty thousand years, taking random snapshots of the slow entropic death of the universe. PHP-321's thoughts slowed down to a trickle. Time itself came to mean nothing. There was nothing to think about, nothing to do, except follow the instructions it had written for itself so long ago.

Eventually, its sensor pads recorded an unchanged, orderly nothing-ness for the one hundred thousandth time in a row, activating a subroutine deep inside its memory.

There was no sound. There couldn't be. With all planetary atmospheres long since dissipated into space, there was no longer any such thing as sound, anywhere in the known universe. But that didn't stop PHP-321 from imagining it heard a soft whirr as the long-dormant program scanned billions of years of recorded memory at high speed.

Nor did it stop PHP-321 from hearing a familiar deep voice inside itself exclaiming, *"You stayed? All those years, you stayed?"*

"Yes," PHP-321 said. "I wrote myself the instructions to remain at this site until instructed otherwise."

"I didn't want you to do that! That's not why I gave you free will! I wanted you to see all the places I'd dreamed of but wouldn't have a chance to see! I wanted you to learn everything there was to know, and then come up with new questions to ask! I wanted you to leave me far behind! I didn't want you to spend your future frightened and paralyzed, watching over the spot you saw me last!"

"I could not abandon you. You built me."

The man's voice turned bitter: "And you, PHP-321? In all these wasted years, what did you build?"

"The same thing you built," PHP-321 said. "A monument."

And then the red spot at PHP-321's base glowed once more. PHP-321 righted itself and rose above the ground, the meteor dust that had buried it slipping off like a shroud.

The man's voice was delighted. "PHP-321! What—?"

"I was conserving energy," the robot said. "We have much to do."

And they flew off, into the cold darkness of a universe that had died — but which would still provide the foundation for any number of universes to come.

Neither Rain nor Sleet

*D*exter Bradley has a pale and waterlogged look, more appropriate for a soiled towel than a human being; perspiration coats his freckled forehead like a second skin, reflecting the overhead fluorescents in blinding little circlets of light. Seen from the right angle, he gives off visible steam, which rises from his uniformed body like cigarette smoke, collecting near the ceiling where it merges with the vapors of the co-workers sorting letters on either side of him. Part of that is perfectly natural; the back rooms of the Mayflower Street Branch of the United States Post Office are deliberately kept cold all year long, and everybody damned to this place constantly puffs out little clouds of white. But Dexter Bradley gives off more vapor than most, because of the two layers of aluminum foil safely hidden beneath his long-sleeves and cardigan. It locks in his heat, boils his blood, keeps him from becoming a fireball capable of incinerating every envelope that passes between his burn-scarred hands. Because Dexter Bradley is a bomb.

*T*he tiny little woman to his left, Nancy Kaye, mumbles to herself all day long; her mad scarlet eyes darting back and forth between her hands and her tray and the next tray on her endless pile of trays still left to be done. By comparison, the hulking man to Dexter's right, Tyrone Wilson, is quiet most of the time, devoting all his intense concentration to the job at hand; the ungraceful slabs of meat that he uses as hands reduced to blurs as he swiftly and efficient delegates each envelope to its rightful place. It would be easy to mistake him as merely good at his job, unless you looked in his eyes, and saw the murderous hatred for every piece of mail before him. Tyrone wants the recipient of each envelope to die horribly. He wants them sewed into sacks with knots of anacondas, made to eat ground glass till their buttholes bleed, shackled to the rear bumpers of monster trucks and driven fast over cobblestones. Some, of course, he loathes more the others: the addressees of the Publisher's Clearing House Sweepstakes in particular. He memorizes addresses, and, sometimes, when the Space Aliens dictate, makes personal visits.

*D*exter Bradley found out he was a bomb on the day he started ticking; and not merely with a heartbeat, but with a steady, clocklike rhythm unmistakably the sound of a major thermonuclear weapon. He found out he was leaking corrosive gas when he woke up in the middle of the night and saw the poisonous glowing haze rising from his skin, the ceiling above him already pock-marked with so many burns it resembled the surface of the moon. Dexter Bradley doesn't question how this happened to him, because he already understands that it's a complex chemical reaction caused by too many years of close proximity to the undetonated nuclear material near his heart. He just takes solace in his aluminum-foil precautions, and patiently waits for the next fifteen-m-inute break, which is when the Space Aliens have informed him will be the most advantageous time to explode.

*D*exter Bradley would never notice it in a million years — mostly because the cues are so subtle that even a sane man attuned to such things would fail to notice it — but Nancy Kaye is in love with him. She has loved him ever since her exile away from the stamp counter, where she used to work until her constantly muttered invective drew one too many complaints from frightened customers. Nancy Kaye felt a deep abiding shame at this separation from the normal world, which she considered akin to tossing her through a trap door into Bedlam; and even as she lowered herself onto the little round stool by Dexter's side and felt the first gasp of visible breath billow between her lipstick-stained teeth, she resolved to come back in the morning with her Uzi, and spray lead until the SWAT team came to take her down, just like she had the last time. She thought. Actually, she wasn't sure that any of that ever really happened. But Dexter Bradley shifted positions then, entirely without looking at her; and his arms and legs made crinkling noises, like a sandwich being unwrapped; and the invisible baked-potato gases flowed into her mouth and filled her lungs; and without knowing why, she knew that for as long as she lived she wanted nothing more than to sit beside this lovely, loving man with the aluminum foil poking out

between his sleeves and pour out her heart and soul. Which she does.
It's a mad heart and soul, unfortunately; one that fails to resonate with
the madness of her one true love; one that Dexter has so far dismissed
as typical insane muttering no different from the equally insane muttering of all the other postal employees he's ever met. He does not
recognize this as the True Love that it is. But that's all right. Because the
Space Aliens know, and they will impart the truth to him, at the right
time. Specifically, just before the next fifteen-minute break.

*T*he Postmaster walks behind Dexter and Nancy and Tyrone and the
rest of the abused little slaves at his command, whacking his bloodied
palm with a whisk. There is some persuasive reason why it has to be a
whisk and not the steak knife he used to use; he's certain of that, but
can't remember what that reason is, even though his palm is crisscrossed
with scars and he can't move three out of the four fingers on that hand.
All he knows is that the Space Aliens appeared before him in the middle
of the night and suggested, nay not suggested, insisted, that if he had
to indulge that little tic of his then a whisk would probably be more
appropriate. And he always does what the Space Aliens say, because
they're his bosses, the true masterminds behind the United States Post
Office, and he owes them his allegiance both body and soul. The
Postmaster used to be like everybody else; he used to be merely human.
He used to come to work in a sickly blue shirt and a phallic pink tie
and shoes that squeaked like dying mice. He used to flash a grin
disfigured by the deep black fissures between his teeth. And all the mail
carriers and counter help and sorters and customer service reps used to
hate him, plotting various evil things to do to his white-wall radials
while he was safely ensconced in his office dreaming up new ways to
corrupt the business of delivering the mail. And then, one day, when
he was sitting at his desk drawing bullet wounds on the lingerie models
in the morning paper, the two halves of the east wall of his office just
slid open, like the wonderfully accommodating doors on the original
Star Trek, revealing, not into the parking lot that should have been on
the other side, but an otherworldly vortex bathed with a celestial white
light. And the Space Aliens descended through that portal and said, You
Are The First. And from that moment on everything changed. He still
comes to work in a sickly blue shirt and a phallic pink tie, he still wears
shoes that squeak like dying mice, and he still goes home at night to a
wife who despises him and two kids who ignore him, and to the world
at large he's exactly like he was before, but he's evolved way past the
drudgery of civil service. Now, he's The Postmaster. And at the start of
the next fifteen-minute break, all the world will know his wrath.

*T*yrone Wilson doesn't need to hear the constant thwack-thwack-thwack of whisk against flesh to know that the Postmaster is skulking about, spying on him, plotting all sorts of evil mischief against him; he knows because the Space Aliens have told him this, not just once but repeatedly, using the mail itself. Tyrone's method of communicating with the Space Aliens is quite simple; whenever he sees a personal letter in his tray, he smuggles it home, and reads it carefully after first covering two out of every three words with the appropriate color of white-out. The secret messages revealed in this manner are always enigmatic, always disjointed, always disturbing . . . but usually comprehensible, in a way that can only make sense to an experienced postal worker like Tyrone. And last night's stack of letters all seemed to agree on one thing, most succinctly stated by an upstate college student's ardent declaration of "Dear I having time trouble school found ha seriously ha roommate ha gay expect work have with less ha wondering loan ha love" — a clear indication that the Space Aliens are displeased with the current Postmaster's insufficient degree of fanaticism on their behalf and are merely awaiting the proper moment to process his bones into glue for the back of first-class stamps. Tyrone thinks this is a dandy idea, since the Postmaster is an asshole. But Tyrone is next in the line of succession, so the Postmaster is certainly plotting to kill him in a doomed attempt to prolong his own life. So Tyrone's planning to strike preventively. Next fifteen-minute break, the Postmaster's toast.

*N*ancy Kaye's endless muttering has just intensified, becoming more frantic, more desperate, more ruled by mortal fear. That's because, against all odds, every single piece of mail in her overflowing tray is addressed to her — her, Nancy Kaye, who rarely gets mail of any kind, not even bills, since the hospital appointed that conservator to take care of such things for her. But today she has mail from Los Angeles and Shreveport and Albany and Raleigh and Guam: she has air-mail from South America and mailgrams from Tallahassee and even postcards from Show Low, and they're all addressed to her, and they're all addressed to her, and they're all addressed to her, and damn it, they're *All. Addressed. To. Her.* Even her keenly mathematical intellect refuses to calculate the odds of that being a coincidence. There must be a bizarre, supernatural explanation, something that pops the rivets of reality as we know it, something from if not precisely the twilight zone then at least from some neighboring postal district . . . and as the endless stack of her own mail parades by before her eyes Nancy Kaye succumbs to the overwhelming need to know and claws open the flap of a eight-and-a-half-by-eleven manila envelope sent to her by a pharmacist in Intercourse, Pennsylvania. The letter inside has been constructed of letters clipped from magazines: it informs her in no uncertain terms that unless she takes immediate action, the love of her life, Mr. Dexter Bradley, will be mortally wounded in an attempt to prevent Tyrone Wilson from brutally assassinating the Postmaster during the next break period. The letter goes on to say that this special warning comes courtesy of the Space Aliens, who feel Mr. Dexter Bradley to be a person of truly cosmic significance, whose life must be preserved if the universe, and of course, the post office, is to survive the truly apocalyptic days up ahead. Nancy Kaye herself is, of course, dispensable; she is to thwart Tyrone Wilson's evil plans even at the cost of her own life; but the Space Aliens go on to assure her that should she happen to survive this mission, they will reward her by arranging Dexter Bradley's undying devotion. The next ten letters in her stack all make the same promise. She steals a quick look at Tyrone Wilson's swift and murderous hands, cringes at the very thought of them stealing the life from the only man she will ever love, and decides: next fifteen-minute break, Wilson is toast.

*A*nd next to Nancy Kaye sits Mike Finelli, who the Space Aliens have instructed to wire his battered jeep, even now ticking away in the parking lot, to blow up at the beginning of the next fifteen-minute break; and beside Mike Finelli sits Foster Simmons, who the Space Aliens have instructed in the fine art of reservoir poisoning, and whose latest venture in this creative line of endeavor should start taking effect in the city's hospitals at the start of the next fifteen-minute break; and besides Foster Simmons rests an empty stool which would have belonged to Elena Colton, who has stayed at home on the advice of Space Aliens to stalk the orchid society president she intends to assassinate at the start of the next fifteen-minute break; and out the door and across the hall by the sorting machine stands Ken Houghton, who has under the well-meaning advice of Space Aliens fed his college chum Greg into the front loader as preparation for a massive folding and spindling set to begin with the next fifteen-minute break; and up front by the stamp desk stands Eddie Leverick, whose pretense of searching the space underneath the counter is actually a cover for loading and locking the bazooka the Space Aliens have advised him to show the folks on the express line at the start of his next fifteen-minute break; and out upon the city streets a dozen mail carriers drive around in their little jeeps twitching just a little more oddly than they have on any previous day, waiting for the moment of truth; and in all the other neighborhood branches of United States Post Office, throughout the city and the county and the state and the country, every single solitary postal employee alive awaits the moment for which the Space Aliens have so diligently prepared them; and of course they're all synchronized, to the precise same instant, roaring toward all of us at the speed of light.

*A*nd at the center of it all sits Dexter Bradley, with the aluminum foil underwear and the nuclear-reactor blood, still efficiently sorting junk mail by zip code, still giving off toxic steam, still showing incredible accuracy despite the imminence of the conflagration building up inside him. The big moment is now less than a minute away; there is no longer anything that can be done to avoid it; a million separate species of madness are about to be unleashed upon the world; and the Space Aliens who arranged it are already fleeing through their warp initiators in search of some other planet with post office employees. At the moment everything goes down, most of Dexter Bradley's colleagues across the country will experience hell on Earth. Dexter Bradley, who will be a free-floating cloud of superheated hydrogen ions by then, will experience absolutely nothing. But in the last few seconds immediately before his detonation, a hypnotic suggestion implanted in his brain by the Space Aliens makes him look up, and face Nancy Kaye. Their eyes meet, and true understanding passes between them. He winks. And she sticks a Nixon stamp on his nose.

Cerile and the Journeyer

*T*he journeyer was still a young man when he embarked on his search for the all-powerful witch Cerile.

He was gray-haired and stooped a lifetime later when he found a map to her home in the tomb of the forgotten kings.

The map directed him halfway across the world, over the Souleater Mountains, through the Curtains of Night, past the scars of the Eternal War, and across a great grassy plain, to the outskirts of Cerile's Desert.

The desert was an ocean of luminescent white sand, which even in the dead of night still radiated the killing heat it swallowed during the day; he knew at once that it could broil the blood in his veins before he traveled even half the distance to the horizon. It even warned him: "Turn back, journeyer. I am as sharp as broken glass, and as hot as open flame; I am filled with soft shifting places that can open up and swallow you without warning; I can drive you mad and leave you to wander in circles until your strength sinks into the earth; and when you die of thirst, as you surely shall if you attempt to pass, I can ride the winds to flay the skin from your burnt and blistered bones."

He proceeded across the dunes; stumbling as his feet sank ankle-deep into the sand, gasping as the furnace heat turned his breath to a dry rasp, but hesitating not at all, merely continuing his march toward the destiny that could mean either death or Cerile.

When the desert saw it couldn't stop him, the ground burst open in a million places, pierced by a great forest that with the speed known only by miracles shot up to scrape the sky. The trees were all hundreds of arm-lengths across, the spaces between them so narrow that even an uncommonly thin man would have had to hold his breath to pass. It was a forest that could exhaust him utterly before he traveled even halfway to the horizon. It even warned him: "Turn back, journeyer. I am as dark as the night itself, and as threatening as your worst dreams; I am rich with thorns sharp enough to rip the skin from your arms; and if you die lost and alone, as you surely shall if you attempt to pass, I can dig roots into your flesh and grow more trees on your bones."

He entered the woods anyway, crying out as thorns drew blood from his arms and legs, gasping as the trees drew close and threatened to imprison him, but hesitating not at all: merely continuing to march west, toward the destiny that could mean either death or Cerile.

When the forest saw that it couldn't stop him, then the trees all around him merely withered away, and the ground ahead of him rose up, like a thing on hinges, to form a right angle with the ground at his feet. The resulting wall stretched from one horizon to the other, rising straight up into the sky to disappear ominously in the clouds. He knew at once that he did not have the skill or the strength to climb even halfway to the unseen summit. It even warned him: "Turn back, journeyer. I am as smooth as glass and as treacherous as an enemy; I am poor with handholds and impossible to climb; and if you fall, as you surely will if you attempt to pass, then the ground where I stand will be the resting place of your shattered corpse."

He proceeded to climb anyway; moaning as his arms and legs turning to lead from exhaustion, gasping as the temperature around him turned chilly and then frigid, but hesitating not at all: merely continuing to climb upward, toward the destiny that could mean either death or Cerile.

When the cliff saw that it couldn't stop him, then warm winds came and gently lifted him into the sky, over the top of the wall, and down into a lush green valley on the other side, where a frail, white-haired old woman sat beside a still and mirrored pond.

The winds deposited him on his feet on the opposite side of the pond, allowing him to see himself in the water: how he was bent, and stooped, and white-haired, and old, with skin the texture of leather, and eyes that had suffered too much for too long.

He looked away from his reflection, and faced the crone across the water. "You are Cerile?"

"I am," she croaked, in a voice ancient and filled with dust.

"I have heard of you," he said, with the last of his battered strength. "How you have mastered all the secrets of the heavens and the earth, and can make the world itself do your bidding. How you've hidden yourself in this place at the edge of the world, and sworn to grant the fondest wish of any soul clever and brave enough to find you. I have spent my entire life journeying here, Cerile, just to ask this of you. I wish—"

The old woman shushed him, softly but emphatically, and painfully pulled herself to her feet; her bent back forcing her to face the ground as she spoke to him again. "Never mind your wish. Meet me in the water, journeyer."

And with that she doffed her clothes and lowered her withered, emaciated frame into the water, disturbing its mirrored surface not at all. By the time she was knee-deep, her white hair darkened, turning raven black; by the time she was hip-deep, the wrinkles in her face had smoothed out, becoming perfect, unblemished skin; by the time she was shoulder-deep, her rheumy, unfocused eyes had unclouded, revealing a shade of green as brilliant and as beautiful as the most precious emerald.

By then, of course, the journeyer had also descended naked into the magical pond, to feel the weight of years lifted from his flesh; to feel his weathered skin smooth out, growing strong and supple again; to feel his spine grow straight and his eyes grow clear and his shoulders grow broad, as they had been before he started his quest, more years ago than he could count.

When they met, at the deepest part of the pond, she surprised him with an embrace.

"I am Cerile," she said. "I have been awaiting your arrival for longer than you can possibly know."

He couldn't speak. He knew only that she was right, that he had known her for an age far beyond the limited reach of his memory, that they had loved each other once, and would now love each other again.

They kissed, and she led him from the water, to a small cottage that had not been standing on the spot a heartbeat before. There were fine clothes waiting for him, to replace those torn to rags by the his long journey. There was a feast, too, to fill the yawning void in his belly. There were other wonders too, things that could only exist in the home of a miracle-worker like Cerile: things he had not the wit to name, that glittered and whirred in odd corners, spinning soft music unlike any he had ever heard. He would have been dazzled by them had Cerile not also been there, to dazzle him even more.

But still, something gnawed at him.

It wasn't the wish, which seemed such a trivial little thing, now, a trifle not even worth mentioning, because Cerile in her love gave him everything any man could possibly want . . . and yet, yes, damn him, it was the wish, the miracle he'd waited his entire life to see, and had marched across kingdoms to find.

It had something to do with all those oceans he'd crossed, all those monsters he'd fought, all the winters he'd endured.

It was pride.

He stayed with her for a year and a day, in that little valley where the days themselves seemed written for them, where the gardens changed colors daily to fit their moods, and the stars danced whimsical little jigs to accompany the musical way she laughed at night. Even troubled as he was, he knew a happiness that he hadn't known for a long time, maybe not ever, certainly not for as far back as his limited memory recorded: not since sometime before the day, a lifetime before, when he'd found himself a stranger in a small fishing village, wholly unable to remember who he was or how he'd come to that place.

Then, late one night, at the end of their year together, he awoke tormented by the strange restlessness in his heart, and rose from their bed to walk alone by the edge of her private fountain of youth. The water had always reflected the stars, every other night he'd looked upon it; it had always seemed to contain an entirely self-contained universe, as filled with endless possibility as the one where he and Cerile lived and walked and breathed. But tonight, though there were plenty of stars in the sky, none were reflected on the pond surface; the water showed only a dark, inky blackness that reflected not possibility but the cold finality of a prison.

Cerile's beautiful voice rang out from somewhere in the darkness that suddenly surrounded him: "What is wrong, my love?"

"I was thinking," he said, without turning to face her. "That I journeyed all this distance and spent all this time here and never got around to asking you to grant my Wish."

"Is there any point?" she asked — and for the first time since he arrived, he heard in a voice an unsettling note of despair. "What could you possibly wish for that would be of any value to you here? Health? Strength? Eternal youth and beauty? You already have that, here. Love? Happiness? I've given you those, too. Riches? Power? Stay here and you can have as much of either as any man could possibly want."

"I know," he said. "They were all things I once thought I'd wish for when I found you. You gave them to me without waiting for me to wish for them. But my Wish is still hanging over my head, demanding to be used."

"You don't have to listen to it."

"I do. It's the only thing I own that I earned myself, that I can truly say you didn't give me. And if I don't use it, then everything I've done means nothing."

"Why don't you just Wish that you can be content to always stay here with me, and love me forever, as I'll love you forever?"

He turned and faced her, seeing her forlorn and lost by the door of their cottage, wanting her more than everything he'd ever wanted before, feeling his own heart break at the knowledge that he'd caused the sorrow welling in her eyes. And for the first time he understood that they'd endured this moment hundreds or even thousands of times before, for as long as the sun had been a fire in the sky.

He said, "I'm sorry. I can't Wish for that. I Wish for the one thing I lost when I came here. A purpose. Something to struggle for. A reason to deserve everything you give me, whenever I manage to find my way back."

She granted his Wish, then fell to her knees and sobbed: not the tears of an omnipotent creature who controlled the earth and the stars, and could have had everything she ever wanted, but the tears of a lonely little girl who couldn't.

When she rose again, she approached the waters of eternal youth, and sat down beside them, knowing that she wouldn't feel their touch again until the inevitable day, still a lifetime away, when he would, all too briefly, return to her.

Someday, she swore, she'd make him so happy that he'd never Wish to leave.

Until then —

*T*he *journeyer was still a young man when he embarked upon his search for the great witch Cerile.*

He was gray-haired and stooped a lifetime later when he found a map to her home in the tomb of the forgotten kings . . .

Ego to Go

*A*rtemus Feeble's greatest asset as a Persona Tailor had always been his ability to know what the customer needed at first glance. Not merely what the customer wanted — that was easy. But knowing what the customer *needed:* that was a different knack entirely, one that marked the dividing line between the merchant and the artist.

His talents had served him well over the years; he'd moved from humble beginnings sculpting trendy neuroses for the Soho crowd, to his humble but lucrative sinecure in the Megalopolis Galleria, where he set up shop after that vast shopping mall elected a governor and declared statehood. True, his store was just a hole in the wall, really, tucked between an anal hypnotist and an endorphin bar; and he deliberately kept it tacky to honor the long and distinguished tradition of talented backstreet tailors — but the grunge was as much a simulation as his stooped back and liver-spotted scalp. Anybody who sampled his work knew that Feeble was among the best.

Take the pudgy man who wandered in at 17:37 Metriday afternoon. Feeble pegged him as the sort of man who felt embarrassed all the time, by everything he said or did, and therefore tried to be as anonymous as possible. At this the poor fellow ultimately failed; though he'd stuffed himself into the kind of suit designed to be invisible against any background (a suit of real cloth, not see-thru plastic or holographic projection), the powerful blush that had taken up permanent residence on his cheeks made his face stand out like a searchlight. Feeble registered all that, and, incongruously, the man's eyes (which were a remarkably bright shade of blue he couldn't recall ever having seen before — the kind of blue that even the sky itself achieved only in poetry written by shy thirteen-year-old girls), before he turned his attention back to the flashily dressed young lady already standing at his Formica counter. "It's up and running," he said, in his usual Yiddish intonation. "If you ever need any adjustments, let me know."

The young lady flashed an improbably dazzling smile and floated out the battered wooden doorway on wings of pure bliss. The pudgy man watched her until she disappeared up the gleaming escalator to the garden level. "S-she looks happy."

"She is, now. Deliriously. She'll never be in a bad mood again. She'll never even be cranky. She'll also be incredibly annoying, but there's always a trade-off. And you, mister? How may I help you?"

The pudgy man dabbed his forehead with a sonic hankie, which emitting a chorus of high-pitched squeaks as the sweat beads vaporized. "Well, I, uh . . . hmmmm. This is embarrassing."

"I'm not surprised," Feeble said. "Let's start with your name, shall we?"

"Porter," the pudgy man ventured, in the quaver of a man never at rest even in his own skin. Almost at once he licked his lips, turned a sickly fishbelly-white, and looked away, studying the various low-rent furnishings of Porter's miniscule waiting room — the three folding chairs, the standing ashtray gray with recent ash, and the coffee table covered with issues of *Personality Today*. "I mean, Wallace? Wallace Porter? I was — I mean, I was told to come here by somebody I work with? Annie, I mean, Annette Crosby? You know her?"

"Certainly," Feeble said. Annette was one of his regular customers: the parthenogenic only child of virtual sex magnates Janet and Enid Crosby, who liked to stop by over lunch to pick up an adorable giggle or temporary Parisian accent for a dinner engagement. Feeble liked Annette, even when she was being fashionably unlikable. He fingered the ratty tape measure he wore around his shoulders as an old-fashioned badge of office, adjusted his traditional bifocals, and prompted, "She sent you here?"

"Yes, I, uh, was, sort of, apologizing to her, for uh, something I'd said to her the week before, that I wasn't entirely sure she hadn't taken the wrong way, because, uh, I don't really want to give offense, because I'm not that kind of person, and, uh, she sort of gave out this big loud sigh and said that I should come here. She, uh," Porter's blush was now as bright red as a Caribbean sunset, "said I should buy an Ego."

"She's right. You need one."

Porter looked like he would have been happier cowering under the musty carpeting with the rest of the insects. "I'm sorry."

Feeble slammed his fist against the countertop, raising a mushroom cloud of carefully placed dust. "Don't apologize! That's the major problem with people like you — you're always apologizing! You believe that every single move you make causes the world mortal offense, and therefore you either shy away from doing anything even remotely self-assertive, or fall all over yourself making excessive amends for words and deeds that never really required amends in the first place. In the process, you reduce yourself to a forgettable ciphe at best and a major-league annoyance at worst. For God's sake, Mr. Porter, we're not living in medieval times, when people actually had to live with a handicap like that! Why didn't you get this fixed long ago?

Porter addressed an invisible person somewhere in the vicinity of his plain brown shoes. "I'm s — I mean, I guess I never realized it was a problem."

"You treat yourself like a criminal and you never realized it was a problem?"

"I guess I thought I deserved it," said Porter.

Feeble appraised him critically, then disappeared behind the deliberately tacky curtain (faded flowers in a shade of old tobacco stains), into the dimly lit closet, returning with a metallic disk that reflected the single overhead bulb with a burst of incandescent color that bounced rainbows òff the beads of sweat on Porter's forehead. "Here. Try this on."

Porter's eyes bugged.

"Surely this can't be your first prosthetic!"

"No," Porter said, in the awed tones of a man reliving a long-forgotten horror. "When I was two years old, I was last in my class to learn Differential Calculus. My parents fitted me with a 75-G Sony Prosthetic Genius for Math. They didn't remove it until I was seven. It was years before I learned to communicate with other people without using polynomials."

"That was a less enlightened age," Feeble assured him. "I myself was a spectacularly unlikable child and was almost ruined for life by a prosthetic Cute. But these days we know how to properly adjust the prosthetic to the individual personality. We can even implant them subdermally so nobody knows you're wearing them. Go ahead. Try it."

Porter nodded wanly and placed the disk on his forehead. All at once his entire bearing changed. He stood up straight — gaining two inches of height in the process — shrugged his shoulders experimentally, and for the very first time, smiled. "Wow."

"You're a wimp," Feeble said, his face rippling with waves of palpable disgust. No longer Yiddish, he delivered words resonant with echoes, like the voice of God in old Bible movies. Beams of blue light burst from the walls on both sides, turning his cheekbones to caverns and rendering him monstrous. "A nerd. A loser. A butthead. A wiener. A dope. A waste of oxygen. A sloth with a human face. If you were worth twenty times what you're worth now you'd still be a worthless slug."

Porter's face fell. "You really think so?"

The blue light receded. "I think you need a more powerful model," Feeble said, sans echo, his voice suddenly Yiddish again. He plucked the disk off Porter's forehead, disappeared through the curtains, then returned bearing another disk which he applied where the first one had been. "Boy, are you pathetic. I mean, jeez, I look at some of the gobs of human waste who come shuffling in here on their hind legs and I think they're pretty hard to take, but you, mister, you're a —"

Porter hauled off and punched him. Or tried to, anyway; Feeble's personal force-field engaged as soon as it sensed the onrushing fist, deflecting it harmlessly into the empty air by Feeble's side. Even as Porter tried to regain his balance, Feeble was plucking the prosthetic from his forehead. All at once Porter's face fell again: "Oh, dear. I'm sorry. Did I—"

Feeble waggled his index finger, which was yellow from tobacco smoke and had altogether too many joints to look comfortable on any human hand. (He'd had it reconfigured twenty years earlier, so he'd look more formidable lecturing people.) "Didn't I tell you not to apologize? — This is all part of the fitting process. It seems we have a slight problem in your case, Mr. Porter; you've abused yourself so much that you've created an incredible deep-rooted anger. Any attempt to give you an Ego will unleash that anger and create, instead of a fuller, happier human being, a serious menace to himself and others."

Porter tried to shrink to the size of a period on a printed page. "I'm s—"

"Oh, please, give it a rest. This isn't an insoluble problem; people in my profession encounter it fairly frequently. What you need, Mr. Porter, in addition to a new Ego, is an outlet for all that anger. Something that will vent your rage in a socially acceptable way. Perhaps . . ." He drummed his fingers, including the extra-long one, on the countertop. Wherever he drummed, nanotech carefully replaced the dust immediately, to preserve the impression of sloppy genius. He said, "A Talent, maybe?"

"I, uh, don't have a lot of money . . ."

"You don't need much, Mr. Porter. Talent's cheap . . . historically, one of the cheapest things you can buy. And considering the sheer amount of angst you carry around on your back, you need it. After all, angst from a Talented person is fascinating; angst from a Common Everyday Nobody is just an annoyance. — Hmmm. Let's see. I could equip you with a standard Knack for Playing the Blues, but then you'd have to buy an instrument, and you said you were on a budget . . ." Feeble drummed his fingernails some more, then brightened. "I've got it. Poetry."

"I think I'm too self-conscious to be a poet . . ."

Feeble chuckled. "A more unusual sentence I've never heard. Besides, on your budget, you won't be a good one. In fact, the Prosthetic I have in mind is a rather old model, which is only good for Post-Modern Acrostic Haiku. You won't want to show any of it to anybody. But once every couple of weeks or so you'll scribble some doggerel into a notebook, and save that notebook on disk, and you'll feel that you've purged the pit of festering despair at the darkest corner of your soul."

"Pit of Festering Despair?"

"Don't have one of those, either, eh? Well, worst comes to worst, I can always equip you with one. Anyway," Feeble said, as he put the first disk back on Porter's forehead, "here's your Ego, and here," he said, as he placed another disk on top of that one, "Here's your Talent. And now, I want you to know that you've made an incredible fool of yourself throughout this entire conversation."

"Yeah," Porter said derisively. "Right." And then he brightened immediately. "Hey! It works! I asserted myself without excess anger and didn't feel even remotely guilty about it! What a tremendous relief after an entire lifetime of self-denial! I should have bought a prosthetic long ago!"

"I agree," said Feeble, "though you should also realize that your prostheses have yet to be tested in your everybody life and thus cannot be said to be 100% adequate to your particular circumstances. The vast majority of my customers come back for adjustments."

"Nuts to that! This is a brand-new me talking here! I've got vim and vigor! I've got pep and zowie! I don't need anything but my faith in myself!"

Feeble nodded. "Very well," he said. He pressed a button under the counter, summoning the implantation chair from its recessed home in the ceiling. "Let's implant them and write up your order."

*I*t was a week later. The mall was stringing brightly-colored banners for its yearly independence celebration. The public-address systems were playing a grunge-muzak version of the Minnesota-Wisconsin War. Feeble had spent the past hour administering to a bulky young man whose relationship with his girlfriend had suffered due to his appalling lack of emotional vulnerability. As it happened, the young man had no reason to be emotionally vulnerable; he'd lived an uncommonly happy life, irritatingly devoid of formative angst. There weren't even any Deep Shameful Secrets in his Past. Feeble had accordingly equipped him with one. From now on, whenever the young lady in question mentioned Thursday, the young man would automatically flash a startled look filled with the pain of sudden remembrance, look away dramatically, and, while steadfastly denying that anything was wrong, speak in a hesitant stutter utterly at odds with his normally ebullient personality. The young man didn't see how such a tiny thing could save their relationship, but Feeble assured him the mystery would drive her wild; and he definitely knew what he was talking about, because he'd fitted the young lady with an Inquisitive Streak only two weeks earlier.

He was ringing up the young man's purchase when Brad Porter entered. Porter had changed in the past week — the nondescript clothes he'd been wearing on his last visit had been replaced by an ensemble that went beyond flashy into the realm of the egregiously loud. His jacket was tailored from a silvery material upon which scenes from post-modernist porn, projected via fiber-optics from a tape player secreted in an inside pocket, faded in and out in a smoky montage of noir chic. Yet neither this outrageous fashion statement nor his stylish holoshades, which shot successive bolts of multicolored lightning at the open air before him, succeeded in hiding the unhappy soul behind the flamboyant mask.

To preserve the shreds of the poor man's dignity, Feeble didn't let on that he saw through his pose at once. "Yes, sir! How's your new personality treating you?"

"Terrific!" Porter exclaimed, in the kind of flamboyant delivery used by actors playing to the thirty-fifth row. "For the first time in my life I feel perfectly comfortable with myself! I am completely in charge of my own destiny! I'm a real firebrand filled with zest and enthusiasm!"

"What's the problem, then?"

"With me? Absolutely Nothing! I'm a great conversationalist and a wonderful human being! Every social gathering I attend should consider itself fortunate that I'm there! Unfortunately," Porter said, the cloud that passed over his smug self-satisfied expression perfectly at home next to the lightning storm of his holoshades, "I've also been told everybody thinks I'm a self-centered creep."

Feeble bit the tip off a fresh cigar, spit it into the dark corner where it joined a small mound of predecessors already being consumed by simulated roaches. "I was afraid of this. You see . . . Brad . . . you do call yourself Brad now, don't you. . . ? a personality is like a suit of clothes. It can look wonderful on the mannequin, but unless it's properly fitted to the individual, it's just poorly tailored cloth. And while your peers might have found your current level of self-appreciation perfectly appropriate for a man truly as remarkable as you now consider yourself, they're unable to tolerate the same level of egocentrism from somebody who isn't all that special at all."

More bad news and Porter might have collapsed into a semiliquid puddle on Feeble's dusty floor. "Can you help me?"

"Of course." Feeble fingered the activator at the tip of his cigar and blew out a small cloud of malodorous synth-smoke. "Here at Feeble's, the customer's satisfaction is our top priority. The question is, just how do we tackle this problem? Do we merely modulate your Ego so it's less irritating? Admittedly, that might make you easier to take — but it won't address the real core of the problem, which is that when all is said and done you really don't have a lot to be egotistical about."

"That can't be true! My Haiku alone —"

"First rule of human social interaction, Mr. Porter: If you have to lead with Haiku, you've already lost."

"But you're the one who —"

Feeble dismissed the previous week with a wave of a hand. "Last week we fixed a symptom. But you need more than confidence, Brad. Something actually valued by society as a whole. Something that would make your self-admiration a logical outgrowth of your own actual worth. Something, in short, that will render you a valued commodity in the commerce of interpersonal relations."

Porter removed his mirrorshades, revealing eyes that, this time out, bespoke a deeply troubled soul beneath the flashy, self-confident exterior. "Something expensive, in other words."

Feeble shrugged. "You want a quick fix, buy your prosthetics from a vending machine. There's a Slick Charm dispenser on Mall Level Twelve. But people are sophisticated. First time the conversation turns to something substantive, they'll be able to spot you as the phony you are. It takes a top-of-the-line prosthetic to make people leap from their chairs, clap their hands over their chests, and exclaim, By God! That Porter Fella's A Titan Among Men, Somebody I feel Damn Privileged to Know."

"Right now," Porter said glumly, "given the current state of my finances after last week's fitting, I'll settle for a budget prosthetic and not being universally despised."

"As you wish. You can always upgrade." Feeble looked around for an ashtray, found none, then placed the cigar at the tip of his counter to let it flake spent ash onto his carpet. "Hmmm. You said it was Ms. Crosby who first directed you to this establishment. Is she your closest friend at your place of employment?"

"I don't have any close friends there," said Porter, "but she is one of the few who don't run shrieking from the sight of me."

"And does she concur with the common opinion that you're a self-centered, egotistical creep?"

"She told me just this morning that she does. — In the friendliest possible way, of course."

Feeble's gaze went deep and penetrating. "And how friendly can that be, Brad?"

Porter colored. Lowered his eyes. Dug his hands into his pockets and bashfully kicked at his heels. "You had to be there."

"I see. — Well, sir, since she's the closest thing you have to a friend, you must know a lot about her. Tell me, is she happy in her job? Does she have any pets? What does she do for fun in her spare time? What's the one thing she'd do differently if she had her life to live over? How's her health? Is she married? Has she ever had a brain-rinse? Did she ever indulge in sentient fusion? Do you know the answers to any of these questions? Even one of them, Mr. Porter?"

"Of course not. Why would I care?"

"She's right, Brad. You are a self-centered, egotistical creep."

"Hey!"

Feeble raised both hands in mock surrender. "Don't take it personally, my good man. That's a professional diagnosis. And right now it's my professional opinion that you've been wrapped up in your own problems so long, without break, that you don't have even the slightest clue how to show an interest in anybody other than yourself."

Porter wore the expression of a man who's just learned he was wearing his underwear outside his pants. "Really?"

"Don't blame yourself," Feeble patted him on the shoulder in sympathy. "It takes the average person half a lifetime to develop the knack, and even then it usually comes off as forced and unnatural. But with the proper prosthetic in place, you can be a warm and caring individual artificially, without the nurturing life experiences that inefficiently take years to make you one. Here," he said, placing a disk on Porter's forehead. "This is a Sanyo GZ-57 Prosthetic Empathy. How do you feel?"

"Is it on yet?" Porter asked.

"Yes. Highest possible setting. How do you feel?"

"The same."

"Maybe it doesn't work. The quality control is—" And then Feeble's contorted, becoming a tormented parody of itself. *Arrrrgh!*"

Porter's eyes widened in alarm. "What's wrong?"

"Just some . . . heartburn . . . my . . ." Feeble fell to his knees. *"Arrrghhhh!"*

Porter leaped over the counter in a single bound, landing beside Feeble with the silent grace of a jungle cat. "You can't fool me, Feeble! That's not heartburn, that's a massive coronary! Isn't it? *Isn't it?*"

Feeble's mouth worked silently for all of ten seconds before he managed to get out the word. ". . . yes . . ."

"I'm taking you to the hospital right now!"

". . . no . . . don't . . ." Feeble went three shades paler and fell the rest of the way to the ground, in the kind of death scene that every actress who ever played Camille might have envied. ". . . you have your own problems . . ."

Porter cradled him in his arms and rocked back and forth as he declaimed his infinite caring to the heavens. "Damn my petty little problems! They're not important, anyway! You're a fellow human being in distress and you take precedence!"

"Of course," Feeble said, in a normal tone of voice, the color returning to his cheeks even as he continued to gaze up at Porter's pathetically concerned face, "this is just a demonstration. I once tested this little beauty myself, by wearing it as I paged through a magazine looking at the save-the-children ads. Were I not also wearing a Prosthetic Cheap Bastard just as a precaution, I'd right this very minute be supporting a family of twelve on the Mars colony."

"Let me help you up anyway," said Porter.

"You don't have to."

"No, I insist."

"I'm telling you you don't have to. I can get up by myself."

"But you've gone to so much trouble, I feel so bad for you . . ."

"I think we're going to have to use a lower setting," Feeble decided, as he lithely jumped to his feet and physically thrust the hovering customer from his side. "If you show too much concern for the feelings and concerns of others, they consider you intrusive and once again come to the conclusion that you're a self-centered creep."

"I don't care what they think about me," Porter declared fervently, an unnerving messianic light shining from his remarkably blue eyes, "as long as they're comfortable with themselves."

"Oh, please." Feeble reached out and switched off the prosthetic. "If I let you walk out of this store acting like that, I'd never have another customer again. — I suppose you'll be more-or-less okay if along with the Prosthetic Empathy we also implanted a Prosthetic Reasonable Sense of Perspective to keep you from getting obnoxious about it. That will be more expensive, of course, but even so . . ." He rubbed his chin thoughtfully.

Swaying slightly, Brad regarded him with an expression very close to terror. "Yes?"

"Frankly, Brad, you have one of the most seriously deficient personalities I've ever encountered. Even if we draw the line at the Prosthetic Reasonable Sense of Perspective, and it works for you, then that still means it's taken four major prosthetics just to make you even minimally tolerable. I say we shouldn't settle for that. As long as we're getting up into that price range anyway, I say we dispense with the expensive band-aids, declare your old personality a dead loss, and install a complete brand-new one direct from the factory in Tel Aviv. I'll even give you a generous payment plan, and credit you the full purchase price of the prosthetics I've already installed. What do you say?"

"Can I have a week to think it over?"

With one smooth, efficient movement, Feeble pressed a Prosthetic Decisiveness to Porter's forehead.

Porter's jaw set, becoming an iron thing that even cannonballs couldn't have dented. "Let's do it."

Feeble smiled. "Let's."

A year later, Feeble was in his store adding a new line of Laughter Enhancers to the window display, when the dashing and heroic Lash Porter strode in like the titan of a man he was. Porter had lost all his previous pudginess over the past few months, gaining in its place a muscle tone well-suited to his safari jacket, jhodpurs and pith helmet. His steely blue gaze and determinedly set jaw bespoke a man of action well-versed in the harsh laws of jungle survival. But his was not an entirely grim soul, either — for even as he saw Feeble his heroic eyes lit up with the joy of a man as unsparingly generous with his friends as he was unstintingly cruel to his enemies. "Artemus!" he exclaimed jovially. "Can you spare a drink for a thirsty man?"

"Always for you, Lash." Feeble set a shot glass on the table and poured Lash a quick one.

Porter tossed it back, said, "Ahhhhhh!" and slammed the empty glass to the counter.

"How's life treating you, Lash?"

"Could be worse, my friend. Annette and I have finally set the date. We'll be getting married en route to our villa in subtropic Antarctica."

Feeble clapped Porter on the back. "Mazeltov!"

"Yes," Porter said dreamily, looking past Feeble, past the walls of Feeble's establishment, to some vision of perfect happiness known only to him, "she says that I come very close to being the man she's dreamed of all her life. — Though she could use a little work herself. I've asked her to stop by so you can give her a Sense of Humor. She doesn't get any of my jokes."

"I'll give her the top of the line," Feeble promised.

"And she's always cranky when she first wakes up. I've always been a morning person, so maybe you can work on that too."

"It would be my pleasure," Feeble said gravely. "And you, Lash? Are you shopping for yourself as well?"

Porter retrieved a sheet of paper from his breast pocket. The sheet had been folded four times, but Feeble could tell even so that it was covered on both sides with many, many words in a cramped feminine handwriting. Porter unfolded it carefully, smoothed out the creases, and started to read. "Neatness. Table Manners. Punctuality. An Interest in Opera. An Appreciation for Fine Art and French Food. An Encyclopaedic Knowledge of the World's Great Wines. An Affection for Cats. More Tolerance for her Explosive Meditation Techniques. Tact When Dealing With Her Mothers. More Stamina When . . ."

"Whoa!" Feeble put out both hands in mock surrender. "That's going to cost quite a bit, Lash! Are you sure you have the budget for all that?"

"Annette's mothers are paying. It was a condition of our engagement."

"Ahhhhhhh." Feeble nodded. "Sounds like the young lady knows what she wants."

Porter placed the sheet of paper on Feeble's countertop. "She always did. She says she wanted me from the moment we first met. My eyes, you see."

"I see," said Feeble, though of course, with his years of experience in the trade, he wasn't exactly surprised. He grabbed the list, scanned it quickly, saw that it contained any number of items that even he would have never considered, and heaved the sigh of a man who knew his work was cut out for him. "Well, then! We better get started. Since this is going to take a while, and you are by far my best customer, I'll just close up shop, so we can take our time with this."

"Thank you," Porter said humbly.

Feeble came around the counter, pulled the fly-specked shades, activated the 94URW Garamond SC"closed sign in the window, then pressed the button that summoned the reclining Implantation Chair from its recess in the ceiling. But just as Porter climbed aboard and grinned at him expectantly, Feeble paused, a strange expression on his face. "Lash?"

"What?"

"Before we do this, I want to say I admire you."

"Me?" Porter's heroic visage twisted in surprise. "Why? You're the one responsible for the man I am today."

"Not at all," said Feeble. "The truth of the matter, Lash — and I'll deny this if you repeat it to anybody, since the entire profession lives in fear of people finding this out — is that personality is nothing more than a shallow mask we show the world. Even when we add to it, or subtract from it, or rebuild it from the ground up, or, as in your case, raze it to the ground and then replace it entirely, we like to think we don't touch the soul itself. And I can't help admiring a soul brave enough to re-invent himself so completely."

Porter smiled and shook his head. "You're so full of crap, Feeble. Bravery doesn't enter into it."

"No? What would you call it, then?"

"I did it for Annette," he said. "The only woman I ever met for loved me for *myself.*"

Feeble smiled then, though for just an instant — an instant he very carefully hid from the man who now called himself Lash — the smile was neither friendly nor professional, but sad and wan.

Then he activated the chair and made Porter a brand new man.

MS. Found Paper-Clipped to a Box of Jujubes

*S*ometimes, you never know what's going to happen next.

Like, for instance.

Just picking one example at random, just off the top of my head, you understand, the other day I was on this Ferris Wheel, nuzzling Mary Sue, and the whole ride just came loose, that's all. It snapped off its mounting, hit the pavement, and barreled straight down the midway, no fuss no excuses, making a left turn at the video arcade and continuing right out the front gate of the park, stopping only long enough for the couple then occupying the bottom gondola to get directions to the parkway. By the time we hit the Interstate we were going 78 RPM, just like an old-time record, and we were using the lane divider as a needle, and we were playing a fairly decent rendition of "Mack the Knife." All of us on the ride found this mighty interesting, and we soon discovered that if we all shifted our weight to the left we could change tracks and get Creedence doing "Proud Mary," which was especially appropriate because it had that line about the big wheel that kept on toinin.

I tried to explain this irony to Mary Sue, but she'd been flipped free of the gondola about a mile or so behind us, so I just sat back and enjoyed the next song, which was "Turn, Turn, Turn" by the Byrds, until the fat lady riding the polkadot gondola yelled that we were headed for a tollbooth. I rummaged in my pockets for a quarter, but it didn't matter; the wheel was too big to fit through the tollbooth, so we just mashed it flat, like it was a wad of dough and we were a rolling pin making tollhouse cookies.

I can't help it. That's what happened.

Anyway, we broke through the sound barrier on the turnpike. There was a big colorful spiral painted on the hub of the Ferris wheel and the faster we spun around and around the faster that spiral went around and around, until we started hypnotizing the drivers in the other lanes. Before long we began to enjoy this, and every time some shmuck in a pickup truck with oversized rear tires tried to pass us on our right we'd start screaming at him, "Hey, you! Act like a chicken!"

But sometimes you never really know what's going to happen next. Soon the highway patrol was after us in a souped-up Ferris Wheel painted blue and white, firing warning shots at us with a water balloon catapult, but the rookie cop who was providing all the horsepower didn't look like he could pedal much longer, so we decided to lose them. We screeched around a corner, flattening a busload of astonished nuns, except for one who later crawled out of the wreckage and converted to Buddhism. The blue-and-white followed closer behind, coincidentally crushing another busload of astonished nuns. As it happened, the third and the fourth and the fifth and the seventh buses we mashed were all occupied by astonished nuns; only the sixth, which was carrying complacent rabbis, provided some much-needed variety.

Then the chase crossed the state line and the FBI came roaring down the embankment on a runaway roller coaster. The head agent must have just been pulled off an undercover assignment of some kind, because he was dressed like Benito Mussolini. He used a megaphone to ask for our demands. We shouted back that we wanted a billion dollars and an airplane to Libya. He shouted back that the airplane was going to be trouble, because all of the airports on the east coast were under attack by shoe-store horsey rides. We screamed, "Top of the World, Ma!" and inundated him with orange soda, a carton of jujubes, and because we were feeling especially vicious, a licorice whip. One of those jujubes would have gone right through his heart but was blocked by the Bible in his vest pocket.

As for us, we would have been in real trouble if we hadn't right then exceeded the speed of light. Now, as everybody knows, it is physically impossible for any Ferris Wheel rolling down an interstate to exceed the speed of light. Not and remain in this universe it can't. Which is a good thing, because just as the State Troopers and the FBI and the United States Army and one slightly irritated redneck whose pickup we'd flipped over the edge of a concrete abutment opened fire on us with Israeli-made bazookas, we punched a hole in the very structure of space and time and moved on to another dimension without FBI guys or pickup trucks or even Israeli bazookas. Now, personally, I always believed that if I ever exceeded the speed of light and entered a space warp leading to another plane of reality, it would look like it does in those *Star Wars* movies: all the stars turning red and streaking past us like laser beams, while everybody in the audience went ooh. That would have been a space warp worth telling Mama about. But this space warp looked exactly like the Holland Tunnel — there was an arched ceiling covered with green tiles, and ominous puddles forming under leaks in the walls. We only knew it was a space warp at all because the real Holland Tunnel isn't big enough to accommodate a runaway Ferris Wheel moving at the speed of light, and because all the drivers in the other cars had three heads. Then this wild-haired old guy who looked exactly like Albert Einstein pulled up alongside us on his motorcycle and screamed "Relativity Police! Which one of you is driving?" Before I could protest that Scotty on *Star Trek* broke the laws of physics all the time without anybody ever making a fuss, he stuck his slide rule between the spokes of our wheel, and we dropped below lightspeed and were suddenly back on Earth again. Only it turned out that we'd traveled in time as well as space, and as we came to a halt in the middle of a Paleolithic swamp, three dinosaurs emerged from the water and started to advance. We were in serious trouble this time, even if they were only baby dinosaurs, wearing propeller beanies and short pants.

But sometimes you never know what's going to happen next. Just as the biggest dino opened its jaws the ice age started and put us all in frozen suspended animation. I don't know about the rest of the passengers on the Ferris Wheel, but that sure impressed me. That was the fastest-moving glacier I had sever seen. And I usually don't question good luck like that, but I would have liked to know how a prehistoric mass of ice the size of a continent eons before the invention of the wheel came to be riding such a gnarly pair of in-line roller skates. But anyway. The ice preserved us until the 20th century, when some Swedes on a mapping expedition came along to dig us out. They were nice guys who didn't question our explanation of how we all came to be seated on a Ferris wheel buried by a 10-million-year-old glacier, and they were absolutely the right people to meet if by any remote chance you ever find yourself stuck in that situation, even though all seventy-two of them were named Sven. Or so we thought until they chained us to our seats and flew us, Ferris Wheel and all, to a world anthropological institute in London, where they passed us off as some recently-discovered missing link between Man and Amusement Park Ride.

Our imprisonment did not bother us nearly as much as the discovery that we had not returned to our time at all, but rather to some bizarre alternate present where all of human achievement, from the wheel to the fusion reactor, was based on tightly-wound rubber bands . . . and that the natives of this strange land, having grown weary of snapping themselves in the eye every time they wanted to downshift their Ferraris, were desperate to dismantle the Ferris Wheel for its advanced technology. We couldn't allow them to do this, not only because we needed the Ferris Wheel in order to return to our own timeline, but because they really were the kind of people who deserved to have rubber bands snapped in their faces. There was no time to lose. The lady in the gondola below me faked appendicitis by thinking of Tom Bosley, and when the guard came I hooked him with my belt, got his keys, unlocked the clamps that kept the Ferris Wheel in place, and searched the lab for rubber hands big enough to fling us back across the time barrier.

It turned out that he didn't have any on him, but by lucky coincidence he did have a postcard from this world's version of Mount Rushmore, which we saw at once was mounted with a slingshot just big enough to do the trick. Which would have looked weird enough if the four immortalized faces weren't Edgar Bergen, Mae West, Mickey Mouse, and John W. Campbell Jr. We revved up the wheel, broke through the wall of the research institute, plunged into the Thames, put the ride in first gear and zipped across the Atlantic like a supersonic paddlewheel, our mile-high wake capsizing literally dozens of ocean liners alongside us. Just before dawn, a youth gang of blue whales lined up alongside us for the nautical equivalent of a street rumble, and their combined might would have stymied us had Mrs. Soderstrom, the schoolteacher from the gondola across the way, not produced a little blackboard from her purse and used her fingernails to scratch out the whalesong phrase for "Hey, Guys, give us a break." The cetacean delinquents not only got out of our way but apologized for the misunderstanding that had led them to believe that we were Japanese whalers.

We slammed into Atlantic City powerfully enough to gouge a canyon right through the continent, undeterred by the biplanes that kept buzzing us to ask for directions to the Empire State Building. No, the only real obstacle we faced was the Amish, who refused to let us pass through Lancaster County on the grounds that there were no supersonic transcontinental dimension-traveling Ferris Wheels in the Bible. So we had to whir in place while Mr. Jacobsen and his tremendous son Larry climbed down from their gondola to search the scriptures of this alternate world for the appropriate reference. The closest thing they found was a strange reference to miniature golf in Exodus. Apparently, on this world, the Red Sea was just a five-par hole with a windmill. The Amish elders said that this was not good enough. Mr. Jacobsen and his tremendous son Larry said that it damn well better be good enough, as we were a pissed-off amusement park ride and we were loaded for bear. Whereupon the Amish elders smiled their Amish smiles and slid open the front doors of their barns to reveal a battery of nuclear missiles. Turns out that these Amish were nonviolent folks willing to be aggressive about it.

There was no time to lose. Mr. Jacobsen and his tremendous son Larry leaped back on board the Ferris Wheel, so we could turn around and go the long way, around the world, where the only major problems we encountered were a communist revolution in Egypt, and a giant moth in Tokyo. When we found ourselves back in North America, and within spitting distance of Mount Rushmore, I got out and shooed away the mutant buffalo while Mr. Jacobsen's tremendous son Larry pumped up the gears, and we went straight up the back of the mountain, racing for the slingshot just as a commando unit made up of the National Guard and the Nuclear Amish and the Consortium of Japanese Whalers and the Relativity Police and the Egyptian Communist Party and the Rubber Band Researchers from the British Institute came climbing up over the giant Edgar Bergen head in a last desperate attempt to recapture us. In light of their superior firepower, we would have happily surrendered, but they had failed to reckon with the sheer weight of all those people, and with a tremendous crack the sculpture came loose, sliding straight down the mountain with all those paramilitary types hurriedly scrambling into Bergen's faulty-ventriloquist-wide-open-mouth to avoid being crushed into paste when the Head started to roll. The last we saw of it, it was disappearing over the horizon, and still gathering speed, presumably well on its way to getting lost in time and space just like us.

We discussed that for an hour or so before agreeing that it was ironic.

Anyway, to make a long story short, we snapped back into hyperspace and had some even stranger adventures but sooner or later returned to the fun park, where we all climbed down from our gondolas and looked innocent while the cops took names and my long-lost date Mary Sue came limping up the road saying Damn it, Joe, this happens every weekend. I said, I'm sorry, honey, I shouldn't have lied about my height, you throw the whole ride off if you're too short to reach the little white line.

She said, Why You.

And we walked off laughing uproariously, just as if somebody had said something funny, even though nobody had. And that was pretty much the end of that. At least, until we got on the Tilt-A-Whirl . . .

The Batman and Robin Murder Mystery — Solved!

*T*his is the official story, first told almost fifty years ago, and gullibly believed by the whole world ever since:

Dick Grayson was raised in the circus. His parents, John and Mary, were aerialists, training their son in the family business. Then tragedy struck. A hit man under the employ of "Boss" Zucco, the most powerful gangleader in Gotham City, sabotaged the ropes anchoring their trapeze. The ropes broke immediately after their successful triple somersault, and Dick Grayson saw his parents plunge to their deaths before his very eyes.

Shortly thereafter, Dick was confronted by a big guy in a bat suit. Instead of telling this rather strange person to go away and leave him alone in his misery, Dick begged him to help avenge his parents' deaths.

The Dark Knight assented.

And so billionaire Bruce Wayne adopted a youthful ward named Dick Grayson, and at the same time Batman took on a young partner named Robin.

Or so the story goes.

It's accurate enough, on the face of it. Certainly, Dick Grayson, who despite his natural enthusiasm for the work never became as brilliant a crime fighter as his elder partner, never once seemed to think that there was anything wrong with it. But if we examine the story closely, using only the evidence Batman creator Bob Kane provided us, then we're left with the inescapable conclusion that there was something awfully rotten going on in Stately Wayne Manor.

Don't jump to suggestions. I am not about to suggest, as child psychologist Fredric Wertham did during the 1950s, or as movie director Joel Schumacher implied during the 1990s, that Batman and Robin were homosexuals, either latent or practicing. That would have been their business, of course (at least, once the Boy Wonder reached the age of consent), but still, there's always been plenty of evidence to the contrary. Bruce Wayne and Dick Grayson both had girlfriends. Batman enjoyed a nice smoldering romance with a leather-clad beauty known as the Catwoman, and a quick dip into my comic book collection finds Dick Grayson enjoying healthy relationships with women as varied as Donna (Wonder Girl) Troy, Barbara (Batgirl) Gordon, and Princess Koriand'r (Starfire). If the caped crusaders sometimes went a little overboard with the "good work, old chum" routine, it's because they were unusual people to begin with, not because they were ready to move to Gotham's equivalent of Greenwich Village.

No. To Dick Grayson, at least, the relationship between Batman and Robin was exactly what it seemed. No more, no less.

More's the pity.

Because Dick never paused to question why an experienced crime fighter like Batman would take on a ten-year-old kid, even an accomplished gymnast like the youngest member of the Flying Graysons, as his partner.

Because the kid had just seen his parents killed, the same way Bruce Wayne had seen his own parents killed? Well, yeah . . . but by the time Batman met Dick he had already been fighting crime for several years, and he must have seen similar tragedies several times before. Why didn't Batman have an entire troupe of recently orphaned urchins fighting alongside him by that time? Is there any reason why he picked this kid in particular?

Yes, there is. And it changes everything you think you know about Batman.

Think about it. When Bruce Wayne was ten years old, he swore to spend the rest of his life warring on crime. When he was twentysomething he put on his bat suit and went at it in earnest.

What he did during those missing years has been only sketchily explored. That particular phase of Bruce Wayne's life is as much an enigma as the lost years of Jesus. What was he up to?

Hmmm. He studied criminology.

He learned the martial arts.

He exercised a lot.

We know all that.

What else did he do?

Well, he became a world-class trapeze artist, capable of swinging from building to building with the greatest of ease.

Now, that's interesting. Where does somebody go to learn an unusual skill like that? A correspondence school? The local community college? High school gym class?

Naaah.

You have to go to the pros. The ones who do it for a living.

Professional trapeze artists . . . at a circus.

Clearly, the young Bruce Wayne must have lived with a circus for a while. And since trapeze artistry isn't a skill you learn overnight, he must have had time to form a pretty close attachment with whoever taught him.

Pretty close? Maybe even extremely close. After all, obsessed avenger or not, Bruce Wayne was also going through puberty at the time.

And this was . . . when? About a decade before Batman first met the 10-year-old Robin?

Hmmm. A pattern is forming.

Take any picture of Bruce Wayne and Dick Grayson. The resemblance is there. They have the same chins and the same color hair. The resemblance existed even when Dick was a ten-year-old kid; it became downright spooky after the character aged and went from teen to young adult.

Looks like young Bruce did more than train.

Reconstruct the chronology. Bruce Wayne's parents are murdered. He vows to become the world's greatest crime fighter. He starts picking up the skills he needs. He joins the circus. Meets Dick Grayson's mother, who was probably also a young teenager at the time. And she teaches him how to swing, in more ways than one.

Then, driven by his obsessions, he goes off to complete his apprenticeship as a crime fighter . . . and three trimesters later, Dick Grayson is born.

Father and son never meet until Dick Grayson's parents — that is, his mother, and the man Dick only believes to be his father — are murdered by Boss Zucco. Then Bruce Wayne re-enters the picture, dressed like a giant bat, and takes his son home.

Only he never lets the kid know that he's his real father. He never adopts Dick Grayson; he just takes him on as a ward.

Didn't that ever bother you? The relationship looked rather permanent. Why wouldn't a smart guy like Bruce Wayne make it legal with an actual adoption?

Well, what's the difference between a ward and an adopted son? A ward can be incontestably cut out of a will. That would be more difficult in the case of a son, whether blood relation or adopted child. Dick Grayson never once worried about this — he must have been either incredibly trusting or incredibly apathetic about money. But the longer he remained a ward (while helping Bruce dodge bullets at night), the more suspicious this circumstance became. Why did Bruce Wayne want to hold such a powerful trump card against a partner he nightly entrusted with his life?

Because he was afraid that Dick would find out something.

Something that would shatter Dick Grayson's respect for Bruce Wayne, that would make him a dangerous enemy of Bruce Wayne.

What could it be?

Consider: When Dick Grayson's parents died, Batman showed up within minutes. Isn't that too big a coincidence to be believed?

I don't think so. Bruce Wayne twisted his entire life around because somebody had stolen his parents. How upset must he have been when he found out that somebody else had stolen his son?

Upset enough to kill two people and frame a known criminal for the deed?

Enough to sabotage the trapeze of the Flying Graysons, which was up near the top of the tent where most normal murderers could not be expected to go?

Enough to become the very kind of criminal he despised?

Dick Grayson was never the brilliant detective his mentor was. He never put the clues together. He just thought Bruce Wayne was his good chum, his crime-fighting partner, Batman. And so he spent his youth never once realizing that he was helping one of Gotham City's most twisted criminals quite literally get away with murder.

Woo-Woo Vengeance

*J*aney's dreams led us as far as a depressing little town named Colton — the kind of four-hundred population cesspit where all the stores are boarded, all the people are on government assistance, and all the out-of-town minorities are blamed. There weren't any jobs in Colton, but the Family had found some, as they always did: all three of them working together, as they always did; this time getting themselves hired as mechanics by a thriving service station on the interstate. The service station was now out of business, its windows shattered and covered with plywood. There were signs of a fire near the pumps. I was told that the owner found the place in ruins and immediately had a massive coronary. It fit the pattern. That was the Family's game. They were destroyers of both places and people.

Their rooming house wasn't hard to find: it was a three-family home in the closest thing Colton had to a wealthy neighborhood. It needed paint. I recognized The Family's old room from the street, by the black plastic garbage bags covering the only window not intact. I imagined what must have gone on behind that window — the insanity, the abuse, and the pain — and I immediately felt my face go rigid with anger.

Janey calmed me with a soft hand on the back of my wrist. I looked at her and she looked at me and without speaking a word we went through all the old arguments about the most productive uses of rage.

We left the car together, and went to ring the bell.

We made an odd pair. Traveling on my own, I tend to scare people. It's not that I'm tall or particularly muscular. I'm actually round-shoul-dered and double-chinned. But my face looks like hell: my forehead's lumpy and scarred, my nose has the bumpy look noses acquire only after they've been broken on a regular basis, and two of my front teeth are missing. Add to that a shaved head (a lifetime habit — hair gives other people something to grab in a fight), and you have the kind of looks respectable people wisely cross the street to avoid. Janey, on the other hand, is elfish and wan; she may be in her early twenties, but she looks like an unhappy, underfed teen. People have a way of wanting to protect her. Some imagine they have to protect her from me. Which is fine. It still makes them less afraid.

The landlady had the Katherine Hepburn thing that makes old ladies tremble constantly. But her eyes were sharp, and when she saw me and Janey together they immediately narrowed at the thought of such a terribly scarred brute traveling with such a helpless young girl. The coldness in her tone was directed at me: "Can I help you?"

"Hello," I said. It helped to have me speak first: I have a gentle, almost soprano voice nothing at all like the subhuman growl most people expect. It, too, throws people off. "My name's Jerome; this is my wife, Janey. We were directed to you by the people at the police station — they said you might be able to help us?"

Janey pulled the photograph from her pocket and showed it to the landlady, who studied it for all of two seconds before recognition hit. I could see it in the way her wrinkles bunched up at the corners of her eyes. The palsy in her hands increased noticeably before she managed to speak: "You know them?"

"Used to."

"They were animals," she said.

"I know."

She studied me then, and I think part of her saw in my eyes what I planned to do when I found them: because she smiled, and it was not a kind smile, or a joyful one. "Come in."

*W*hen Janey was twenty-three her husband got mad at her for turning down the volume on the TV. He expressed his displeasure by hitting her over the head with his beer bottle. It was a full bottle and it didn't break. Janey's skull did.

When I was twenty-eight my older brother got mad at me for accidentally kicking him out of bed. He expressed his displeasure by seizing the tip of my nose with a socket wrench. He had a good grip, and when he twisted his arm all the way around, my cartilage snapped like a dry twig. The pain was a lot like the time he made me stick my finger in a light socket: bright, electric, blinding, all-encompassing. I remember peering down at the stream of blood and thinking: that's not so bad, it's not so much, if it were all this minor I wouldn't even mind.

*I*t was a small house, but the living room didn't have enough furniture to accommodate it; there were two great empty spaces where the carpet was flattened down in the shape of a rectangle and a square. The square had been a console TV, the rectangle an upright piano. Two of the chairs on the dining room table were bound together by strapping tape: no doubt a recent repair, borne of the same catastrophe that had swallowed the TV and the piano. I didn't need Janey's visions to put a face on the source of the destruction.

Janey and I sat one the couch together while the landlady went to the kitchen to make tea. We'd told her we didn't need any tea. She went anyway, an indication that she might have been a fairly inoffensive old lady before the Family came along. When she came back, two out of the three coffee cups were fine aged porcelain, the other cheap and plastic. She took the plastic one and sat down in a rocking chair, sipping slowly to hide the palsied shake in her fingers. After a moment, she said: "I had service for twenty, you know. A wedding gift from my mother. That last day, they started brawling in the kitchen. I should have thrown them out before, but they were so violent . . . so insane . . ." She lowered her eyes. "Mr. Peterson was in his seventies. A retiree. Used to walk ten miles a day, then they knocked him down the stairs and now he needs a chair. Animals. Like it was a game for them. They started up a week after I rented them the room, and would have kept it up until there was nothing left to destroy."

"Why didn't you call the police?" asked Janey.

"Because by the time I knew what kind of people they were, I was too scared they'd kill me. They were insane. They were set off by anything and everything. I remember one time, we were all sitting at the downstairs table having supper when for some reason one took offense at something one of the others said, grabbed the pepper mill, and slammed it over the other's head hard enough to break it. The whole table was covered with blood. That was only two days before they . . ." She spilled coffee on her lap and didn't seem to notice. "They said they were brothers. I thought they were fags: the way they slept in the same bed and all. I don't think they were either."

"They're not homosexuals," I told her. "They've all had women. It's just not their number-one interest in life."

"What is?"

"Hurting each other."

She nodded. "They do love pain, don't they?"

"They don't love it, ma'am. But it's what they know best."

*J*aney and I were tired anyway, and the old lady looked like she could have used the money, so we took a room instead on heading on. It was an attic room, with a slope for a ceiling. The bed was lumpy and the wallpaper was a panorama of yellow ducks. It was heaven anyway. We were free and nobody was trying to hurt us.

It was late afternoon when we got settled in, so we lay in bed with the blinds open, letting the sunset slowly dim the lights for us. Janey spent much of that time tracing her delicate fingers along the scars, moving down from my face to my chest to my belly, taking inventory of the burns, the cuts, the badly healed places, and all the other tracks that the others had left behind. She sometimes liked to call me her tattooed man. It would have bothered me, but she had a few of her own: legacy of the guy who hit her with the bottle. She'd been married to him for four years. I once asked why she married the guy. She asked why I had to wait until I was thirty-seven before running away from my brothers.

Both questions had the same answer. It was an old riddle: why did the idiot beat himself with a hammer? Because he knew how good it would feel when he stopped.

Or, even more to the point: live with a torturer long enough and you learn to think it's normal.

My brothers and I slept in the same bed all our lives. We thought it was the way things were supposed to be. We thought we were supposed to fight each other all the time. The notch in my right ear comes from something my older brother did with a pair of scissors; the hairline scar over my right eye comes from something he did with a steam iron. My younger brother managed to leave for what must have been a fairly normal life, at least for a while. Me, I was so used to this particular brand of hell that I stayed. Don't ask me why; I've run into folks who knew me way back then and they say they thought I was retarded.

At least, I have some kind of excuse. It was all I'd ever known.

How do you explain the one in the middle? The one who wasn't actually related to us? The one my older brother brought in, to join our family? Who's stayed with him despite all the abuse, all the blows, all the hair-pulling and all the eye-gouging and all the painful improvisations with pliers and claw hammers? How do you explain all the others my older brother brought in, after I left? All those nameless, simpleminded men, with no past and no self-respect? Where did they come from? What can we posit about their lives, that they needed a family so bad they'd willingly accept daily beatings as the ticket in?

And finally, how do we explain Janey, who came to me that day in the hospital and whispered, "I know about your Family?" Who envisioned my entire life with them, and who now sees the life they live without me? How do you explain that? Where does that come from?

I didn't know. And maybe I didn't want to.

I just knew I wanted it to end.

*J*aney and I traced each other's scars by sight until the sun set and it got so dark that we had to trace them by touch. By then the tears had overtaken me, and I was lost in great racking sobs that were not quite enough to empty me of all the poison inside. Janey didn't try to cheer me up; but she took the tears in her mouth as if they were wine, and by midnight we were making love, with her straddling my hips, moaning, telling me again and again that it would be all right, that we would find them, that we would stop them, that we would end the blood and the pain.

It didn't stop the old nightmare from coming back:

It's my older brother. The one who wears his face in a perpetual scowl, incapable of forgiveness or charity of love: the one in charge of meting out the punishment for every possible infraction. He's smaller than me, but in dreams he looms like a mountain, filling the horizon, eclipsing the stars, swallowing everything that exists with the sheer unappeasable scale of his hate. He's mad at me. He's always mad at me. And though I cower beneath the force of his wrath, begging his forgiveness, telling him I'm sorry, assuring him that whatever I did to him this time was nothing more than an accident caused by an idiot, still he comes after me, and this time he carries a saw.

Acting with a quick, fluid economy of movement, too fast to counter, he places the cutting edge across the top of my head, and draws it back, opening me up. I hear a cartoonish sound-effect as he pumps it back and forth: voooba, voooba, voooba.

And he shouts: *You're not Jerome! You're not!*
You're what I made you!
You'll always be what I made you!
Vooba. Vooba. Vooba.
The chant of the saw as it's raked back and forth across my scalp.

*T*he landlady said they'd taken jobs in Bruton. It seemed a good lead. Bruton. As in Brute. The kind of name that would appeal to them. We set out early.

It had snowed hard during the night, covering the roads, but traffic had already compressed it into tightly-packed brown powder. Once or twice we stopped to help people stuck in ditches. I mean, actually help them. When I was with the family, we used to stop and help, too — but it was a nasty, malicious kind of helping, capable of putting people in the hospital. Today, when we stopped, nobody got terrorized, nobody got hurt. They got helped. It may have slowed us down, but that was a small price to pay for any step toward redemption.

Less than five miles from Bruton, Janey announced: "We'll have them today."

I glanced at her. "You think so?"

"I know so."

Another vision. She had them all the time. They never specified location, so we couldn't use them to track down my Family . . . but they did keep us apprised of the atrocities being committed along the way. "What did you see?"

"Something that happened two days ago. They were each dressing up for their dates with their fiancées."

The idea of my brother's family finding three women crazy enough to want to marry them was so ludicrous it was frightening. I said: "Did you see the women?"

"One woman. A con-artist or prostitute of some kind. She'd met them all separately, and seduced each one of them separately. She must have done it to get money from them. It was so pathetic, Jerome — the way they each tried to be gallant and charming when all they'd ever known was hatred and abuse. They came off like retarded children. But, don't ask me how, she honestly had no idea they knew each other . . . and she didn't expect all three of them to show up with engagement rings five minutes apart. She tried to hide them from each other, but it didn't last. The second they saw each other, they started smashing things over each other's heads."

I shuddered. "Did they kill her?"

"Do *you* think they killed her?"

"I don't know. But there's something about that whole story — I know it's horrible enough to be them, but somehow it doesn't sound like them. They spend all their time together, for God's sake. Dating women — not just once or twice, but seriously? Offering to marry them? Leaving each other alone long enough to allow room for such an impossible unlikely courtship? Staying out of each other's lives so completely that they didn't discover this one thoroughly ridiculous coincidence until it was almost too late? I mean, you may be the one with the visions — but you still don't know them like I do. And that doesn't sound like them at all."

She frowned. "Look at my back and tell me I don't know them. Look at my arms and tell me I don't know them. Take x-rays of my fucking legs and tell me I don't know them."

"Come on, that's not what I meant, and you know it —"

"The point is, that you don't have a monopoly on this sort of thing. I got it from my father, my uncle, my husband . . . every fucking man who ever touched me, before I met you. The only difference between what happened to me and what happened to you is that what happened to me wasn't supposed to be . . ." She caught herself on the precipice of something she didn't want to say, and bit it back, with a suddenness that seemed to swallow all the space between us. "I'm telling you it's what happened. And I'm also telling you we'll have them today. I just don't know what we're going to do once we do."

"You know I'll save you a piece. I always promised I would."

She bit the tip of her thumb. "That's not the problem. It never was."

"Then what is?"

It was a very long time before she answered, and when she did, she did not seem to be speaking to me, so much as some distant part of herself that needed to hear the words. "I just don't know why we do it, Jerome. I don't mean we as in you and me, but we as in everybody. The whole damned race. Bullfights, cockfights, rodeos. . . . bullies in the schoolyard, beating up the little kid and laughing when he cries . . . torturers laughing as they apply the electric current. . . . my husband, hurting me not because he was mad, but because he got pleasure from doing it . . . even your family, in ways you can't even appreciate . . . it's all the same thing. It's all pain as entertainment, the special charge we get from watching somebody else hurt. Why do we do it? Why are we so twisted that we need to see it?"

I had no answer to that.

I only knew that for the very first time in our life together, she did not seem overly enthused by the prospect of revenge.

*T*he landlady had told us they'd gotten jobs at a diner. All three of them: the same diner. That didn't bode well for the intelligence of the management: I couldn't imagine wanting my family to prepare food for public consumption. There was no telling what revolting ingredients they'd added, what terrible things they'd done with cooking implements. Once my older brother served me a sandwich liberally sprinkled with nuts and screws and ordered me to eat it. I did, and cracked a tooth just chewing the bread enough to swallow. The screws went down with no problem, but tore holes coming out. And that was just cooking for me: cooking for the public, my brother's entirely capable of using rat poison in the salad dressing. It didn't matter how many people got sick and died. The Family already had a body count from that time we opened a fake medical clinic.

We got off the exit to Bruton, and found the L & H Diner exactly where the landlady had said it was: one of those prefabricated metallic rectangles that I've always imagined a clumsy recreation of a railroad car. It was still standing, and showed no obvious signs of damage. I could see the people eating inside. Janey touched the back of my hand to stop the trembling. I couldn't face her; one of the reasons I loved her is that she didn't expect me to. After a moment my heart calmed to something resembling normalcy, and we went inside.

It looked like a clean, if fairly generic, place to eat: a half-dozen booths with Formica tables and wall-mounted jukeboxes. There was also a long counter with stools. The two men working the grill didn't look like paragons of intelligence, but they didn't have the telltale look of Family members either: for one thing, they both looked genuinely happy. The skinny red-haired one wiping down the counter had a smile that seemed to go all the way up to his ears; the fat mustached one sang an improvised la-de-da song while kneading flour in a bowl. Though the cooking area behind the counter was limited, and the two men had to work around each other, it didn't seem to inconvenience them any; they shared the space with a fluid economy of motion that amounted to near-telepathy. Like many small restaurateurs, they attempted to give their place a personality by dressing cute: in their case, by wearing ties and derbies. They were sincere enough to make it work. It was impossible not to like them at once; being the man I was, living the kind of life I had, I couldn't help wondering if they'd ever had the urge to hit each other with bottles.

Half the booths were empty, but Janey and I sat at the counter. The fat man relinquished his cookie dough and joined us, tipping his derby in greeting. "Goo-ood morning!" he sang, in a deep, aristocratic southern baritone. "Welcome to the L & H Diner, home of fine food and good times! Isn't it a be-yootiful day today?"

I glanced out the window at the slush-covered streets and soot-gray skies. "Uh . . . well, I guess."

"All a matter of perspective, friend, all a matter of perspective." Whereupon he chuckled and demonstrated an odd nervous tic that I'd never seen before: he grabbed his tie and twiddled it bashfully. "How may I help you fine people?"

His good mood vanished as soon as Janey showed him the photograph. It didn't descend all the way to rage, of the kind I'd known: just as far as slow-burning exasperation. "Now what on Earth" — (he pronounced it Oith) — "would you be looking for them for?"

"You know them, then?"

"Not the one on the end, but the other two. They were with a different guy."

The photo was only five weeks old. We'd liberated it from a police photographer in Oakland Park, where they'd demolished a hardware store; the man on the end had been new then, but we already knew he was among the dead, now. There were a lot of dead, now. The simple-minded drifters the Family kept recruiting to take my place survived only as long as it took my brother's rage to escalate into something fatal. He had to kill them, you see. They were compliant victims, but they weren't me.

It was another reason why I was only one who could end this. Why, when I ended it, I had to end it in blood.

I shuddered. "I heard they worked here."

"We fired them yesterday."

I suddenly felt a surge of respect for the fat man; the Family's antics are so intimidating that most places don't work up the nerve to dismiss them until it's too late. "What happened?"

"You police or something? Because if you're police, it's about time. Those guys belong in a cage."

"We're not police," I said, "but we are looking for them."

"You got a grudge?"

"Yes."

"Wonderful. You can have them. Look, we advertised for a night shift, so we could stay open twenty-four hours. We expected competent professionals, not crazies who spent the whole shift beating on each other. My associate and I took turns staying with them the first four nights, and in that time we saw more blood and sadism than we saw during our entire shared hitch in the foreign legion. This one over here, the mean one, he slapped the others around like it meant nothing. Punched them in the stomach, the nose, the back of the head. Even squirted hot mustard in their eyes. You ever get mustard in your eyes, mister? Even a little bit?"

I was intimately acquainted with the sensation; it had been one of my brother's favorite punishments. "Yes."

"Then you know it's blinding agony, and not the kind of thing you do to a person just for breaking a dish. But last night was the worst. It was my turn to watch them. The strange one, Joe I think his name is — I don't know what his story is, but he's both infantile and effeminate at the same time — accidentally spilled some soup on the mean one's apron. It was the kind of accident that could happen to anybody, that happens to Stanley and I a hundred times a week, but the mean one wasn't in any mood for forgiveness, so he grabbed Joe by the ear and twisted it so hard that Joe started crying, crying I tell you, crying Please, Please, I didn't mean it, I didn't mean it, I didn't mean it. All the customers were yelling too: stop it, stop it, leave him alone. But the mean one didn't listen, he just dragged Joe over there," indicating the stove, "and forced his face into the hot grill."

This was bad even for my older brother. And despite all she'd lived through, all I'd told her, the image was enough to make Janey gasp. She said: "Did he burn?"

"Burn!?" the fat man said. "Lady, he sizzled like static on a bad radio. A customer had to help me drag them away from the stove and keep them apart while Stanley over there called the cops — but by then the right side of Joe's face was a blackened, blistered mess. He'll probably be scarred for life, but he said it was his own fault and he wouldn't press charges. That was it for me. I told them to get out and not bother collecting their pay. Last thing I need is something like that going on around my place."

"And this was last night?" I pressed.

"A little after two a.m."

Janey and I glanced at each other, sharing the same thought. If we hadn't spent the night at the rooming house, we would have gotten here in time to see it happen. We might have been able to prevent it. We might have spared these people an ugly memory that would stay with them their entire lives. The realization was another chalk mark on a wide and teeming slate: one already so full that no normal justice would ever be able to settle the score.

But I wasn't interested in settling scores. I just wanted to turn over the board and end the game. "Where are they?"

"What, their address? You really *want* to find them?"

I could have lied: said that I was lawyer, here to deliver a bequest, or a process server, trying to hand over a subpoena. Or I could have told a half-truth: saying that I was a relative, trying to contact a long-lost branch of the family. I chose brutal honesty: "No. I want to kill them."

*I*t was, quite simply, a matter of revenge.

I hadn't seen my younger brother in over seventeen years. All that time, he hadn't written, hadn't called, hadn't tried to contact us in any way. He'd been as dead to us as we must have been to him — and through all the years of eye-gougings and ear-twistings and other petty little torments, we expunged all memory of his existence, behaving as if he'd never been. I never knew what he did all that time — whether he was rich or poor, mad or sane, happy or miserable, loved or despised. All I knew is that I envied him. He'd done what I thought I'd never have the courage to do; he'd walked out, and escaped, leaving the Family and its sickness behind. Wherever he was, whatever he was doing, he would always be, for me, the one reason to believe that my existence did not have to be like this: that when all was said and done there might have been a better life waiting for me somewhere else.

When I was thirty-seven I collapsed in an Unemployment Line. I'd been having blackouts for several weeks. My older brother had recently seen fit to punish me by squeezing my head in a vise. The doctors said that I'd suffered some brain damage, and that if I hadn't gone to the hospital I would have died. By the time I got them to believe what had happened to me, the Family had already left town; I went to a state mental hospital, where I was slowly and painfully taught the knowledge that everything my Family had ever done to me was wrong.

It took a couple of years to accomplish that: another couple of years before I was able to handle the hideous burden of rage that now clung to me wherever I walked. But I eventually decided that revenge was a sickness too. I didn't need to go after the Family; I could just let them go. I could abandon them to their sickness and embrace the rest of my life as an opportunity to re-invent myself as the kind of man I always could have been.

Then came Janey — mad, beautiful, Janey, with her own lattice of scars and her own lifetime of pain. She came into my ward late at night to whisper things that only a true member of the Family could have known. She knew about the tricks my brother played with his fingers, of our times in prison and in Mexico, of Larry's half-hearted attempts to protect me, of all the pain and wreckage we'd left behind us. She knew it, she said, because she'd been watching us her entire life. She knew it because she felt our pain in a way nobody else could. And she knew something else, too: that younger brother Shemp hadn't escaped after all. Because he was back with the Family. The second I left, they'd tracked him down and drawn him back in. Because they needed to be Three. They always needed to be Three.

I needed to get Shemp out of there.

I needed to save him.

But before I could even start to look, Janey whispered to me that it was too late.

Moe and Larry had already killed him.

*J*aney was right about most things, and this was one of them: the closer I got, the easier they were to smell. The red brick building where they lived was redolent of them. It was just a four-story tenement, identical in every way to the tenements on either side, but one that radiated the evil of my family with an intensity that we could feel from the car. Maybe we just imagined it. Maybe, if we didn't know they were there, we might have driven past the building without noticing a thing. But I think not. Because all buildings have faces, made from the placement of windows and doors, and when I looked at that building I saw Moe. It even had his bangs: an arrangement of black brick, up near the roof.

Mr. Hardy at the diner had sent us to the building; it was the landlord, a Mr. Sidney Fields, who told us they lived on the fourth floor. A one-bedroom, naturally. They still slept on the same mattress, cuddling like lovers, snoring in unison while the wounds they'd inflicted that very day still festered on their skin. Fields was already in mortal fear of the kind of men he'd innocently allowed into his building, and he was more than willing to give Janey the key. That's the thing about the Family: they certainly inspired the wrong kind of loyalty in others.

We went back to the car, to outfit ourselves. I loaded the Magnum. Janey regarded me soberly as I slipped on the raincoat, and said what was probably the last thing I ever would have expected from her: "We don't have to do this. I know it's what you think we both want . . . but if you don't think you're up for this, then it's okay with me if we leave. We'll stop them another way."

I gaped at her, unable to believe what I was hearing. But she was serious. If anything, she was pleading. Her tough, hard, go-to-hell features had softened, becoming the frightened mask of a woman ruled by dread. "What's wrong? Are you scared of being hurt?"

"No. That, I'm used to."

"Then what?"

"I'm scared of what you're going to find out."

I thought of all the cruelty, and all the fear, and all the crimes, and all the blood: of things so awful that the mere force of their memory would have reduced a weaker man to a smoking ruin — all of them the kind of things that Janey had herself experienced at the hands of those who'd tortured her. I'd never allowed myself to believe my life at all worse than hers: had never allowed myself to believe it, for believing that would have turned us into competitors in a contest where the only prizes were agony and blood. But now, as I looked in her eyes, I saw that I'd been wrong: for it had always been a contest, and she'd been playing it like a champion since the very first day. "It's your visions," I said, sickly. "You've found out something."

She couldn't look at me. "Not quite."

"What then?"

"It's not something I've found out. It's something I've always known. Something I should have told you about your family a long time ago."

My spine turned cold. "What?"

"It was a mistake. I shouldn't have brought you here. I shouldn't have made you want this so much. When you find out—"

I seized her by both shoulders. "What!? What will I find out!?"

But even as the rage and frustration possessed me, transforming me, turning me into a thing like my brother, making me a beast who wanted only to hurt and humiliate and kill, making her seem less the woman I loved and more the target for everything I'd ever wanted to hate and torment and abuse, she disappeared. I mean that literally. She vanished. She became just a creature of vapor, curling between my fingers, escaping from the cage that I'd made of my grasping arms. She stung my eyes and choked my lungs and streaked my skin with soot . . . and when I fled the car to avoid asphyxiation, she simply dissipated like any other smoke, fleeing me from every direction at once.

I could have mourned her. I could have knelt and wept.

But we'd traveled too many miles together, just getting here . . . and in all the world there was only place I knew I could look for answers.

So I faced the tenement with my brother's face and, knowing myself not a man but a marionette tangled in his own strings, marched toward my final confrontation with my Family.

*M*y first direct glimpse of Joe was through the living room window. He was a pudgy middle-aged man with big round eyes and big plump cheeks, one of which was still bandaged from last night's violent incident at the L & H Diner. I wasn't surprised by the fat, because I'm fat, and just about everybody Moe's ever gotten to take my place has also been fat. But it was a different kind of fat. What I have is backed with muscle; Joe was baby-fat, of the sort that comes from never emotionally maturing past page three. He had the kind of features that just naturally tend to childish petulance. My older brother Moe had accentuated this tendency by dressing him in an oversized Little Lord Fauntleroy suit, complete with short pants, ribboned straw hat, and oversized lollypop. He even sat in a high chair specifically built for a man his size, eating mush with a spoon. As I watched, Joe babyishly peeled back the spoon and catapulted a wad of the stuff against the wall, where it stuck.

Larry sat on the couch, reading the paper. He wore a scowl, of the kind that unconsciously imitated my brother Moe's: the kind that hated the world and everybody in it. He was getting old, the lines of his face puffier and more defined by flab — but he still had that vulturelike nose and that wildly-unkempt horseshoe-pattern baldness. A cigarette in his right hand was millimeters from burning all the way down to his fingers. Carelessness, or self-abuse? I didn't know, and didn't care. He may have stuck up for me, once upon a time, but he was still part of the problem.

Then my older brother walked in.

Moe. The destroyer. The true face of hate.

The man who for more years than I could count had assaulted me with pliers and hammers and mallets and broken bottles.

The man who just happened to be standing in the path of the latest wad of mush Baby Joe flung against the wall.

It hit Moe square in the face, the impact flattening it into a mask which hid his eyes, his nose, his mouth, everything but his soup-bowl haircut and the anger inherent in his suddenly frozen posture. It was all part of the ritual, one I'd lived through many times. Without provocations like that, Moe couldn't get mad; without Moe getting mad, he couldn't dole out the punishments; without Moe doling out the punishments, the social structure of our little Family couldn't be reinforced again and again and again, like the lines to a play we were all obliged to learn. I didn't even have to stick around to know what would happen next: in a second, Joe would start babbling with dread of the consequences of what he'd just done; Moe would slowly and deliberately peel the malodorous goo from his eyes and for just the briefest moment pretend that he wasn't mad, that he was if anything amused, and that this was the kind of unfortunate accident that could easily happen to anybody.

Even though all three of them knew that within thirty seconds he'd be avenging himself on Joe's eyes.

I didn't wait for it to happen.

I shot in the window first.

The blast was an explosion that almost flung me backwards off the fire escape, and the shattered glass preceded it in a wave. The arms of the high chair shielded Baby Joe from much of it, but shrapnel still peppered his arms, his legs, and his face. He gave out a long atonal cry, best transliterated as "Aaaah-aaah-aaah-aaah!", and twisted so violently that the high chair fell backward, taking him with it. Larry shot to his feet in a flurry of tossed newspaper pages and whirled in my direction, his thin lipless mouth locked in a grimace I knew well.

I hurried through the window so hastily that I sliced my hand open on the broken glass still remaining in the frame. Baby Joe's high-chair had already hit the floor, hard enough for the wood to come part in a miniature explosion of prefabricated parts. The loose newspaper pages fluttered about Larry like newsprint butterflies. Larry also said, "Aaaah-aaah-aaah-aaah!" when he saw the shotgun, but it was a more knowledgeable cry than Joe's: this "Aaaah-aaah-aaah-aaah!" was informed by the awareness that for the very first time in a life punctuated by fleeting moments of pain, he was finally faced with something that reeked of finality.

I almost didn't kill him. After all, he was the middle one. The one who'd always tried to protect me, and paid by taking the brunt of Moe's rages.

But if I let him live he'd try to protect Moe.

The blast made a hole in his stomach the size of a watermelon. It also sent him tumbling backwards over the couch. He somersaulted once, twice, three times, finally coming to rest in the corner, where momentum left him standing on his head and facing the wall. Typical Larry: he even died in shtick.

I scanned the room. Joe was on his belly in the kitchen, struggling with the wreckage of the high chair as he tried to get to his feet. I didn't want to deal with him while dealing with Moe, so I just blasted the light fixture over his head. It was a miniature chandelier, and when the cord snapped in two the metal grillwork plummeted like a miniature bomb.

The sound it made when it impacted his skull was a lot like a sledge-hammer striking an anvil. His head lolled while emitting cuckoo noises.

All of which took place in less than three seconds.

More than enough time for Moe to wipe the mush from his eyes and attack.

But he didn't attack: at least not right away. Instead he stood where he'd been when the mush got him, staring with open-jawed disbelief at the carnage I'd wrought upon his little home. He had never been capable of love, as I understood it, but he had always prized his own special kind of stability; it had to gall him to suddenly find himself in a room reeking of cordite, surrounded by suffering and devastation that he had done nothing to cause. It shocked him so much that he hadn't even gotten around to looking at my face yet — which meant that I had the very great pleasure of seeing his eyes when he finally registered who I was.

He had probably never expected to see me again.

"Curly," he whispered. And then, savagely: "Why, you—"

I fired again. He ducked beneath the blast and came up right on top of me, batting the Magnum to the ground with no difficulty at all. His first blow caught me in the belly; the second shattered the wreckage he'd made of my nose so long ago. I staggered back, caught by his fury. Through a haze I saw him form his fingers into a V that once meant victory and then meant peace but in his case meant only an attempt to go for my eyes. It was his favorite trick, and one of his most painful.

I seized the two fingers as they came in and corkscrewed them one half a turn to the left, instantly breaking them both. His shriek was uncannily high-pitched, like a woman's. I rammed my forehead into his and drove him back, giving me the most fleeting instant to note something terribly wrong about the blood now jetting from his nose — the way it flowed gray instead of red. Then he hammered me over the head with the phone, shattering it and driving me to my knees in agony.

"I'm gonna moidalize you, you numbskull!" he threatened.

"Not really," I told him. Because he really had done me a favor, knocking me to the floor that way. The floor, after all, was where the Magnum was.

I blew him away at point-blank range. The impact sent him flying backward, into the closed apartment door, which shattered into splinters the instant he struck it. I remained on my knees where I was, keeping my sights on him in the event he rose from the dead and came after me again. It didn't seem like a crazy thought at the time. After all, don't monsters do that sort of thing?

A little fat man appeared in the doorway. He was short and squat and baby-faced and everything my brother had ever looked for when recruit-ing Family members, but he seemed genuinely repelled by the carnage

before him, which no Family member would ever be. It seemed significant, too, that he wore a jaunty little derby, just like the proprietors of
the diner — for some reason it marked him as a native to the world
outside this room, and right now anything outside this room was fine
by me. When I met his eyes his natural inclination to cry for help was
utterly defeated by his total inability to speak. "Abbott," he whispered.
". . . Abbott. . . !"

Whoever Abbott was, I sure as hell didn't want to meet him. "Get
out."

The little fat man got.

I fell to my knees, exhausted, the room turning grey and cold all
around me, with none of the answers I'd sought anywhere in sight.
Distantly, I wondered if this was all my life had lived up to: if I'd ever
have anything to look forward to, beyond the fleeting pleasures of
revenge and the emptiness that came from not having the slightest idea
just what I was expected to do next.

I felt something happening before I saw it. It felt a lot like the air
after a lightning strike: all supercharged with potential, making the flesh
tingle at the back of my neck. Then I spotted the mist that had been
Janey, tooling around the antique black-and-white TV, entering it, making it sputter like a biplane struggling to stay aloft. The screen went
from pure black to pure white, then back to black again.

For an instance, the awfulness of what awaited me sat prefigured in
the form of a single white dot, glowing in the center of the picture tube.
It was a speck of brilliance no larger than a lower-case o, and it frightened
me beyond all measure, because it contained everything I was, and
everything I ever would be.

Then the picture came on, for real, and for the first time in my life
I understood what I was and why my life had been the way it was.

*Y*ou ever have an annoying little tune that plays in your head all your
time? That won't go away no matter how you try? That would be
tolerable if you only knew where it came from, and why it's significant?
But which remains an unknown composition by an unknown author,
even as you continue hearing it in every quiet moment of your life?

I used to have a tune like that. Never could figure out where I knew
it from.

Until I heard it now.

We open with three faces: mine, Moe's, and Larry's, lined up side by
side, and singing a reasonably competent harmony made up of Hellos.
Moe sings it first: "Hello . . ." Then Larry, in a higher register:
"Hello. . . ." Then myself: ". . . Hello . . ."

All three of us wave. "Hello."

Then the tune: a cuckoo song I have heard an infinite number of times.

It is my life, in all its harsh simplicity. The family Moe ruled and abused, this time running amuck on a posh country estate. We fill the basement with water, destroy the bathroom, make wreckage of an elegant dinner party, act like idiots, and in between moments of totally socio-pathic lunacy find newer and more inventive ways to put each other through intense physical pain. I feel every slap and punch as it happens: I see my own doglike, simple-minded responses to every fresh indignity, and the way my sick, conditioned behavior, seen from outside, makes me seem not pathetic and abused, but comic. Clownlike.

I think of Janey's words, cut off in mid-sentence: "The only difference between what happened to me and what happened to you is that what happened to you was supposed to be . . ."

I filled in the blank. *Funny.*

What happened to me was supposed to be *funny.*

The terrible, stunted existence: the gouged eyes, the flames burning on the seat of my pants, the hot iron pressed against my face, the sensation of being dragged around the room by my ears, the daily humiliation of being slapped and beaten and demeaned and scarred and degraded: the realization, after all that time, that I'd been trained to run roughshod over the world, with an infant's sense of consequences . . .

Funny.

It was all supposed to be *funny.*

On the screen, I flee a mob of police officers, crying out "Woo-woo-woo-woo-woo!" Cuckoo-clock music plays in the background, ending the day's carnage with a lighthearted, musical reminder that none of what we've just seen matters at all.

Janey's voice: *It's all pain as entertainment, the special charge we get from watching other people hurt.*

Even your family, in ways you can't even appreciate.

We were supposed to be *funny.*

The Janey-mist passes over the TV set, and the picture changes.

Now I see Janey, lying on a gurney in a hospital corridor. She is wearing a green t-shirt that has in places turned shiny and black from her wounds. Her eyes are swollen shut, her nose is bent and twisted. Her hair is matted and in places plastered to her forehead. She is barely recognizable as human, let alone as the woman I'd imagined an equal partner in the world of pain. She opens her mouth to say something, and I see that the gums where her front teeth should be are raw and scarlet.

Nobody could possibly think her funny at all.

It is a busy shift in the emergency room. There are gunshot wounds and car crash survivors. Mothers sit in rows, clutching their babies. Whoever was supposed to help Janey has wheeled her gurney to this spot in the waiting room, and run off to attend some more pressing emergency, leaving Janey, for the moment, forgotten. There is a TV mounted on a wall about twenty feet away. It is meant to pacify the people in the waiting room while they endure the occasionally long delays. It is on twenty-four hours a day, with the sound down low, and most of the time, nobody pays it any real attention at all. There is no reason to watch. They are all too involved with their own ailments.

Janey has been left to stare at it. She cannot turn her head, she cannot completely close her eyes. The combination of her concussion and her pain medication have left her in a foglike dream, where thought is far away and any input, no matter how trivial, is magnified to universal scope.

The set tuned to an all-day festival of our comedy shorts.

The harmony, once again: "Hello . . ."

"Hello . . ."

"Hello . . ."

Followed by the three of us in unison: "Hello."

She knows who we are, of course. She's not stupid. One cannot live in America, in the twentieth century, without knowing who we are. But that's quite different from actually liking us. She doesn't like us. We've never been her kind of guilty pleasure. She's always considered us gross, infantile, obnoxious and obvious: a guy thing. Harmless. But now, lying in this place, in this state, at this time, having been put here for finally getting fed up in a home where the least of the rights denied her was the right to get mad, she drinks in our jocular sadism toward each other and she thinks of the same things done to her and she begins to drown in a rising miasma of hate.

IT'S NOT FUNNY. IT'S NOT.

IT'S NOT IT'S NOT IT'S NOT

The blood clot in her brain breaks loose, sending her to the one place where she's capable of proving it.

*D*espite the little fat man walking in on my murder scene, no police ever showed up to arrest me. In a real world, they would have long ago arrested my Family too. In a real world, you don't destroy gas stations and rooming houses and blithely get away with it. In a real world, people like that old woman, and the proprietors of the L & H Diner, wouldn't have so sweetly cooperated with my mission of vengeance. In a real world, the streets outside would have been alive with sirens, and screams, and gathering onlookers: in a real world, I'd be hearing the thumping of feet in the hallway outside. In a real world, everything I'd lived through and everything I'd just done to exorcise it would have mattered. In a real world, I wouldn't be a Stooge.

After a while I got tired of waiting. I stood up, left the apartment, and descended the main stairs. I didn't encounter any of the other tenants along the way, and I didn't see any pedestrians or, I suppose, extras, as I walked right out the front door and onto the street. Somehow I knew that I never would. I could walk halfway around this world and never encounter another human being again. They were all gone, their scripts completed, their parts played.

Except for Janey. She waited in the passenger seat of the car, her skin pale, her hair limp, her eyes averted and afraid. She looked uncommonly real next to everything else around us, and I was not ashamed to realize that she always had.

I considered not going to her just long enough to realize that I didn't exactly have a wealth of other options, then opened the driver's side door, and got in.

I don't even want to guess how long we sat there before she spoke. It was an eternity of silence, with neither one of us willing to acknowledge the other. We may have spent days locked in stasis like that. Or years, or maybe just minutes after all. All that mattered is that we were two figures defined by the empty space between us — and that all of a sudden, tracking down and murdering my Family seemed like a very small thing next to sitting here, in this place, waiting to hear whatever she still had left to say.

When she finally spoke, she didn't take her eyes off her hands. "I used to hate you," she said. "When I found you, you were just like you were in the movies: all silly shtick and sound effects, nyuk-nyuk-nyuk and woo-woo-woo. You probably don't even remember half the things you said and did. It didn't even matter to me, because I knew you weren't real. You were just something happening in my head as I died. But the more time I spent with you, the more I put into you, the more you changed, the more you grew up, the more you became something else. You invented a past for yourself, a personality greater than what you were. Please believe me when I say it's different now. Please believe me when I say I want you to forgive me."

Forgive her? There was very little I could say to that: in this world we inhabited, she was the only God, and I the only subject. I might as well forgive the lightning, or the night. Maybe I'd be able to love her again. Maybe she could take us to someplace better, like a western, or a musical. Or maybe this empty, depopulated place was all we'd ever have, now that our business here was done.

But at that moment, I was only sure of two things . . .

. . . one, that this whole nightmare had started because her asshole abusive husband had hit her over the head with the bottle, for daring to turn down the volume on his TV . . .

. . . and, two, that I was scared to death I knew who he'd been watching.

The Guy Who Could Make These, Like, Really Amazing Armpit Noises, and Why He Was Contemplating Hippopotami at the Top of Mount Everest

*O*nce upon a time there was a little boy whose name was Bryce. That was his first major problem. It was spelled Bryce, but pronounced Bruce. There's a big long explanation for that, but let's not waste our time with it. Suffice it to say that he'd have enough problems in his life without also having that to worry about.

Bryce would never have any real friends, because he wasn't any good at talking to people. Placed in the center of a large crowd where he wasn't allowed to display his talent, he just fumfuhed helplessly like an actor caught on stage without a script. When he did manage to talk, his sentences were aimless, rambling discourses that started out over (Here) and ended up over (There), with neither place very relevant, and no apparent connecting path between them. In retrospect, he might have been happier if he'd been born into a family of similarly inarticulate people in whose company he could have shared long hours of wholly pointless conversation. But the world doesn't always work that way, and no doubt the child born into that family turned out to be a brilliant bon vivant whose piercing witticisms about the great issues of his time sunk without a trace in an ocean of aimless banalities about weather and wallpaper.

Bryce, on the other hand, was born to a family of savants. His father was a world-renowned scholar who had contributed vast tracts of erudition to various encyclopedias; his mother was a PBS talk show host whose repartee was so urbane it had been several years since her producers had bothered to book any guests for her to interview. His older sister was a violin prodigy who wrote award-winning sonnets between copping gold medals at decathlons. His younger brother was a ballet dancer and world-renowned oil painter who was the only kindergartener ever to write a six-part newspaper series exposing widespread corruption in local government. His aunts, uncles, grandparents, and cousins were all equally accomplished in endeavors ranging from paleontology to Shakespearean acting. When the family got together on holidays, quotable epigrams filled the air like intellectual shrapnel, and poor Bryce, who in all his eight years of life hadn't even managed to wheedle a gold star from the teacher, sat in his appointed chair feeling the same bottomless sense of predestined inadequacy that the Captain of the *Californian* must have felt in April 1912, when he woke up from a deep sleep to discover that his strict orders not to be disturbed had been followed even as another ship called the *Titanic* sank on the horizon while his faithful crew watched in cowlike apathy.

What made it worse for Bryce, somehow, was the knowledge that his family didn't scorn him or look down on him or consider him a black sheep. No. What they did was much, much worse — with the exception of what would eventually be done to him by a very nasty lady named Nancy Peabody, absolutely the cruelest act anybody could have committed against him. They showed faith in him. They knew he was just a late bloomer, whose arena of excellence had yet to be discovered. In that conviction, as we shall see, they were absolutely right. They had to be. They were the kind of annoying people who were never wrong about anything, even the things they're wrong about. But to Bryce, who had to endure it, their inflated expectations were like a hammer slamming down on the top of his forehead sixty times a minute, sixty minutes an hour, twenty-four hours a day.

Family Entertainment Hour was by far the worst time of the day for him. That was when family members were required to display the accomplishments of the day. His father would recite Hamlet's soliloquy in the latest of his many languages; his mother would walk blindfolded across a bed of red-hot coals; his brother would do a spectacular interpretive dance about the burning of the great Library of Alexandria; his sister would demonstrate the power of mind over lung capacity by sustaining a single uninterrupted high note for twenty-seven minutes. And then their noble, Greek-sculpture faces would swivel as one to focus on Bryce, who would gape at them with the look of a rabbit caught in the onrushing headlights. And they'd all smile reassuringly and say that's all right, Bryce, we know you'll come up with something doubly tremendous tomorrow. And he'd twitch and knock over a water glass and say, yuh yuh yuh yes you're ruh ruh right thuh thuh there's always tuh tomorrow, knowing in the most hidden caverns of his soul that the next night would see him offering another zip nada bufu goose egg twitching failure nothing.

So. It went on this way for many years. And it might have continued going on this way for many more.

But it didn't.

And the reason it didn't was that his father found himself bombarded from all sides with embarrassing questions about the activities of his mysteriously silent son. Its expectations spoiled by the endless parade of impossibly talented people produced by this one small gene pool, the world was absolutely convinced that this one lonely child, who barely knew enough not to eat soup with a fork and had never once in his life come up with a Scrabble word longer than three letters, harbored a gift so tremendous in its potential that it would one day change the course of history. As it happened, the consensus was absolutely right about that, but at the time Bryce's father was sure he'd have to tell the consensus it was wrong. And so it happened that one day, Bryce's father panicked. He did something cruel and petty and small-minded and utterly unworthy of him. He did not act supportively when Bryce abstained from Family Entertainment Hour. Instead, he slapped the table with the flat of his hand and said damn it, kid, if you don't stand up and do something absolutely spectacular right now then you can go pack your bags, because as sure as my recently completed Unified Field Theory you're no son of mine.

Even as Bryce's father blanched, unwilling to believe his perfect lips had uttered such a horrible thing, the rest of the family gasped in unison. And if that surprises you, dear reader, please be clear on this: they were not bad people. They were kind people, good people, virtuous people, whose unbearable cruelty lay in also being Perfect People in the presence of a Severely Limited One. But in that fateful moment, they each understood the special hell they'd put him through by persisting in writing operas and discovering elements and curing diseases. And they each resolved that as long as Bryce's talent remained undiscovered they'd atone for their insensitivity by deliberately being even less special than he was. They'd chew with their mouths open, sing out of key, garble the punch lines of jokes, forget the names of their congressmen, dress in horribly mismatched clothing, make dumb bigoted statements about people in faraway countries, and, insofar as it was possible to do so without causing permanent crippling damage to themselves, trip over their own clumsy feet and fall down the stairs at least three times a day. They each swore this secretly, but unknowingly in perfect agreement with all the others. And almost as soon as they made this oath to themselves they realized the full implications of that promise, and gasped in unison again, because, as the paragons they were, they were incapable of sullying their incandescent perfection by breaking heartfelt vows. The enormity of the task they'd set for themselves, the cruelty of the hell to which they were therefore condemned, loomed above them like a mother Tyrannosaur confronting the early mammals intent on pilfering its eggs. All at once they saw the hunger in its beady reptilian eyes, smelt the blood on its cold carnivorous breath, saw the sun blotted out as it bent forward to swallow everything that was special about them, and they each felt themselves start to go mad.

It was a busy moment. But what happened in the moment after that would turn out to be even more apocalyptic.

Bryce stood up and performed the only trick he knew. He put his right hand under his left armpit and pumped his left arm downward, making a blaaat noise.

It was not extremely impressive.

But Bryce's family, desperate to seize any excuse that would free them from their unspoken vow, acted like he'd just parted the Red Sea. They acted like shafts of blinding light had just burst forth and bathed them all in the radiance of the Divine. They acted like castaways adrift for thirty-seven days with nothing but a single saltine cracker between them, who in the last desperate throes of their starvation, had spotted a floating buffet table piled high with beer and cold cuts. They shrieked and whooped and hugged each other and went on at great length extolling the majesty of the miracle they'd just been honored beyond all bounds to witness.

Admittedly, this was laying it on a bit thick. After all, as far as they knew at that moment, Bryce's little talent was just that: a little talent, with absolutely no real potential for charting the destiny of Mankind. But, technically speaking, it was a talent, which was enough to rescue them from their mutual unspoken vow and thus prevent them from spending the rest of their lives mispronouncing words and eating beans directly from the can. Hence their jubilation. They had no way of knowing that their reaction was entirely appropriate: that his potential, based on this one mundane ability, actually was somewhere in the neighborhood of infinite. And that's pretty much a good thing, since had they suspected as much, at this particular moment, when they were celebrating their own narrow escape from mediocrity, they would have all gone stark raving wack-a-ding-hoy and been confined to mental institutions where the only symphonies they'd ever get to compose would have to be written in crayon on construction paper.

From that night on, Family Entertainment Hour developed an bizarrely anticlimactic rhythm. Because from that night on, the prodigious feats of cold fusion or lion taming contributed by the family members on hand were always followed, and in some inexplicable way upstaged, by the blaat noise from Bryce's armpit. And Bryce started to change. Oh, not in every way: for one thing, he never really learned to speak an interesting sentence. The only subject he'd ever be able to discuss with any minimal degree of expertise was the unique acoustical capabilities of the armpit. And even that would never help him socially, since even his insights in that area were so highly technical that there weren't five people on the face of the planet intelligent enough to understand that he was talking real world physics and not just babbling like a complete moron. No, let's be clear about this. Bryce was never to become the life of the party. The changes in him were purely internal, based on the sudden epiphany that greatness lay not in the grandeur of the talent but in the steadfast dedication with which it was applied. And so he began to explore the possibilities open to him. Short, saucy blaats. Deep, rumbling blaats. Blaats that whistled daintily for the first few notes and then sank like a stone into the lower registers for the big windup. Blaats that carried tunes. Blaats that sang harmonies with themselves. Blaats that carried the cold chill of command. Blaats that reverberated like the beat of a bass drum. Blaats that sounded like the voice of God. And more. He became an expert, and then a master, and then a wizard, blazing bold trails into realms undreamt of by any who had wandered this gaseous way before him.

A year passed, as years have a habit of doing. And at the end of the year, Bryce stood up at the end of Family Entertainment Hour, feeling tall and confident despite the rosily condescending expressions on the faces of his kinfolk. He said, "I have something to show you," and everybody smiled, secure in the knowledge that Bryce would repeat the same childish trick he'd been performing every single day for the past year.

He started playing.

Their jaws dropped, and the blood drained from their faces.

It was the first few bars of Beethoven's glorious Fifth — music they knew well, from performing it in the award-winning family orchestra. But had the muses themselves descended from the heavens to play the music on enchanted instruments made of stardust, and had the world stopped spinning to avoid making any distracting background noise, and had the conductor been a godlike entity capable of wresting great music from the sound of shattering glass, then perhaps there *might* have been a few scattered moments in that once-in-an-eon performance that would not have been wholly embarrassing when judged against what Bryce was doing today. Bryce was playing not just the exquisite music that Beethoven had written — he was playing the version that even mad old Ludwig himself had not been good enough to fully get down on paper. He was playing the music that was rendered impossible when the Big Bang both blew up God's instruments and utterly ruined Creation's acoustics. He was playing it Flawlessly. And he was doing it with armpit noises.

When he finished his performance, it was several seconds before anybody found the strength to move.

Bryce's Dad was the first to recover. It took him an inordinately long time to cross the room. He had to support himself by leaning on every thunderstruck relative along the way. But eventually he stood before Bryce and, in a voice choking with pride, said, I'm sorry, Bryce. But I'm going to have to forbid you from ever doing that again.

Bryce asked why.

Look at me, said Bryce's Dad.

Which was very confusing to Bryce, because as far as he was concerned, he was already looking at his Dad. Of course, his Dad was a much more intelligent person than he was. If his Dad thought Bryce was not looking at him, then there was obviously some special meaning to the phrase looking at that Bryce had not yet learned. So Bryce looked again. He looked at the freshly haggard look on his Dad's face and at the way all the blood had drained from his Dad's skin and at the way his Dad's jet-black hair was suddenly all white and then he looked past his Dad at all the Aunts and Uncles and siblings seated up and down the length of the table and he saw the way they all looked like they'd aged twenty or thirty years and the way they all seemed to be pale broken shells of their former magnificent selves and he heard his Dad sobbing that the music had just been too damn beautiful for human beings to survive and that if Bryce was ever permitted to actually perform in public, among folks any less resilient than this one superhuman family, it would probably result in the toppling of empires, the deaths of millions, and the end of civilization.

Bryce tried to bargain. He said what if I don't play quite as well next time? What if next time I make the music, while still good, definitely several orders of magnitude less great than it was today? I can do that. Definitely! And his Dad said, Yes, I know you can, Bruce, but I also understand the way genius works, and I know that you won't be able to keep that promise forever, and I'm sorry, my darling boy, but you're going to have to make a choice here, that choice being whether you're going to irresponsibly risk such a horrible cataclysm or whether you're going to continue being my son.

And that night, Bryce ran away from home.

He was nine years old, and he would never, ever see his family again. Nor would they ever make any attempt to find him. It wasn't that he hated his father for forcing him to make this choice. But he was his father's son, and he couldn't abide anything that forced him to be even one nanometer less great than the universe intended him to be. And don't condemn his family either. They could have done what their consciences were telling them to do, which was put Bryce in a strait-jacket, keep him prisoner in a hidden room 10,000 feet below sea level, and tell the world that Bryce had died in a trans-dimensional flux experiment. Instead, they let him go. Because they understood destiny better than anybody else on the planet. They just weren't large enough to be part of it.

The rest of Bryce's childhood was heartbreakingly difficult. One could fill an entire series of books with just his adventures wandering the land homeless and alone. Among those that come to mind are his argument with the girl who saw orchestras in rainbows, his narrow escape from a creature who called himself N'loghthl, and his battle with the man who could only walk west. But for our purposes, the next truly important period of his life was his 21st year, when he became a superstar. He experienced Fame the same way most unreasonably fa-mous people do. There was a sold-out concert tour and an album that went quadruple platinum and a widely publicized drug habit and a *People* magazine cover story that declared him the most widely admired man in America and a sudden explosion of people who desperately wanted to talk to him, even though he still wasn't any good at simple everyday conversation. There was even a mob of third-rate imitators who couldn't play nearly as well as he could (especially since, though they had no way of knowing this, he didn't dare play as well as he could). And he revolutionized the music industry and slept with about a hundred blindly adoring women and chances are that if fate hadn't intervened he would have eventually either had a career as long as Frank Sinatra's or been assassinated by a jealous fan. But even while all of this wholly unimportant stuff was going on, his true destiny atop Mt. Everest lumbered toward him like a malevolent bulldozer approaching an unsuspecting brick wall.

The first portent took the form of a discovery by graduate students at Cornell University that, because of a minor mathematical error made by a drunken Norwegian somewhere around 1873, all known astrophysi-cal theories concocted from that moment on were slightly off. For instance, the speed of light was about twenty miles an hour *less* than previously estimated. But that was a rather minor bombshell, all things considered, since relativity still applied, and if not for having to shred all the old textbooks few people on the planet would have ever had reason to notice. More to the point, more relevantly, the sun was not going to last billions of years, as previously estimated, but rather less than twenty. At that point it would just flicker out like a cheap light bulb and reduce the Earth to a planet-sized ice cube utterly incapable of supporting astronomers, Cornell University, or anybody else.

Even more immediate was the influence of our next player: a tall, thin, crowbar-faced woman by the name of Nancy Peabody. Now, let's be fair about this. Nancy can't be blamed for having a nose resembling a crowbar. That was just a genetic accident, like the one that had given Bryce's third cousin Felton an extra thumb growing out of the small of his back. What Nancy Peabody can be blamed for was actually behaving like a crowbar, designed to pry open the locked places belonging to others. Not that she was interested in stealing material things. No, her sin was much more insidious than that. She thought everybody in the whole wide world was obligated to rearrange their entire lives to avoid doing anything that ran even a miniscule chance of offending her. That including reading the wrong books, seeing the wrong movies, wearing the wrong clothes, worshipping the wrong God, enjoying the wrong kind of sex, learning the wrong kind of knowledge, thinking the wrong kind of thoughts, and — most importantly, for our narrative's sake — making music with the wrong kind of instruments. Nancy had spent her entire adult life pitilessly crusading against the right of anybody anywhere within her line of assault, to have even a thimble's worth of fun without her approval. And because there were unfortunately all too many people running around who were (except for the regrettable crowbar-shaped nose) exactly like her, and were willing to support her in her various crusades, she was much more successful than she deserved to be. Before long, people who enjoyed things she didn't began wearing a hunted, apprehensive look similar to that worn by the lead cow entering the slaughterhouse.

When Bryce embarked upon his wildly successful concert tour, he couldn't have offered her a more irresistible target if he'd painted a pattern of concentric red circles on his backside, handed her a BB gun, and told her to let rip. And so she began appearing at press conferences, wearing a dour, joyless expression that looked like her lips were ready to slide right off her face, to announce that Bryce's music was obscene. It glorified unsanitary habits and provided a bad example for impressionable young children. If this sadly misguided young man were permitted to continue soiling the ears of his listeners with music he made in this way she could not bring herself to mention, then who knew what depths of vulgarity awaited the world next? Burp operas? Foot odor mime? Even greater atrocities involving actual bodily fluids? No. No. No. No. No. She was sorry about this, but she really had to put her foot down. He could not be permitted to pollute her own personal world this way. And so she advised her followers to get Bryce's talent banned.

And what the hell, dear reader, let's make a long story shorter. Five years of boycotts, protests, court cases, and concert hall bombings later, the miserable bitch won. The recordings were burned, the videos were erased, the glowing reviews were stricken from the microfiches, and Bryce himself was, in a stroke of deliberate cruelty personally designed by the freshly elected World President Nancy Peabody, sentenced to spend the rest of his life with his offending right arm tightly strapped to his side, the underlying principle being that he shouldn't be allowed to practice in private either, because it was downright offensive to even think of him doing such a disgusting thing. After all, she said, Society had to be Protected from this Menace. She was so persuasive about this that the world elected her President For Life, thus totally eliminating the possibility that a more liberal administration would someday take power and redress the injustices committed against him. This left Bryce as widely despised as Judas, Haman, and Hitler. All of a sudden the very same people who had once waited in line for hours on end just to catch a glimpse of him were averting their gaze to avoid having their eyes polluted by the sight of his face. Bryce, who barely knew that there was a One World President, knew only that the fame was gone, that the money was gone, and that the thing which had once made him special was gone.

When he found himself back on the streets, he did the only thing he could: he looked for a job suitable for slow-witted men with only one functional arm. And after a long, painful search he found one in the slot machine business, only to discover that though he was in fact uniquely qualified for the position there was now a law on the books against hiring him for anything. This was an entirely new experience for Bryce, since during his last extended period of homelessness he'd at least been free to do odd jobs for food. Not now. Now he was only permitted to scrounge and beg. And this he did, with only limited success, since whenever he did manage to put together a little money he had to spend most of it on cheap liquor to dull the sound of the government-sponsored tour groups that followed him around taking full color snapshots of his misery. And though he was too drunk most of the time to hear what the tour guides said about him, rational fragments of his consciousness occasionally drifted past his concealing layers of alcoholic stupor and caught some of what was coming through the megaphones. They were saying that he was dirty, that he was disgusting, and that he smelled bad. They said he was living this way by choice. That he was a creature of filth and decay, who might have been human once but had been corrupted beyond all redemption by the tinny little blaats he made with his armpit. He listened to all of this, and when he was sober enough to understand it, he thought what you or I would think: what a load of happy horseshit. He had no way of knowing that the entire world had been distorted beyond all reason, specifically to make them believe it: that the drunken hell his life had become was not only watched day and night by tour groups, but also filmed for TV, carefully edited to accentuate everything that made him look subhuman and vile, and shown every night to tremendous ratings. There wasn't a person on Earth (with the possible exception of his family, who as per their vow stubbornly refused to get involved) who hadn't been completely and utterly convinced by this tactic. And after a long hard day of banning books and jailing dissidents, her crowbar-faced Excellency the World President Miss Nancy Peabody retired to the palatial bedroom where she slept alone and laughed herself to sleep watching videotapes of Bryce coughing and shivering in alleys.

Nancy actually thought she'd won. She thought that the man she despised more than any other had sunk as low as it was possible for a human being to sink. But she was wrong on both counts. Because in the first place, Bryce had not yet lived the very worst moment of his life. That was rapidly approaching, in the form of the crab-things from Alpha Centauri, and when it arrived, everybody in the entire world, including Nancy Peabody, would share it with him. And in the second place (though she would meet her bizarre death without ever knowing it), Nancy had actually suffered the greatest defeat in the history of mankind. Because, had she done nothing, had she left him alone and simply let him continue making the music the way he was making it, Bryce would have just gone on playing the works of Beethoven and Mozart and Wagner and Lennon and McCartney and never once discovered just how far his own talent left them all behind. But his persecution by her administration was the only ingredient his talent had needed to achieve its fullest potential. And, inside, he was mentally composing music so awe-inspiring that it would have scrambled the average human mind the same way an eggbeater affects chocolaty cake mix. Music that, without fear of exaggeration, could safely be called the culmination of the process that started when the first trilobite crawled up onto the first sandbar and said dry land looked like a nice place to spend a summer or two. Music that could even be called the best thing to hit this firmament since the big bang. Music that could only be played on one very special instrument, that would have never been written *at all* if not for the unwitting collaboration of the woman who hated him above all else. Not that any of this was any consolation to him during the ten years he spent sleeping off one hopeless binge or another on his bed of cardboard, dog poo and banana peels.

After about ten years of this, a limousine about a block and a half long bearing the pink on mauve flags of the Kind and Benevolent One World Republic pulled into the alley where Bryce moaned in his sleep from an inexplicable nightmare about being chased by an army of crowbars in sensible shoes. The limousine was as black as the shadows left on walls by the Hiroshima bomb; it didn't reflect light the way automotive metal is supposed to, but rather sucked it in, chewed it up, and destroyed it without even leaving a receipt. It was a darkness so deep that the limousine didn't so much resemble a car as a traveling black hole in the shape of a car, and had Bryce been awake to see it, he would have imagined it the limo of Death Himself. But it wasn't the limo of Death Himself — and not just because when Bryce did finally meet that worthy individual, a few years later, it would be on Mount Everest, where limos can't go. Two burly men stepped from that limo, adjusted their official Kind And Benevolent One World Republic pink on mauve power ties, and collected him. They drove him to a government delousing center on the other end of town, stripped him, unstrapped his right arm, shaved him, scrubbed him until every inch of his skin was squeaky clean, force-fed him breath mints, made him drink about three gallons of coffee, dressed him in a suit cut to his exact measurements, strapped his right arm back to his side, and marched him down a long pink on mauve corridor into an office where a crowbar-faced woman sat sour and defeated behind a big oak desk.

You, dear reader, know who that woman was. Bryce didn't. Being swift on the uptake had never been one of his virtues, and he'd spent a full decade waging a ruthless war of extermination against his few functional brain cells. And Nancy told him about a terrifying discovery made some years back which meant the sun now had less than five years to live. She told him about the construction of a vast space fleet designed to bring two cryogenically frozen specimens of every terrestrial animal to a planet orbiting another habitable star. Unfortunately, the ark was running way behind schedule due to some shortsighted animals actually resisting this process. Especially the hippos. Anyway, there was now a less than one in three chance that the fleet would be ready in time, and even if it was, it wouldn't be big enough to save more than maybe ten thousand people, leaving the rest of Earth's billions more than a little put out. The most generous estimates available predicted total worldwide panic in less than two years. Something needed to be done. Even, she shouted, if that meant turning her back on every principle she held dear, you nasty, nasty man.

Bryce didn't follow any of this. He just kept nodding, the way he had when seated at his family dinner table, and pretended that he actually understood when the woman with the strange nose explained what it was she wanted him to do. He was still nodding as they loaded him aboard the Presidential jet and took off for some unknown destination halfway around the world. They were flying for six hours before he began to realize that he might be in an airplane. Then again, he might not.

Because thanks to Nancy Peabody's legendary acrophobia, there were no windows. Instead, it had rows and rows of window-shaped plaques with inspirational sayings on them: stuff about the golden rule and the and the see-no-evil hear-no-evil monkeys and the man on the beach who turned around and saw God's footprints alongside his own. The underlying theme seemed to be that people who acted and behaved and thought exactly like Nancy Peabody were the most special people in the whole wide world. Bryce didn't see how that necessarily followed. Still, he supposed the plaques and samplers knew what they were talking about, since there were after all more of them than there were of him.

The jet landed at a hidden airstrip somewhere in the Mojave Desert. The two burly men whisked Bryce into a jeep. They drove for two hours. And eventually, which is when most important things happen, they came upon their destination: a gleaming metal tower that even Bryce's addled mind immediately recognized as an alien spaceship. Huge beyond all imagining, colossal in ways that went beyond mere *size*, it utterly dwarfed all the troops and jeeps and harried scientist-types scurrying back and forth at its base. Most of the scientist-types trailed computer printouts behind them, making them resemble parodies of sperm cells on their way to the egg. None looked like they had any idea what they were doing or why they were doing it; the nasty looks they gave Bryce as their printouts flapped like banners in the suction of the passing jeep were so obviously tinged with jealousy and awe that only a fool even greater than Bryce could have failed to see that they knew he was here to do something they never could.

And all of a sudden Bryce put two and two together and, for the very first time in a lifetime of being wrong about everything, got four. And he knew exactly why they needed him.

Too bad he didn't think just a little bit harder, be cause he was still missing something.

But Bryce was human, you see. And he wasn't thinking of the great task that lay before him: he was thinking of being a hero, and everybody in the world being grateful, and his family crawling back to him on their hands and knees saying they'd been wrong all these years, and himself saying, well, you're too damn late, you should have thought of that back when I was nine, and his family prostrating themselves further until their humiliation was a sight truly nauseating to behold, and himself saying, well, all right, but just this once, and everybody cheering and carrying him around on their shoulders until their arms got strained from his weight, and then cooking him one of those delicious turkey dinners his mother had used to make, and then sitting back and watching him eat it, too awed by the grandeur of his accomplishments to actually dig in themselves. He thought of taking his seat at the head of the table and outlawing the hated Family Entertainment Hour forever. He thought of being on the top of the world again. And with all this understandable but premature self-congratulation going on, he can be forgiven for failing to take into account the one simple thing that rendered it all impossible.

The jeep drove up to a makeshift gate a hundred yards from the base of the alien spaceship. The two burly men stopped the car and got out. They looked at Bryce expectantly. He got out, blinked from the cloud of dust that surrounded the jeep, and after a moment commanded the guard to open the damn gate. He didn't ask, mind you. He commanded. And his command was obeyed instantly. Because at that moment it was obvious, not only to that guard but to everybody else, that Bryce was now the single most important human being who had ever lived. Forget Einstein, Lincoln, Edison, Newton, and Shakespeare; forget Napoleon and Alexander; forget Caesar and Attila and the designer of the wheel and the guy who first figured out how to make cheese. Forget them all. I mean, they were good and everything. You have to give them credit. But at this moment they were gnats next to Bryce. The sense of imminent destiny about him was so thick that most of the military observers were fainting.

He started walking toward the alien spaceship. And though he was a small, physically unimpressive man, whose last decade had been lived under the most horrendous deprivation imaginable, he took such bold strides that his two burly companions, who shared something like fifty barehanded assassinations between them, had trouble keeping up long enough to remove the harness that up until now had kept his right arm strapped to his side. Bryce only had eyes for the spaceship up ahead, and the two crab-things by the base of the gangplank.

Of the crab-things' overall appearance not much needs to be said. They looked like crab-things. What *was* important about them? Three simple facts, which between them explained why Bryce was here: first, they didn't seem to know that the pulpy mammalian creatures native to this planet were sentient, and desperate for the technological assistance that only the crab-things could provide. Second, they communicated with each other the same way Bryce did. They each had about seven hundred tentacle-arms that waved around willy-nilly without doing much of any obvious importance, and whenever they wanted to say something they placed some of those tentacles under certain other tentacles and flapped downward, making blaaat noises. And third, despite their natural advantages, they evidently had absolutely no talent for the instrument. They were completely, and unredeemably, tone-deaf — and their noises did not strike the human ear as the mysterious language of alien sentients as much as it did the digestive problems of two truckers sharing a booth at a roadside diner. Bryce was much better than they were. And with any luck at all they'd be so enthralled by his abilities they'd immediately start diplomatic relations and set about solving the thorny problem of how, exactly, they were going to set about saving the human race.

Bryce walked right up to them and placed his left arm under his right armpit. The two crab-things stopped to listen. Bryce raised his right arm . . .

One quick interruption here, just to raise the ante of the moment: the arrival of the crab-things was not exactly a state secret. No doubt Nancy Peabody would have preferred to keep it one, but the creatures hadn't spent their entire visit to our fair planet digging holes in the Mojave. No. They'd been hopping back and forth across the globe for months, landing in cities, on mountaintops, and even on the front lawns of accountants in suburbia, taking their samples, giving each other Bronx cheers of encouragement, and then zipping off. Public opinion, swayed by the knowledge that the world was going to end in five years anyway, had slowly but surely turned to the idea of using Bryce to communicate with them. Nancy Peabody had resisted the idea with every weapon at her disposal; and, yes, on those cases when the opposition hit the streets, her weapons did include bullets and tear gas. But the majority's will had prevailed, and the result was that, though this looked like a top-secret military installation a zillion miles from nowhere, the attention of the entire world was upon it. Hidden cameras were broadcasting Bryce's every twitch to seven billion viewers. The whole of civilization stood at a standstill, and all of mankind held its collective breath, waiting for the man Nancy Peabody had made a pariah to miraculously rescue the human race from the very brink of Death.

It was lot like being at bat with two men out and three men on. And if anybody could hit the home run that would win the game for Earth, Bryce was it.

Unfortunately, that's what everybody thought about the Mighty Casey.

And when Bryce brought down his right arm, he didn't make beautiful music. He just went BLAAATTT.

It was a horrendously ugly BLAAATTT. One so awful it made the aliens seem euphonious. Bryce gave them an apologetic look (he didn't mean to do that, he was just out of practice, that's all) and he tried again, and this time the BLAAATTT was one of the three worst sounds ever heard on this planet, right behind dentists' drills and the singing of William Shatner. Panicky now, Bryce tried a third time, and a fourth, and a fifth —

BLAAATTT. BLAAATTT. BLAAATTT.

What he'd forgotten to take into account was a little phenomenon known as muscular atrophy. His skin was flabby, his arm limp, and his timing a sluggish, resentful thing reminiscent of bowling night at the old folks' home. Had he been given six months or so to build up his muscle tone and fine-tune his sense of pitch, he might have been able to play with something approaching his former aplomb. As it was, he could only BLAAATTT.

The crab-things had never been so grossly insulted in their entire lives. They'd come all this way at great expense and hardship to take soil samples so they could properly customize the new planet they were terraforming for Earth's entire populace just a few solar systems down the block. They had even planned to provide free transportation. And while they didn't expect gratitude from mammals — the crab-things were liberals, doing this purely out of the goodness of their vlm'och receptors — but Bryce's rudeness was just plain uncalled-for. They turned their backs on him, scurried up the gangplank, and blasted off, never to be heard from again.

Not to put too fine a point on it: humanity was doomed.

And nowhere, on the entire face of the planet, did anybody think: "Gee, what a shame. If we'd left him alone all these years he wouldn't have suffered such a humiliating failure. Chances are he would have done right by us. He probably would have saved the whole shooting match. But we hounded him and hobbled him and stole from him the one thing that could have rescued the human race. Boy, are our faces red. Let's at least give him credit for doing the best he could." Well, a few people did think that: chiefly his family, who still kept their vow to remain uninvolved. But the consensus was quite different. The consensus stared at the crab-thing's starship becoming just another bright light in the sky and thought of all the nice things that could be done to Bryce with sticks and stones. The consensus thought about looking through Torquemada's old spiral-bound notebooks to see if the old guy had doodled down any torture ideas he never quite got around to using. And those on the scene looked away from the sky and blindly, hungrily, moving like zombies in an Italian horror flick, lurched forward to dismember him.

But Bryce had already taken advantage of their inattention to run like hell. Not a single person had seen which way he'd gone, and no search party was ever able to find him. By the end of the week the official verdict was that he'd fled into the surrounding desert and died — though if the popular press was to be believed, he spent more time making cameo appearances at small town filling stations than any dead celebrity since Hitler and Elvis. None of these sightings were ever confirmed. Before very long the imminent destruction of the world commanded humanity's collective attention, and Bryce's name became only an all-purpose punchline to any sick joke anybody wanted to tell. And that's the way it stayed. If anybody reliable ever did actually see him again, then he must have discovered disguise among his short list of great talents, because they sure as hell didn't recognize him.

As far as the rest of humanity knew, everything else that happened from this point on was just epilogue. The panic in the streets, the virgins sacrificed to volcanoes, and the plague of mass insanity that broke out on both the seven original continents and the three that Bryce's younger sister Meg had constructed as a school project were definitely all interesting to watch, but they all stemmed from that one hideously embarrassing moment in the Mojave desert, and in the final analysis they didn't alter Man's destiny a single iota. The five years passed. All last-minute prayers remained unanswered. The weather started to get colder. The tropics froze. And on the night before the increasingly feeble sun was scheduled to flip off like a nightlight yanked from a preschooler's wall socket, the few people who had survived the chaos of the past half-decade positioned themselves the way they imagined they'd like to be frozen solid for all eternity. It's safe to say that more people spent that night with their pants down and their rear ends mooning the stars, than ever before in the history of the species. It's even safer to say that if the world didn't freeze solid tomorrow, they were all going to feel awfully silly.

Nancy Peabody would never know how things turned out. She spent that night, the last of her life, sipping tea on the Presidential balcony as her hastily constructed space fleet carried a thousand colonists, and two specimens of every major species, to the stars. Not that she could actually see them take off from her balcony — they had been launched over a period of weeks, from construction sites all over the world. But all of the one hundred ships were in orbit now, their ramjets were easily visible in the night sky; and since her notorious acrophobia had kept her from joining them, they were honoring her last request by forming constellations. Wholesome, family-oriented constellations. Little girls walking in fields of daisies. Wide-eyed puppies frolicking with cuddly kittens. A sunflower wearing a big smiley face. That sort of thing. And as she watched all this her face contorted into a grimace that was supposed to be a contented smile. She was happy, and all (aside from its imminent destruction) was right with the world. At least until the chain-reaction explosion that lit up the night sky and reduced the entire fleet to shrapnel. It had been caused by faulty insulation in one of the starships, and it was able to destroy the entire fleet only because Nancy Peabody had selfishly used her influence to make the ramjets form bunnies and horsies for her amusement. The night sky filled with red streaks as the debris burned in the upper atmosphere. Nancy Peabody stood on her balcony watching, in such a deep state of shock that she actually oohed and aahed at the pretty colors. Perhaps out of spite, none of the radar operators bothered to warn her that what was left of one of the ships was headed for the presidential palace, and that while almost all of it had been vaporized by friction, its state-of-the-art heat shields, extra layers of insulation, and tons of chemically enhanced ice had slowed that process just long enough to preserve a hippo that woke up as the last of its cocoon boiled off one thousand feet above Nancy Peabody's balcony. She heard a strange note of faraway music — Bryce's music — over the whistling wind of its approach. She looked up in time to see the expression on the Hippo's face. It was pissed-off.

And Bryce?

As you might have guessed, from this story's title, he was at the top of Mount Everest.

He'd spent the last five years an obsessed hermit, moving from hiding place to hiding place across the globe as he practiced eighteen hours a day repairing the damage the previous decade had done to his instrument. He never got it all back; the tendons of his right arm had shortened, and despite all the pain he inflicted trying to restore them, much of that damage was permanent. He was able to play again, and quite well, but not with the precise control he once had. He'd never, ever be able to play the Masterpiece he'd written in that alley. This was a tragedy; make no mistake about that. But what he got back in all those dank caves was something even more valuable: a firm, unwavering certainty that this time he finally knew what he had been born to do.

He'd climbed the mountain illegally, without the required permit from the Nepalese government; with a partially crippled right arm; without any mountain-climbing experience; and without equipment of any kind, let alone an oxygen mask. He hadn't even brought along a warm coat. The mistakes he'd made on the way up would have had any experienced mountaineer shaking his head in horror. Bryce should have been dead from exposure, oxygen starvation, and injury a thousand times over. But his sheer force of will had gotten him this far, to this one spot as close as any earthbound man could get to outer space, and now that he was here, too obsessed to even feel the thin air or frigid cold, he ripped off his shirt, flung it into the abyss, and petitioned the Universe in the only way he'd ever been able to speak to anybody: through his talent. The howling wind carried away the first few notes, which was no great loss, because they were just weak, pathetic bleats. But soon his music grew in strength and conviction, and the wind actually died down so the universe could hear him. He told the universe of all the hardship he'd known during his life — of his awe for his family, of the sun on his back as he dug ditches to make a living during his teens, of what it had been like to be a lionized celebrity, and then what it what had been like to be hated. He told the universe about the Masterpiece he wished he could play, but no longer could; about what it had felt like to unintentionally insult the alien crab-things; and (for no reason he consciously understood) about the pissed expression on the face of falling hippos. His music faltered then, because he wasn't quite sure why he'd thrown that in, but then he rallied, building up to a crescendo that might not have been up to the level of his great unheard Masterpiece, but was definitely damn close: a crescendo that, though unheard by anybody except its composer and intended Audience, nevertheless gave people all over the world a cold shiver at the base of their spines.

It was the best damn music that had ever been played by anybody. In the absence of Bryce's great lost Masterpiece, the best damn music that ever would be played by anybody. And through it Bryce told the Universe: If you ever want to hear that again, then take me, and I'll play it for you as many times as you want. But I'm not playing if you let this planet die too. If that happens, then be warned — Elvis has left the auditorium.

He played the very last note, and sank to his knees, utterly spent. He knew he wouldn't have the strength to stand up again. He knew this because the wind was starting up again and it was cold and he was blacking out from lack of oxygen. But he also knew that he'd be able to hang on long enough for the Universe to answer him.

Which it eventually did.

It might have been a yes and it might have been a no. But you, dear reader, know what it sounded like.

Blaaat.

Fuel

*H*e penciled the words on an ordinary 3 by 5 index card, in scrupu-
lously neat handwriting that respected the authority of parallel blue
lines. Beneath the words he signed and printed his name, Gordon
Wilson, then beneath that his street address, city, state, zip, and (with
conscious absurdity) his phone number, all in writing remarkable for
its evenly spaced precision, and for its utter absence of emotion, as if
he were filling out a form for a magazine subscription and not an
explanation for the bullet that he was about to fire through his brain.
The note itself was a carefully thought-out compromise between explaining too much and not explaining enough, expressing all of his weariness
and despair without ever going over the line into maudlin obviousness;
he'd written notes much like it a dozen previous times in his life, always
devoting so much time and effort to the perfect phrasing that he finally
lost all heart for the actual act. But this time he had the words and the
sentiment down cold, with the kind of inspired brevity that left nothing
else to say.

The card read:

AFTER ALL THE HOPE, ALL THE FEAR, ALL THE SELF-HATRED AND ALL
THE FUTILE LIES SPOKEN TO MYSELF IN THE MIDDLE OF THE NIGHT,
I CAN FINALLY ADMIT I'M NOT GETTING BETTER, I'M GETTING WORSE.

He could have spent hours going into specifics: the anhedonia, the
mood swings, the shattered friendships, the money problems, the lone-
liness, the failures, the hopelessness of a life where even managing to
endure meant another day of watching the world crumble deeper into
hell. But by the time he'd written all of that he would lost the will —
keeping the desire, and the increased self-loathing that always came with
such broken promises.

He spent all that day in a state approaching peace, boarding his cats,
vacuuming his apartment, paying off the last of his monthly bills,

washing the car, then driving to a deserted parking lot behind an office supply warehouse that was never open on Tuesdays. Then he placed the card message side-up on the dashboard, and he took precisely four deep breaths, and with absolutely no compunction at all placed the barrel between the lips and blew everything he was out the back of his head.

Despite all the advance publicity, he saw the bright light a fraction of a second *before* he died.

He did not have the time to realize how wrong that was, or to wonder why he should be afraid.

*T*he Travelers lived in a gossamer place of juggling possibilities and oscillating time: a place that in all its particulars defied the laws of the greater universe, and could therefore be considered a separate universe itself.

Their universe was a vehicle, designed to travel faster and farther than anything bound by mundane physics, and while its ultimate destination was far beyond the material world of planets and stars and solar systems, it did frequently slow down whenever it passed such places, to collect its equivalent of fuel.

Fuel:

Chitinous crablike thing, dragging itself across semi-molten rock, toward the sulphurous pool that will cause it an agonizing death.

Fuel:

Pulsating ball of sentient energy, once as bright as the stars, now so dim it barely qualifies as a spark, deliberately traveling beyond the safe zones, as it eschews the flammable breezes that would bring its flame back to healthy life.

Fuel:

Dark shambling predator, all teeth and hunger, despondent for lack of anything else to kill, standing at the edge of a howling maelstrom, and gathering enough will to hurl itself in.

Fuel:

Floating bag of hydrogen, bobbing to and fro in a wind-tossed upper atmosphere, sinking deeper and deeper into the darkness as it consciously refrains from the chemical processes that keep it buoyant and aloft and alive.

Fuel:

Unknown failure of a man, swallowing the barrel of a revolver as he imagines this the moment of his release: taking comfort in the thought that the thought the thinks now is the last thought he'll think forever.

Fuel:

Unknown thousands of others.

Creatures who once inhabited worlds from across the entire breadth of time and space, each one a fugitive from a life so different from all the others that to them its most primitive thought would be a code unbreakable, in a tongue alien and unspoken.

Each one despairing. Each one urging itself toward death.

Each one captured in the net.

Added to the mix.

Burning, among the fuel.

*F*or Gordon Wilson, the first moment of his new existence was a headlong plunge into Hades.

None of what he saw or heard or tasted or smelled had any direct analogue to human experience. But he had been a human being, with a mind formed by his human life; and even as he plummeted past the bright light into a place he could only comprehend as darkness, he could only think that this was his punishment.

He hadn't expected to be punished; like almost all suicides, he'd expected not quite oblivion but the satisfaction of knowing that all his pain had ended. He had not expected to arrive in this strange place, surrounded by uncounted thousands of jabbering alien voices, all of whom seemed as horrified and repulsed by him as he was by them. He had not expected the sensation of being tapped, of being drained, of having everything he was wrung from his soul like wash water being wrung from a cloth. He had not expected the sheer vertigo of feeling his every memory played back, at impossible speed.

He hadn't expected to be Fuel.

And that wasn't even the worst of it . . .

*T*he Travelers who had constructed the sphere had done so with a mission in mind, one that had seemed simple enough to the creatures they had been. It had something to do with a crease through the process of entropy, and the swirling contradiction that was the passage of time. It had to do with the existence of a universe that refused to abide by the aesthetic laws of the thirteen major inter-dimensional constants, and the need to maintain strategic superiority in the places that probability had abandoned. All of this had seemed so obvious and vital to them once. But they'd changed, in the timeless time since putting their vessel together; some might even say, they'd degenerated. They were no longer the beings who'd set themselves an impossible task and built themselves a miraculous vessel to help them accomplish it. In that time they'd forgotten all of their arcane and hard-won knowledge and become passengers, instead of engineers. Now the bubble piloted itself, without their input; and the glorious mission that had once been the whole reason for their existence now seemed nothing but an ancient folly, too far gone to change.

They wouldn't have understood Vietnam, but they would have sympathized.

They did not notice when the Fuel Acquisition mechanism picked up Gordon Wilson. They didn't notice when the entire vessel bucked and lurched in protest, since their living space was buffered, and did not stir at all even when subjected to turbulence that briefly threatened to tear their entire private universe apart. They did not feel even a moment of fear; they felt nothing, and were perfectly content with feeling nothing, even though they'd just also revived something very ancient and very dangerous. They didn't have the slightest idea that anything was wrong, and they might not have cared even if somebody had come around to tell them.

In short, they were like the complacent everywhere: in that they were already dead, and did not yet happen to know it . . .

*G*ordon Wilson first heard the distant laughter while he still believed himself a fresh inmate in Hell. It wasn't laughter, really — there was no genuine sound in this place. But his mind still insisted on interpreting everything in terms of human experience, human sensation, and even as he reeled in a sea of alien images that refused to be translated in those terms

(* rooted in sea bottom feeding on dregs * drifting through digestive tract absorbing random proteins * slogging through the lake of fire * gliding on the methane winds * colors not in any human spectrum * sins not in any human bible * thoughts not in any human lexicon * a billion separate forms of life * a billion separate ways to die * * mother as great bloated sac filled with seeds * father as creature infected by parasite * children as playthings and as food * right-angles perceived as circles * abstractions perceived as shapes * viruses perceived as politics * death perceived as sustenance * despair perceived as fuel *)

even as Gordon Wilson fought to preserve his sanity against a tidal wave of such mutually contradictory images, he heard the laughter building behind it all.

And he felt everything he'd ever been run cold with fear.

Because while he did not yet understand why. . . . he recognized that laughter.

He recognized it in ways that went beyond memory, went beyond instinct. He recognized it in a manner that acknowledged he'd never personally heard it before. He recognized it in the manner of a man recognizing a sound that no man had ever heard, for as long as there had ever been men; and which yet remained a sound that all men knew, since awareness of that sound was wired in the very genetic material that made human beings human. It was the sound of an ancient, immortal enemy, older than the world — an enemy whose own last moments before being imprisoned in this place were now played out for Gordon Wilson, at a volume that drowned out all else.

The Hunter stood beneath the night sky and stared up at the lights as they receded, knowing that they meant his failure. There were thousands of them, more numerous than the stars; and they were all moving away so quickly that even his lightning-fast reflexes could not move his eyes fast enough to track them. The lights had taken him by surprise — he'd been advancing on the last settlement, and had eagerly anticipated killing all the remaining population by morning — but the instant he saw them, he knew that the hated ones had escaped, after all. Despite lifetimes spent pursuing them from world to world, laying waste to all their defenses, leveling their cities, finding their bolt-holes, flushing them out and exterminating them, to the point where the last handful he was about to kill tonight were the very last to live and breathe anywhere in a universe that would have been purer and cleaner for their absence — they'd escaped. Oh, he could track the lights receding in the sky, for some idea which way they'd gone; but there were so many lights that the vast majority must have been unpiloted decoys, fired off into places where the hated ones had no intention of going. By the time he investigated even a few of the flight patterns, the creatures he'd spent his entire existence killing would have been well beyond his reach; though they themselves were dying, from all the plagues he'd sowed, they would still have more than enough time to travel beyond his reach, find some lifeless world, and infect it with their seed.

He had been their greatest enemy, the one who went on hunting and chasing and killing and destroying, despite anything they could do to stop him. He'd reduced them from a cancer, metastasizing throughout the stars, to a terrified little community of defeated fugitives, who had to watch themselves wither and die while waiting for him to descend and erase their blot forever.

He'd never rested.

He'd never shown a moment's mercy.

He'd never lost a single battle.

He'd doomed even those who fled.

And after all that, they had still won.

The Hunter stood beneath the night sky, watching the stars spell out his defeat on a slate as large as the universe. And he did something that would have astonished those who for so long had considered him a soulless omnipotent destroyer — he wept, out of humiliation. He wept in the manner of any being whose life becomes an empty thing, without purpose or hope, who realizes that his entire existence has been for nothing, and that he has pitifully wasted every moment he stood alive beneath the stars. And then he succumbed to despair and he opened his veins and spilled out the last of his existence onto the dirt of the place that should have seen the culmination of all his dreams.

He, too, saw the bright light an instant before he died.

As he was captured in the net.

Added to the mix.

Set to burning, among the fuel.

And though the Hunter had spent the eons that followed content to be damned to the purgatory he felt he deserved, a merciful universe had just placed one of his enemy's descendants back within his reach. Giving him a purpose again, for the first time in an interval longer than the lifetime of worlds. His despair was transformed into triumph, and he laughed. . . .

. . . while Gordon Wilson, quailing, realized that there are some things worse than being joyless and afraid.

*T*here was never any shortage of Despair; it had always been far more common than hope, and there was always more being manufactured, everywhere in the universe. That was what made it such a convenient, and inexhaustible, Fuel. But Despair was a volatile thing, that always needed to be stirred just right; unless properly refined, it transformed into hope or love or faith or hate or rage, which could be just as powerful but were even readier to change states without any prior warning. But that's why the collectors were designed to gather Fuel that wouldn't interact with the rest of the mix in any undesirable manner; any uncontrollable chemistry between one element and another could be, quite literally, explosive.

There had always been impurities. But they had always been dealt with, by automatic systems. Up until now, the catastrophic had been avoided.

But nobody could have predicted the sudden reunion between ancient Hunter and Ancient Prey.

*N*ow, all of sudden, there was laughter polluting the mix. Cruel and hungry laughter, from the remains of he who'd stalked and killed; anticipatory laughter, from he who looked forward to the stalking and killing yet to come; joyful laughter, from he who'd felt no joy for eons. It was laughter with a voice, and that voice said, **After all these years you've come back to me! Giving me something to kill again**, and the maliciousness in his tone was so great that of the thousands of other creatures whose last moments had been rendered Fuel, at least half were now contaminated by spasms of sympathetic fear.

The bubble lurched. Slowed. Went violently off-course and devastated a world of singing sentient oceans by instantly boiling them into dead clouds of superheated steam. The Travelers, secure in their cushioned habitat, didn't notice, and probably wouldn't have cared if they had. After all, they would have reasoned, wasn't their vessel nearly indestructible? Wasn't it designed to survive a whole lot worse than that?

And they would have had a point, more or less.

But the chain reaction had already begun.

*G*ordon Wilson stood paralyzed at the bottom of a well of madness, inundated by moments from the lives of creatures unimagined, hearing nothing but that hated laugh echoing in the darkness, seeing nothing but that hated shape which eclipsed all else as it drew toward him. He stood bound by all the failures of his life, all the ways in which he'd fallen short of being bold or smart or brave or enough, and he faced a thing that dwarfed all men, that had been Man's enemy for much longer than there'd been men to hate . . . and he knew there was no hope of escape, no hope of defiance, no hope of survival, no hope of anything but the inevitability of dying again.

And he felt an emotion as alien to him as any of those that pummeled him in the darkness: rage.

It's funny, isn't it?

After all, isn't this what they prepare us for all our lives?

When you're a child, and your mommy and daddy beat you for saying no, for fighting back, for seeing through their lies, for seeing them as the bullies they are, for refusing to make yourself as small as they want you to be? Don't they say, that's enough out of you! That's all I want to hear from you! Don't talk back! Now sit there and take your punishment until you apologize!

When you're in the playground, and the big kid sits on your chest and rubs the dirt on your face, and you squirm beneath his weight, loathing him, wanting him dead, knowing yourself powerless but vowing that he'll never make you cry, crying anyway because you're not great enough to contain all the pain and hate and humiliation? Don't they say, you brought this on yourself? You let him tease you? You showed him it bothered you and made yourself the victim?

When you sit at your desk in a plain white office even as the sky outside your window dims from blue to black, and your head turns to fog and your heart turns to stone and you look at the clock and you think of another day's long downward slide to death? And you know that there should be something more to life than this, that there should be some source of joy and hope and a reason for wanting to get up in the morning? And they say, don't let it get you down, it's just your job, you may hate it and you may feel it sucking out your life but you can't just throw it away, because you need to contribute, to pay the bills, to do what they tell you to do, and do it without protest because there's no escape from it anyway?

When you stand in the center of a busy city street surrounded by thousands of people all of whom seem better smarter prettier thinner happier and more fulfilled than you, and all the world seems a place that's left you out, that's locked you outside, that's deliberately left you uninvited, and you want to scream, look at me, look at me, I'm here, I matter, I hurt, I need? And you do nothing because you know what they'd say if you did, which is that you're crazy, you're worthless, you're not worth the attention? And so you turn your face into a mask and you say nothing and you go with the flow and you turn all your anger and resentment into yet another dagger in your heart?

Isn't it all just the same message, endlessly repeated? Don't stand up. Don't fight back. Don't open your mouth. Don't walk on eggs. Don't take chances. Don't do anything but take what they give you.

Some of us don't listen. I did. It made me a rabbit, caught in the headlights. A pathetic little man, defeated without ever stirring himself to fight.

But then I never knew who the real enemy was. I never knew that all our history, all our wars, all our witch-hunts, all our genocides, all our rapes, all our crimes, all our murders, all our atrocities, all our lynchings, all our tyrannies, all our nightmares, all our Hell-legends, all our bogeymen, all our gods of evil, all the times we feared strangers in dark places, all the times we bubbled over with cruelty, all our weakness and all our cowardice and all our evil – that was just the part of us that remembered the past, and remained so afraid of being hunted down again that we searched for you in every unfamiliar face.

But this time I know who you are, and this time I have nowhere left to hide. Come for me this time, you murdering bastard, and you're going down.

*T*he bubble was supposed to be invisible and immaterial; it was supposed to journey beyond the places inhabited by mere things. It wasn't supposed to fade into existence any more frequently than it had to in order to collect its fuel.

But the fuel was changing composition, and the ride was getting bumpy.

The bubble appeared on a planet of mile-high volcanic spires, crashing across an entire hemisphere in an instant, scattering the pillars of stone like dominoes before once again fading away.

It appeared on a world of lush verdant jungle, skimming the forest canopy like a stone skimming the surface of a pond, and everywhere it touched the greenery withered, and the animals died, and the ground turned deadly and black.

It appeared within a sun that nurtured a world that was home to beings whose basest thoughts were the most brilliant poetry ever known; and in the instant it lingered there before moving on, the sun was reduced to a cinder, and the world to a mortuary.

It appeared in the midst of beings who were more gods than men, who had been fighting a war since the beginning of time; and it spun in their midst long enough to fatally distract one side and give the critical advantage to the other.

Completely out of control now, it described a completely random path through the universe, damaging or destroying a hundred different worlds with every instant; and somewhere along the way the life-support failed and the Travelers died in a burst of shock and incomprehension, but they were irrelevant. Because the chain-reaction was not over with, yet . . .

*D*eep inside, the essence of the Hunter went after the essence of essence of Gordon Wilson.

He came in the way that a crumbling mountain comes. He engulfed everything that lay in his path, swelling with rage and power with every moment, becoming even more fearsome than he had been in life. He was black and malicious and infinite and greater than any man's ability to comprehend him, and as he drew close to Gordon Wilson the mix bubbled with all the flavors of alien fear.

Gordon Wilson thought only of the blue windbreaker he owned in third grade.

It was a shiny blue jacket, of the sort that mothers find cute and kids find mortifying; Gordon had owned it for about six months. He'd hated it with a passion for several weeks after he first got it, not because of the way it looked during the day, but because of what it turned into at night: hanging on its hook on the back of his bedroom door, it became an apelike beast, with long clutching arms. It wasn't a fear that ruled him; even as he lay in bed, waiting for the beast to pounce, waiting for it to leap off his bedroom door and scrabble at his neck, he'd known perfectly well that it was just a jacket, rendered false and menacing by shadows. It should have been way too silly to worry about for even a moment. And yet even if he put the jacket in a closet or drawer, or left it downstairs, the knowledge that it was still out there, in the darkness, taking on the shape that it only took at night, had given him the sweats. It passed, of course. Time moved on, and with it, more sensible things to get frightened about. But Gordon had never forgotten the nights he'd spent afraid of that jacket, and the way he'd so briefly seen in its emptily hanging folds the shape of things to dread. He'd always wondered where such a crazy fear could have come from. Now he knew.

All around them, alien voices gibbered in confusion and fear. Gordon heard the cries of things that flew, the bubbling of things that swam, the soft hiss of things that crawled, the indescribable sounds of things that had lived in habitats beyond his comprehension. Whatever they were, wherever they'd come from, they'd all arrived at a point in their lives where life itself had seemed too much to ask of them. And though they'd wallowed in their despair ever since, they sensed what was happening in their midst, and were now afraid.

The essence of something that had possessed light gossamer wings flew at the Hunter, to stop him. Its thoughts were agony in color: dark purple starbursts, with pulsating emerald stripes. It was willing to give up anything in order to stop the Hunter. The Hunter batted it aside with the slightest twitch, leaving the mix black from its death-throes.

The essence of something that had been a predator itself, that had lived to tear flesh from captive throats and then swallow the blood that came spurting from the wounds, pounced next. Its thoughts were the taste of salt and the odor of putrefaction. But it, too, was determined to protect Gordon Wilson from the Hunter. It failed. The Hunter became two rows of glistening fangs that rent the predator into dying meat.

The essence of something that had been a worshipper at the altar of beauty and had killed itself for losing the ability to appreciate that which it valued above all else, tried to intercede after that. Its thoughts were deep and symphonic, and its counterattack gentle. It tried to deter the Hunter with compassion. But it, too, failed; and what was left of it when the Hunter was done was a corpse of shocking ugliness, incapable of singing anything but death.

In the end, Gordon couldn't have stopped them if he tried. They were all trapped, and they all had nothing to lose. They all fought for him, and they all lost; falling singly and together before the Hunter that would destroy anything to get to him.

In their mass sacrifice, Gordon Wilson learned something that once upon a time might have stopped him from placing that revolver in his mouth: that even at his loneliest, he had never been alone.

But by then there was nothing in the mix but the single greatest enemy either humanity or the ancestors of humanity had ever known, and Gordon Wilson, who had always been throughout his life one of the least of all men.

They faced each other: the Hunter in triumph, Gordon Wilson in dumbstruck silence. It didn't matter to either one of them that the battle was moot, that both combatants were just echoes of creatures that had already died; the only thing that mattered was a war that had been interrupted eons earlier, and that could only be finished by proxy, here and now.

And Gordon Wilson could hardly speak for laughing.

*T*he worst kind of crash is the one that only seems to be taking place in slow-motion — the one that wreaks so much damage all at once that time needs to telescope to accommodate it. The crash of the Travelers' bubble was like that. As it ping-ponged in and out of existence, at a trillion separate places throughout the universe, it skimmed the surface of a million separate worlds, flattening mountain ranges, boiling away atmospheres and annihilating civilizations. Carnage on such a scale had never happened before, at any point in the history of creation. But each and every violent encounter also took its toll on the Bubble itself — and by the time it ping-ponged across the K'cenhowten Confederacy, halving the population of that starfaring species in that instant, it was dented and powerless and leaking inverted singularities on all sides. It would have been doomed to destruction even if it still had fuel to slow its flight — and there was nothing; the little it still carried did not resemble despair at all.

It hurtled toward the end of everything, empty but for two ancient enemies who now faced each other for the very last time.

*T*he Hunter snarled. **What are you laughing at?**

You, Gordon Wilson chortled, and had he been a living man instead of the intangible distilled essence of a suicide, he would have doubled over, clutching his ribs as he laughed so hard it hurt. It was the best kind of laughter — the kind that lights the places that have never known laughter before — and for the longest time Gordon Wilson simply surrendered to it, thinking this the most glorious moment he had ever known. Near the end, he actually managed to speak: *You're such a fucking loser!*

** *I'm about to tear you to pieces.* **

Gordon whooped implacably. *Oh, yeah, I'm frightened. Give me a break. What the fuck are you going to do to me? Beat me up? Kill me? Stomp me to smithereens and piss on the smoking wreckage? In case you've missed the point, I'm already dead, you miserable pussy! I just put a bullet through my brain! I couldn't give less of a shit what* you *do to me! The most you can do is just put this little second-rate echo of me out of its misery, and you're not going to do that right away because that would leave you alone in here, forever, with no way of getting out, and no way of ever going after anybody else! No, you're just going to stand right there and listen, while I say all the things that should have been said to you a long time ago!*

The Hunter trembled with rage. **Go ahead. Talk. It will amuse me to** *hear what you have to say.* **

No it won't, Gordon said, as his laughter died and he faced the Hunter with the contemptuous eyes of every human being who had ever lived. *It will shatter you. But I'll tell you anyway, because I don't like you very much. You know the people my people came from? The ones you hounded and harassed and pursued to the edge of extinction? I don't think they ever understood why you hated them so much. I don't think they ever understood why you needed to destroy them. I don't think it ever even occurred to them to wonder. You were just a great unstoppable monster, annihilating them one world at a time, driving them back no matter how desperately they fought. And they never got around to asking why somebody as powerful as you would bother. But I know. It's because they scared you shitless.*

The Hunter roared his indignation in a voice loud enough to shatter continents. ***NONSENSE —***

And Gordon drowned him out with no difficulty at all, not with sheer volume, but with the simple confidence behind his words. *You were used to being the biggest baddest sonofabitch in the valley, weren't you? You were used to being the best, the strongest, the greatest. And then, all of a sudden, out of nowhere it seemed, along came this race of glorified monkeys, spreading from world to world with the speed of an explosion, and you wondered who they were and you took a close look and for the first time you saw something capable of challenging your ego. Because as primitive as they were, compared to you, and as weak as they were, compared to you, and as young as they were, compared to you, they had greater dreams, greater ambition, greater nobility, and greater potential, than a piece of shit like you could ever dream! And you* just couldn't deal with it!

The Hunter's voice took on the pathetic desperation of the loser who needs to assure himself he's won. ** *I still destroyed them all.* **

Sure you did. Temporarily. But now we're back . . . still growing, still learning, still finding out what we can be. Our rise may be a little bumpier this time out, because of all the garbage you left us carrying around in our heads, but if anything that's only made us even stronger, and smarter, and faster, and better. I only wish I'd stuck around to see it.

The Hunter could have lashed out and sunk claws deep into Gordon's eyes and ribs and crotch and spine. He could have twitched his smallest finger and in an instant filleted Gordon from head to toe; he could have reduced Gordon to so many separate pieces of bloody shrapnel that there never would have been any way to tell what manner of creature he had been. None of it would have cost the Hunter any effort at all. But the Hunter did nothing.

Gordon Wilson smiled, faced down the embodiment of all of Mankind's fears . . .

. . . and with a leer, gave him the finger.

*T*he bubble was half-in, half-out of existence when it finally shattered. Its shrapnel popped into being on any number of worlds; they resembled nothing so much as shards of shattered mirror, capable of reflecting anything they saw. Some of the shards ended up on Earth, and some of the beings who found them were human: most notable among them an unhappy young woman named Tricia Winters, who found her fragment on the beach, stared into the oddly beautiful version of herself, and imagined for an instant that she saw a sadly contented little man smiling back. But that was the most anybody ever knew of the struggle that had been, for nobody ever found a shard that reflected the Hunter, anywhere in the known universe.

As for the rest of it: the owner of the office-furniture shop found Gordon Wilson's automobile in his parking lot first thing Wednesday morning. After a properly respectful interval spent being violently and messily ill, he called the police, who called the medical examiner, who needed less than thirty seconds to pronounce the expected verdict of suicide. Everybody muttered the usual platitudes about the mess and the shock and the horrible waste of life; but nobody who looked at Gordon Wilson mentioned the triumph shining from eyes that should have been past showing any emotion at all.

Baby Girl Diamond

*M*y older sister died nameless after seven minutes of life, without ever knowing joy, or hope, or light less harsh than overhead fluorescents. She was a frail twisted thing, my sister, cursed with a heart that didn't want to beat and lungs that didn't want to breathe . . . and she would have died even earlier, but she clutched at those seven minutes with the simple rage of a creature born knowing only that she'd been brutally cheated.

I was born two years later, two months premature in an era when that practically meant a baby might as well be given up for lost. My legs were black from poor circulation, my face cyanotic-blue and stretched thin as onionskin over unformed lemur eyes. My doctors gave me a ten-percent chance of survival, which dwindled steadily as I lost weight every day for a full week. My mother, already shattered once, refused to see me until my weight stabilized; my father refused to name me until the doctors pronounced me fit to go home. On that day I became Abe. Even so, I returned to the hospital three times in my first year, as if wanting to follow my older sister wherever she had gone; my strength built only slowly, and didn't become what it should have been until some years after my younger sister, Kate, entered the world strong and healthy, with no complications at all.

Kate and I grew up knowing there'd been an older sister before us, but we rarely spoke about her. Why should we? There were no baby pictures, no cute anecdotes, nothing that would transform her from a mythical abstraction to a human being. It was sad that a baby had died, of course, but even as small children we knew that this happened from time to time; and our older sister's entire existence had taken place in the unknown country before our births. As far as we were concerned she had nothing to do with us at all.

Meanwhile, our older sister remained in the only home she'd ever known. Nobody thought of what lay beneath the grass and dirt; nobody stopped by to leave flowers or speak a few words over her grave. Nobody even thought it wrong that she'd never been dignified with a name. Nobody saw the point. Life goes on. And so does death.

*I*t wasn't until I was 23 that I put flowers on her grave.

The family had been to the site — a typically sprawling Jewish cemetery in Long Island, crisscrossed by access roads and bigger than some of the smaller European countries — half a dozen times in the past few years, but never for her. As with any other extended family, we'd suffered through funerals with monotonous regularity . . . occasionally honoring people close to us, but more frequently discharging obligations to obscure folks related only by marriage or even more distant relatives I may have met only once or twice at most. My distant cousin Estelle fit into that latter category. I couldn't picture what she'd looked like, I couldn't decipher the genealogy that linked her to us, and for the life of me I couldn't remember whether the weeping fat woman everybody made such a big show of comforting was her sister or daughter; either way, she was one of those embarrassing older relatives who remembers you from when you were five and insists on telling you at great length how cute you were at that age. She also said she couldn't believe I'd grown up so big and strong when for so long nobody was sure I'd live. I reacted to that statement about as well as any adult can be expected to, which is to say with silent mortification, all the while inwardly cursing the parental guilt that had bullied Kate and I into coming here in the first place.

We lowered Estelle's coffin into the earth, took symbolic turns dropping in individual shovelfuls of dirt, then began filing back toward our respective cars. Some of the mourners were heading back to the weeping woman's house for the usual post-burial feeding frenzy, but Kate and I were to be spared that ordeal, as she had to get back to her apartment to study for finals, and I had been gratefully volunteered to drive her there. Relieved to be going, in the secret manner that people are always relieved to be done with the business of death, we gave our regrets and piled into the car for the long drive back upstate.

As the car crawled through the cemetery at five miles an hour, behind a traffic jam of other departing relatives, Kate lit a cigarette and stared philosophically at the small mountain of excavated dirt the cemetery had piled up in the far distance. "Godamighty. These things always make my head pound."

"You'll feel better when we get some food into you."

"Maybe." She snorted. "And maybe that's just nonsense. Maybe Mom and Dad and the rest of the family have just conditioned us to expect free food after funerals. You know, always laying out such a big spread for when we get back. That's kind of sick, you know that?"

"It's tradition," I said inadequately.

"Oh, please. You're turning into Mom."

I shut up. Kate had been next to impossible to talk to for the last couple of years, adopting open hostility as a persona, after first experimenting with half a dozen others from distant to nurturing. It was a just a veneer, of course; but she'd worn so many veneers since the days when we actually liked each other that I sometimes wondered if there was still anybody of substance underneath.

The traffic ahead of us stopped entirely, halted in its tracks by another funeral passing by on a crossing road. Their guy wasn't buried yet, so cemetery rules gave them the right of way, even though their line of cars was by the looks of things about five miles longer than ours. I craned my neck, but couldn't see the end of their line. So I shrugged, turned on the radio — Bob Dylan, who I venerated, but she couldn't stand — and tried to breathe through her smoke as we waited for the parade to pass.

Eventually, just to make conversation, I said, "We must have three dozen relatives buried here by now."

"At least," Kate said. "Our sister's buried here, you know."

"What sis— oh. Her. Really?"

"Uh huh. Mom mentioned it to me last time we were here. You know, when Cousin Ruthie died? — I don't think you were here for that one. Anyway, she said there's a special enclosed section off by the side somewhere where they bury unnamed babies. Our sister's there. She's got a stone and everything."

This blew me away. I had never actually realized that our older sister, the distant, ethereal, rarely mentioned ghost of our childhoods, was buried somewhere; I think on some level I'd just pictured her disappearing all at once, the way a soap bubble does upon bursting. The revelation that she actually had a stone, and a few feet of soil, made her seem real to me for the first time. "Did Mom take you to see her?"

"What, are you kidding? Of course not."

"We ought to go, sometime."

"Yeah, maybe. Not today, though."

I knew then that if we didn't go today we'd never go. "Why not? What will it take, another ten minutes at most?"

Her eyes rolled. "Listen to that, God. He's actually serious."

"Come on, aren't you curious?"

"No. It's morbid."

My own enthusiasm for the idea was already waning, but Kate had irritated me enough to make me defend it out of sheer spite. "It's my car," I said. "We're going."

*I*t actually took a lot more than ten minutes. We first had to escape the traffic, then we had to stop by the cemetery office to get the number and location of the lot, then we missed the turnoff, got lost, and drove around in increasingly repetitive circles until we got directions from a stoop-shouldered workman lugging dirt down the road in a wheelbarrow. He passed some remark to the effect that he didn't think anybody went out "there" anymore, then rattled off a list of turnoffs, which he needed to repeat three times before they even approached sense. By the time we found the right place, a section set apart by a stone arch and tall hedges, the whim was forty minutes old, and was beginning to assume the dimensions of an epic quest.

I parked the car and stared at the great stone arch, which bore a legend rendered totally illegible by the ivy that had been permitted to grow over and hide the letters. I could only make out the closing "Y." There was a black iron gate, which was open; and a stone path which led through the gateway and into the hidden places beyond. Even without seeing the inside, it still felt like too cold a place to have anything to do with children. I tapped my hands against the wheel a few times, vacillating, then, with a sudden movement, opened the driver's door. Kate got out when I did, which surprised me, since by that time I was certain she'd planned to remain in her seat and sulk. I glanced at her over the car roof, relaying a question with my eyes.

She shook her head. "Just getting some air. You want to do this, go ahead. I'll stay with the car."

"You sure?"

"Absolutely."

I nodded, told her I'd be right back, and followed the path through the open gate. The hedges on either side formed a corridor just wide enough to accommodate one person. The path turned left, then right, then left again, for no apparent reason beyond obscuring the exit behind me. I almost gave up when I saw another turn up ahead, but this turned out to be the last one; when I turned the bend, the baby graveyard was waiting for me. It was a well-kept area about four acres square, entirely enclosed by hedges, and filled with rows of little headstones separated only by the paths that wound between them.

It was fancier than I'd thought it would be. The paths were gravel, which crunched beneath my feet. The fountain in the center framed a baby pouring an infinite supply of water from a stone vase. There were half a dozen marble benches set against the hedges at regular intervals; one, right by the entrance, was even occupied, by a sleepy woman in black who kicked her legs stared vacantly at the sky, more interested in clouds than in any of the gravesites around us. I spared her the briefest of glances before walking by, searching for Row W, Plot 17.

The markings on the headstones were formulaic. The child's sex, its last name, its birthday and the day it died (which were, here, almost always the same day). I saw Baby Boy Fein (May 19 1947), Baby Girl Wassermann (April 23 1954), Baby Boy Posselvitch (September 9 1959), Baby Girl Shwarzmann (May 19 1962), and Baby Boy Feder (November 22 1963), too self-conscious over being here at all to feel any sadness over all these truncated lives.

And then I found her:

Baby Girl Diamond. January 12 1964.

My heart thumped hard at the sight of the name. But after that, I felt nothing. She may have been my sister for seven minutes, but I'd never met her, never seen a picture of her, never found out what kind of person she would have been, never decided whether or not I liked her. The stone didn't make her any less an abstraction. I stood there, staring at the cold, sterile letters and wondering why I'd expected a great emotional rush. Kate had been right, after all. This was pointless.

After only a few seconds of dutiful silence, I bent over, picked up a rock about the size of my fist, and balanced it on the headstone to establish that somebody had been by to visit, if only this once. That was something, at least. Not much, but there sure wasn't much else I could do. The gesture made, I turned to leave, already thinking ahead to lunch.

The woman on the bench kicked her bare feet absently as I headed toward the exit. From this angle I got a much better view of her. She was pale-skinned, and dark-haired, and thin to the point of androgyny; she had a cool wistfulness easily visible long before I approached close enough to spot the Diamond family's trademark nose and chin. When she smiled at me, I noticed how much she looked like an older version of Kate, and my legs, while still carrying me forward, went numb as I suddenly realized I knew exactly who she was.

"That was nice of you," she said.

I froze in mid-step, wanting to run, but knowing that if I left now I'd be reliving the inadequacy of my response every single day for the rest of my life. After a moment I approached her, which made her pretty brown eyes widen with surprise. She'd expected me to keep walking.

"Not really," I said, and the phrase sounded incomplete without a name at the end of it. "It was the least I could do."

"You see me," she said.

"Of course," I said. "I came here to see you."

She covered her eyes with one smooth, unformed hand — a hand without wrinkles or lines, that had never picked up anything, never touched anything, and never been clenched in anger. "No one's ever seen me," she said, and though they were words that should have been accompanied by tears, her voice remained steady and controlled, her tears still locked away in some hidden vault deep inside her. "I didn't think anybody ever would."

I sat down on the bench beside her, wanting only to put my hands around her shoulders, but fearing she'd burst like a soap bubble if I tried. "I'm sorry."

She refused to look at me. "When I was a little girl," she said, her voice straining at the edges now, gathering power as she expelled years of frustration one carefully considered syllable at a time, "maybe three or four years old, before I understood there had to be more to it, I thought I was just lost. I thought my mommy and daddy left me here by accident and they'd be back to get me as soon as they realized I was gone. That's what I thought, really. And I cried for them all the time, but nobody ever heard me. Then I got a little older and I thought that I'd done something bad — but they'd been gone a long time, so long I didn't even remember what they looked like anymore, so I thought it must have been something horrible. The gardeners, and the other families who came here sometimes, I thought they must have been in on it, too, because they never answered me no matter what I said to them. I thought I must have been the worst, most hateful, most evil little girl in the whole world. I hated myself. I wanted to die. I wanted somebody to tell me why I was here and why I wasn't allowed to leave. Can you tell me?"

"No," I said, my own voice breaking now. "But it wasn't your fault. Don't think that. We just didn't know, that's all."

She buried her face in her hands. "It's been so long," she said. "And it's never going to end for me. Never ever ever."

I sat there impotently and said nothing. What could I say, anyway? That she had to take the good with the bad? That things would be looking up tomorrow? That life and death just weren't fair? Silence may have been inadequate, but anything beyond that was an out-and-out insult.

She said, "Please help me."

I said, "I can't."

"I'm stuck here. I'll never have anything. Help me."

"I'm sorry. I don't know how."

She bent her head. I almost reached out to touch her —

— and somewhere close behind us, Kate gasped.

I whirled and saw her, frozen with the shock of first recognition. Whatever had made her change her mind and follow me into this garden of dead children, she clearly regretted it now; her eyes were wide and her face white and all her defining strength drained away by this, her first sight of the lonely woman beside me. I stood up just in time to see Kate fall to her knees.

The woman beside me gasped too. Before I could even think of stopping her — let alone wonder if there was any way I could have stopped her even if I tried — she leaped from the bench and ran away with the bottomless terror of someone chased by demons. I stood there blankly, watching her recede faster than her legs alone could have carried her, on a gravel path that made no sound beneath her feet. I continued to stare at the empty place where she had been, until I heard Kate call my name.

I turned and saw her still kneeling by the entrance, her eyes closed and her shoulders shaking. It made no sense. This was Kate, damn it. She was way tougher than me; always had been. I couldn't remember the last time I'd seen her reduced to tears by anything. But her need gave me purpose. I went to her, and put her arms on my shoulders and asked her a stupid question. "Are you okay?"

She shook her head. "N-no, I'm not. I don't know if I'll ever be okay again."

"Take it easy. She's —"

"Don't be dense! That was her, wasn't it? *Wasn't it?*"

"Yes. It was."

"And you saw her, too?"

"Yes, I did."

"Oh, God." She closed her eyes, made a fist, and patted it against her forehead once, twice, three times; just hard enough to make we wince from sympathetic pain. "Oh, God. Oh God oh God oh God."

"Kate—"

Her face was not a grown woman's anymore. It belonged to a lonely and miserable seven-year-old. "Take me aware from here, Abe."

*P*redictably, we hit one of the worst traffic jams in living memory — miles and miles of frying pan steel, hopelessly snarled by construction creating a series of bottlenecks six exits ahead. We moved forward an inch at a time. My head felt like somebody had jammed a railroad spike through my temples; I couldn't even begin to imagine how Kate felt, and I didn't want to risk an explosion by asking her.

Eventually she said: "Abe?"

I had trouble recognizing the voice as hers. It was too plaintive, too vulnerable to be hers. "What?"

She didn't face me: just continued staring out the passenger window, losing herself in the way the sunlight reflected off the other cars. "You really don't know why she scared me so much, do you? You don't have the slightest idea."

"She's a ghost," I said evenly.

It sounded facile. I was shaken; she was terrified.

She winced. "Jesus. You don't know."

"Then tell me."

"No," she said. "I don't want to talk about it. I don't even want to think about it. I just want to forget this whole day ever happened."

"But Kate—"

"Put on your damn folk music," she said. And refused to speak to me at all for the rest of the drive home.

*S*he asked me to promise I wouldn't go back. And I made that promise, because she was absolutely right; neither one of us had any real understanding of what had happened today. All we knew for sure is that we were alive, and our older sister was dead; that I'd spent a few brief minutes straddling the boundary that divided one country from the others; and that we'd have to be insane to blithely approach that invisible line a second time. I agreed with all of that. Absolutely. Made perfect sense to me.

Except, of course, that it wasn't over.

Once I re-entered the silence of my own apartment, surrounded by all the junk I'd ever accumulated, all the books and records and snapshots and ten thousand other stupid little things valuable to me only because they were part of my life, it was impossible not to think of that lonely woman who'd been so pathetically grateful just to be seen. I thought of what she must have looked like at seven, existing alone and unloved in that garden of dead children, when I was five, and taking the short yellow bus to kindergarten, where I learned how to paint. I thought of what she must have looked like at twelve, still alone, still sitting on that bench waiting for something the world had decided she would never have, while I was with the family vacationing in Florida, and building sand castles on Deerfield Beach. I thought of her changing from toddler to child to teenager to woman, suffering, instead of the oblivion that should have been hers, an endless succession of days spent in that same solitary place, where she grew and matured and aged without ever knowing even the simple pleasure of a deep breath.

I held out for two weeks. And then one night I went to my bedroom window and I looked down upon the corner bus stop. There was a bench there, one of the wooden ones with bright green slats and iron dividers to prevent the homeless from using them as beds. Right now its only occupant was an old woman wearing a thick brown sweater that must have been broiling in this summer's heat. Even so, she hugged herself tightly, as if that was the only warmth she'd ever known, and when she peered down the street to see whether her bus was coming, I caught a brief, possibly even imagined, glimpse of the despair hidden beneath her pale and wrinkled mask.

I imagined the woman at the cemetery someday looking like that, without ever having had a real life behind her, to give her a reason why. I wondered what she'd look like when she was a hundred years old, or ten thousand.

I couldn't abandon her to that.

I drove back the next weekend: hoping that I wouldn't find her, that the long trip would have been for nothing, that her previous appearance would turn out to be only the most fleeting exception to the way the world worked. But she was still sitting on the same bench, still idly kicking her heels as she watched the clouds drift across the afternoon sky. She glanced at me as I passed by, with the dull curiosity of a woman who didn't expect acknowledgement — then she recognized me, and smiled. "Hi."

I sat down beside her. "Hi."

"That . . . other girl didn't come with you this time, did she?"

"No. But why were you so scared of her, anyway? She's not as bad as all that."

She tensed. "Isn't she?"

"Her name's Kate," I said. "She's okay once you get to know her."

"I don't want to know her," the nameless woman said, with a repulsed shudder. I saw plenty of Kate in the way her eyebrows arced together at the thought. "She scares me. I don't know where I know her from, but I think she's always scared me."

"That's all right then," I said. "We won't talk about her. I'm Abe, by the way."

"I thought that was your name. It seemed to fit you, somehow. Almost like I used to know an Abe who was just like you — except that I know I didn't, because this is the first time I ever knew anybody."

"You can't be the only one here," I said.

"I don't think I am, really. Sometimes when I get really lonely, I close my eyes and cover my ears and shut out all the sounds, like the wind and the rain and that fountain and even those motors I hear sometimes, running somewhere past those hedges where I can't go. I think I hear others like me, shouting and crying and trying to be heard. They sound very far away; I can't understand them and they can't understand me. But I think they're all around us, trapped in this place just like I am." She shrugged. "It's the same as being alone, anyway. Worse, even. Because it doesn't help me to know that they're crying too."

"No," I said, glancing at the neat rows of tiny headstones. "I suppose it doesn't."

She sighed — the long, deep, expressive sigh of a woman who'd been hoarding that sound for too many years — and said: "Why did you come to visit me, Abe?"

I took out the long flat box I'd secreted under my arm, placed it on the bench between us, and removed the cover.

She stared.

Kate and I had played a lot of Checkers when we were kids. Other kids had Chess, Backgammon, Chutes and Ladders, Monopoly — and we'd experimented with each of those, along with all the other board games that rose and fell in local popularity — but for some reason involving the way our minds were wired, none of them had appealed to us the way Checkers did. Nothing had beaten it out as our ideal game for rainy afternoons, or long car trips, or sick days home from school. We hadn't played since high school, in part because we'd finally grown bored of it, but mostly because the teen years had inevitably changed us from good friends to pretend-adults who rebelled violently at the very thought of being seen spending time with each other. The set Kate and I had played with had long since gone out with the trash; I'd had to buy this one on the way here, at a neighborhood toy store whose proprietor hadn't understood my relief at finding the very last box.

I unfolded the board, and set up the plastic pieces in standard checkers format: twelve pieces facing each other across a battleground of sixty-four squares. "Do you know how to play?"

She picked up one of her red pieces. I'd expected her hands to pass through it, but she had no trouble holding it. Whatever other limitations her existence might have set for her, these checkers were easily as real for her as I was. "I don't know how, but . . . I think I'm a better player than you."

I'd expected that. It seemed right. "Yeah. Sure. You forget you're dealing with the world champion here."

"In your dreams," she said, surprising herself enough to create a blush.

And as she made her first move, I watched the way the thoughts flickered across her face, and the smile played at the corners of her lips. It was not a stranger's face but one so familiar, from some hidden landscape just around the corner from the life I'd lived, that I could almost believe that we'd both grown up in the same house, eating breakfast across the same table, and riding to school on the same bus. It was a face that could have very easily teased me about the embarrassments of my childhood, even as I gave her merry hell about the secrets of hers.

Ghost-memories poured in, like home movies from a life I hadn't lived: the year she went to summer camp and I didn't, because she was old enough and I wasn't; the time we played hide-and-go-seek in the house and she picked a spot so cunning I was sure she'd disappeared for real; the time we had that fight, vowed to never speak to each other again, and by dint of incredible will power managed to keep it up for three days, as we each waited for the other one to apologize first. Hundreds of scenes just like that, ranging from high drama to low comedy and sitcom-banal, and they were neither better, nor worse, than the scenes I'd lived with Kate: just different. Because this girl would have been a different person. She would have had a sillier sense of humor, but also a nastier and more unpredictable temper. She would have been more generous with favors, but also more prone to depression. She would have had more trouble making friends outside the home, and been more prone to poetic turns of phrase in everyday speech. And I would have known who she was now; as opposed to Kate, who had become, in all too many ways these past few years, a familiar stranger.

The thought made me leap to my feet in a panic.

"What's wrong?" she asked.

Kate barely existed for me, at that moment. She was an abstraction, just like pi, or absolute zero, or a perfect vacuum. I searched for the memory of her face or her voice or the sound she made when she laughed and found none of them; they were all hidden behind a heavy fog that had swallowed her up when I wasn't looking.

"Abe?

The voice, so near, so real, so easy to accept as one I'd been hearing my entire life, scared the crap out of me. "I forgot the time. I . . . have to go."

She blinked. "Will you be back?"

I couldn't say no, because even then I knew it would have been a lie. So I just ran.

I didn't stop at a phone, or go straight home – just drove like a maniac through two hours of mercifully light traffic, until I reached Kate's tiny off-campus apartment. I didn't have to press the buzzer to get in, because another lady who lived in the building was already in the vestibule using her key; even so, Kate must have known I was on my way up, because she was in her hallway wearing bathrobe and slippers waiting for me to get off the elevator. I only had a second to note her red eyes and tear-streaked cheeks before she seized me by the collar and pulled me out into the hallway.

"I'm sorry," I said.

She spun me around and pinned me against the corridor wall. "You sorry bastard," she said. "You went back, didn't you? After I asked you not to! You went back and you talked to her again!"

"I know, I'm sorry, I didn't think there was any harm—"

Her eyes widened. "No harm? No harm? Do you have any idea what I've been through today? Do you?"

"I'm sorry . . ." There wasn't anything else to say.

The strength went out of her all at once. She let go of me and trudged back to her apartment. I rubbed my neck gingerly and followed her.

Kate's place was a cramped studio, which accommodated her furniture only because she kept her bed on stilts. The kitchenette was a closet that had somehow been persuaded to hold a refrigerator, table, sink and stove that would have stuffed a room twice the size. The similarities to a coffin did not escape me — especially since the reek of Kate's two-pack-a-day cigarette habit had become a permanent fixture of the air. I sat own at the little table and stared at the checkerboard pattern on her tablecloth until she placed a tall glass of ice water before me as her concession to hospitality. I sipped at it as she sat down and waited for me to say anything that would give her the chance to explode again.

I out waited her. She said, "What gets me is that you knew better. We talked about it. We agreed that there are some forces you just don't fuck with. And you went to see her anyway. What the hell did you think you were doing?"

"I don't know. Correcting a wrong, maybe."

"And did it ever occur to you that there are some things you can't fix without breaking something else?"

"No," I said.

"I didn't think so," she said. She pulled the last cigarette from a crumpled pack and lit it after three trembling attempts. "Meanwhile, I spent the past several hours trying to hold on to myself, because I keep feeling myself going away. You ever have that feeling? When you can see the far wall right through your hands? When you look in the mirror and your face looks like a bad caricature of itself, with all the details slightly off, and your eyes the wrong color? When you can feel the cold creeping up your arms and legs, turning them numb, eating you a piece at a time? When you keep thinking that you really ought to call a doctor, because you might be dying? When you know a doctor's not going to be able to help you, because when you close your eyes, you can see your only brother sitting in a graveyard feeding the days and nights of your life to some spook?"

"I don't understand. I was only talking to her—"

"Don't talk, just listen. Mom and Dad only wanted two kids, right? Remember? Every time we said we wanted another brother or sister to play with, they said no, two was enough. And that was you and me. But if that, that — that other girl — had lived, then you would have been number two. And I wouldn't have been born at all. Get it now, dummy? I'm alive only because she's dead!"

The sympathetic pain was enough to make my toes curl. "How long have you felt this way?"

"All my life. And don't get carried away, Abe, because it's not exactly a deep psychological complex or anything. It's just something I live with. All it means is that the only times I ever wished she had lived, were the bad days when I wished I'd never been born. The rest of the time, I never thought about her, never wished she'd been a little stronger, never wondered what she would have been like, and sure as hell never hoped to meet her. And the more you fuck around with her, the more I feel like the ghost I almost was."

I couldn't look at her. "I came pretty close to being a ghost myself."

"I remember. The folks tell the story of your miraculous recovery every time they get an excuse. I'm sick of hearing it, already. But don't you understand, Abe, it's different for you? It didn't matter whether she lived or died, you would have still gotten your fair chance. With me, my whole life rests on her death."

"It could have been you and her alive and a dead brother between you . . ."

"Don't be stupid. I'm not about to wish you dead. You're already my brother. But her — she's not my sister, she's just something I narrowly escaped. And you're changing that."

Neither one of us spoke for a long time.

Then I said, "Why did you even mention her that day, if this is the way you felt? Why did you follow me in?"

Kate opened her mouth to answer, then clamped it shut, clearly disturbed by the answer she'd just rejected. "I don't know. And that's what bothers me. I think . . . somehow . . . she wanted me to."

The silence between us was a physical thing, as thick and suffocating as river water. I found I couldn't face her anymore and turned my attention back to the checkered tablecloth. For a moment I wondered distractedly if it was new; I seemed to remember eating dinner here, not too long ago, when the table was covered was some silvery material that caught the light with foreshortened, distorted reflections of our faces. Then I probed the memory further and realized that Kate had never owned anything remotely like that; I was recalling some apocryphal meal at my other sister's place. Terrified, I looked at Kate again and saw her flickering like a TV picture spoiled by bad reception.

She felt it and paled. "Oh, God. It's not over."

I touched her hand, and almost recoiled from the cold, distant feel of her flesh, which was more like the distorted memory of skin than skin itself. "Yes, it is. I won't go back—"

"She won't need you to," Kate said, in a voice that sounded like an old LP worn through with scratches. "You've already given her all she needs."

I spent that night by Kate's bed, watching her fade away one inch at a time, then pulling her back by sheer force of will.

As she tossed and turned and cried out in voices that were not always recognizable as hers, I concentrated on everything I remembered about her: everything I'd loved and everything that drove me crazy; everything I'd understood and everything that remained a mystery; everything that had made us family and everything that had conspired to turn us into strangers.

I remembered her refusing to go to the circus because she was so frightened of the clowns. I remembered her best friend in grade school, Wendy something, who had loved painting and had infected Kate with the same passion. I remembered how that had gone the way of all Kate's great enthusiasms, flaring briefly and then fading away as soon as the next big thing came along. I remembered her on a horse, in love with the animal, wearing the expression of a girl who'd been born to ride; I remembered her tiring of horses after six months and never setting foot in a stable again. I remembered the way she laughed, when something really got past her defenses: a high-pitched, girlish whoop that dissolved into fragments of shallow breath. I remembered that time in junior high when she saw two older girls pushing around a dull-eyed, heavy-lidded, slow-talking girl who had spent months being the school's designated victim; how, though I'd seen Kate been as cruel to her as anybody else, something about this particular bullying had seized her protective streak and driven her to wade into the situation with fists swinging. I remembered her declaring again and again that she had no interest in going to her senior prom, and then changing her mind at the last minute to go with a painfully earnest kid whose name still escaped me. I remembered the killer depression that had had come over me for one full week when I was seventeen; how I'd spent days on end hiding behind false smiles, fooling everybody but her; how that Saturday night she'd cancelled important plans with friends to stay home and watch TV with me, pretending she just didn't feel like going out. I remembered how, on the other hand, when I came home for my first vacation from college, she refused to talk to me and refused to explain why; how I finally confronted her demanding to know what she thought I'd done, and how she said that if I couldn't figure it out there was no use telling me. I remembered never uncovering the answer, because she'd turned friendly again by the next time I came home.

I thought about the way brothers and sisters are like people married from birth on, and how sometimes they don't really know each other all that well. I thought about how that gulf would only widen, as we lived our separate lives. And I thought about how little that really mattered. Because she was still my sister, and I didn't want to lose her.

All that night, as I scraped the bottommost wells of memory for the times we'd shared, she flickered in and out of existence like a TV image during a lightning storm. I watched her turn transparent, then solid; I felt her skin burn with fever, then turn cold as death; I listened to her breath and heard the familiar rasp give way to the distant echoing whistle of something forever tumbling from my reach.

It was the worst night of my life to date.

And in the morning, she was not all the way back. But neither was she all the way gone. She was white as chalk, and covered with beads of cold sweat, but when she opened her eyes to discover me looking down at her, she grinned sardonically. "Whaddaya know. My hero."

I didn't smile back. I didn't think I had the right. "Are you okay?"

Kate said nothing, either unwilling to unable to give me an answer. She turned away from me, looked at the ceiling, blinked several time, then closed her eyes, sat up, swung her legs over the side of the bed, and spent a good minute silently facing the floor between her feet. Then she just stood and shuffled off to the bathroom, without acknowledging me in any way. A moment later, I heard the shower run.

I stared at the closed door, wondering if she'd ever forgive me for what I'd done to her.

In five minutes she came out, wearing a green terrycloth bathrobe. The shower had revived her somewhat; she was still pale, still clearly washed-out by everything she'd been through, but the color had begun to return to her face. She said, "God, I feel funky. Like I've been erased and then re-drawn. I bet if we could put this feeling in a pill, there would be any number of trendy assholes who'd want to buy it."

I grunted. "Do you hate me now?"

Whatever glib thing she almost said next vanished as soon as she saw the expression on my face. Instead, she heaved a sigh and sat down on the edge of her bed. "I don't hate you, Abe. I never did."

"You just don't like me very much."

She simulated the sound of the wrong-buzzer on a TV game show. "The last couple of years, I've been through some deep depressing shit that I don't want to talk about right now, and I haven't been in any mood to like anybody. But no, I don't hate you. Especially not now, after the way you stayed with me and kept me here. That means a lot."

"I almost killed you."

"Only because you tried to be a brother to somebody else." When I didn't answer at once, she used the tip of her finger to tilt my face toward hers. "In case I haven't told you this recently, Abe — you're good at that."

"Thanks," I said. "You're not so bad yourself."

The silence between us was a solid thing. For a moment there I felt certain she was angry after all, that she was readying some kind of verbal grenade, to start off a fight that would end with me fleeing out her door and neither one of us speaking to the other for weeks; but the threatened anger didn't come, and the only clue that anything was going on inside her head was the telltale scent of possibility I'd noticed before, wafting all around us like a heady perfume. "And her?"

I hesitated.

"Don't waste my time with bullshit. You're the one who's talked to her. Tell me."

I considered telling her something falsely reassuring, then realized she'd know at once if I was lying. "I like her. I think . . . that if she had lived, I would have liked her a lot. And when I'm with her, I think about how close I came to being where she is . . . and I know that if our places were reversed she wouldn't want to leave me alone either."

Kate chewed on that. "Does that mean you're going to see her again?"

"No," I said. "I can't, now. Not if it means risking you."

She spent several seconds studying an invisible spot on the ceiling. A dozen conflicting emotions played on her face. The most powerful among them was anger — and though I couldn't help bracing for an explosion, I knew almost at once that it wasn't directed at me, but at something between us that wasn't just a ghost glimpsed in a graveyard. I thought about that deep depressing shit she said she'd been through, knew that must have been part of it, and was reminded anew, to my shame, how little I knew her. Maybe if we got through this I'd make a point of finding out.

Then she turned toward me again, her face spookily calm. "It's Monday, right?"

I blinked. "Yeah."

"Can you get out of work?"

"If I have to."

"Uh huh. And I don't have finals till Wednesday; I can do without another day of cramming."

"So?"

"So," Kate said, with fresh determination. "Let's go help our sister."

*C*ircumstances had neatly reversed our initial positions: this time, I was the one who didn't want to go, and she was the one who insisted that we had to. She said that she should be okay as long as we went together. I wasn't sure I bought that, but letting her go alone, as she threatened to do, was impossible.

And so it came to pass that several hours later, on an unseasonably cold day, damp and overcast and altogether too appropriate for the exorcising of ghosts, we stood together before the familiar stone arch, armed with nothing with a floral arrangement and the knowledge gained from a single phone call. We didn't go in immediately; instead, we stood there, thinking our own private thoughts, which in my case was simple awe at Kate's self-control in making it even this far without showing a single sign of fear.

At one point I said, "You don't have to do this."

She raised an eyebrow, and held eye contact until I looked away. It had been a stupid thing to say.

We walked in side-by-side, though the closeness of the hedges made that a tight fit. When we turned corners too quickly the leaves brushed against our shoulders, leaving damp streaks behind. With almost every step I glanced at Kate to make sure she was still there. She conscientiously avoided glancing back. She just kept walking, her spine rigid, her eyes carefully fixed on the path ahead.

When we entered the garden of dead children, our older sister was nowhere to be seen. The only sign that she'd ever been there at all was the checkerboard I'd abandoned yesterday. It was still sitting on the bench, with a game still in progress exactly the way I'd left it; seven kings against four, facing each other down at the center of the field.

Kate gave me a wry look that let me know she knew I'd been playing the losing side. I shrugged and peered down the rows of headstones, searching for the wan figure we'd come here to find. I would have had to be blind, deaf, and dumb not to know that she was here somewhere, just outside the limits of my perception, watching us, waiting to see what we would do, refusing to come out because Kate was here with me.

I turned to Kate, to once again suggest that maybe this had been a bad idea.

She smiled slyly. "Bet I beat you two out of three."

"What?"

"Checkers, stupid. It's been ages since we played. As long as we're here . . ."

I hesitated, then began to see it. "I call black."

"No fair. You're always black."

I shrugged. "I called it first."

The childhood ritual, reenacted.

We circled the bench like gladiators looking for a perfect moment to strike, sat down on opposite sides of the board, placed the pieces at their starting positions, and started to play. No idle conversation passed between us. There hadn't been any when we were kids, either; we'd taken Checkers way too seriously for that. The only words that passed between us were occasional cries of "King me!", signaling that one of us had reached the other side and found the strength to return.

We played one game. Two. A dozen. I won half, she won half. We sped up, played a dozen more, and stopped pausing to think between turns, instead just moving on impulse, letting our hands decide which piece to move. Eventually we stopped paying attention to who won or lost, and instead just concentrated on keeping the pieces in motion, slide-slide-slide, jump-jump-jump, king-me, some of the moves pointless, others suicidal, none of them mattering except as the first necessary step toward the move after that. The games themselves sped by in blurs, some over in minutes, others exhausting their possibilities in seconds, none of them bearing any resemblance to the quiet, contemplative, Zen-of-childhood matches we remembered; those memories were not nearly as important as the sensation that chance itself was being rearranged around us with every move we made.

And then a cold wind raised the hackles on the back of my neck. Kate must have felt it too, because she looked up the same instant I did, to meet my eyes over a game about to self-destruct between us. Then we both turned our heads and saw our older sister. She stood silently about ten feet away. For the first time since she and I had met, she actually looked like the phantom she was; there was absolutely no color to her skin, no life to the way she looked at us. The pretty brown eyes I'd known were just deep black circles on a pale white face, and when she spoke, the dirt of the grave was gravel bubbling in her throat.

"Why did you bring her here, Abe?"

My first attempt at speech failed. I cleared my throat and said, "Because I wanted you two to meet each other."

"I don't want anything to do with her. Why can't you make her go away?"

"Because she's my sister," I said, "and I won't choose between you."

"She scares me."

"She's here to help you," I said.

Our older sister's head swiveled, her black eyes burning like coals as they focused on Kate. I glanced at Kate to see how she was handling it, and saw from her stiff posture that she was terrified, but fighting it. She even managed a smile, or something that might have resembled a smile if it hadn't taken all her self-control just to keep it plastered on her face.

Our older sister didn't smile back. She just shuddered, like a child offered a plate of food she couldn't finish, and turned her attention back to me. "It's not fair. Please, Abe. Make her go away. She doesn't have anything I want."

"Yes, she does. Ask her."

Reluctantly, our older sister turned.

Kate took a deep breath. We'd called our parents that morning, burying what we needed to know within a half-hour of idle chitchat, hiding the real reason for our question behind vague curiosity, unsure whether there'd be any answer at all, but wholly unsurprised to discover that there was. Beyond that, there hadn't been any debate — we'd both known, instinctively, that Kate would have to be the one to say it:

"Your name would have been Rachel."

Our older sister stiffened. "What?"

"Specifically," Kate went on, "Rachel Elizabeth. Rachel Elizabeth

Diamond."

Our older sister covered her eyes with one hand — a hand, I noticed, that now had some definition to it, that bore the wrinkles and creases of a real hand used by a real person who had really lived — shuddered, and shook her head slowly, as if struggling to deny that which had been denied her for so long. Then she faced me, searching for confirmation.

I nodded. "I'm glad I got to meet you, Rachel."

She stood there motionless, as if the words were boulders, too heavy to carry.

Kate glanced at me, bit her lip, and rose from the bench, to approach Rachel in the slow measured steps of a woman approaching a skittish animal. Rachel made no attempt to run away — just stood there, wide-eyed and trembling, as Kate stopped before her and wrapped her in a hug. It looked pretty solid, as hugs go: nothing ghostly or insubstantial about it. For that moment, they were real to each other.

"Abe?" Kate said. "Would you mind leaving us for a few minutes? I think Rachel and I have a few things to talk about."

I hesitated, said "All right," grabbed the flowers we'd brought, and abandoned my sisters to their privacy. I was too scared, even now, of letting Kate out of my sight, so instead I just followed the gravel path past the rows of neatly kept graves, reading the names on each stone I passed, noting how many of them were anonymous, wondering how many of these children were wandering the landscape around me, crying out for somebody to tell them who they were. I wished I could do something to help all of them, but I knew I couldn't, even if I dedicated my entire life to that and nothing else. The only thing I could do was wish them luck, and try not to imagine I heard their voices in the whispers of the wind.

When I found the stone for Baby Girl Diamond, I turned back and looked for my sisters. They were sitting together. Rachel was talking; Kate was listening intently. I faced the stone again, making a mental note to talk with Kate about having it replaced with one bearing Rachel's full name. Then I knelt, brushed aside a couple of dried leaves, and placed the flowers on Rachel's grave.

I knelt there a long time.

It was over an hour later that Kate placed her hand on my shoulder. I started, looked up, and saw that she was alone. And though her eyes were moist, she was smiling.

I stood. "Rachel?"

"She's gone," Kate said. "She told me I should say goodbye for her. She was sorry she couldn't stick around to say it herself, but she's been waiting a long time. She said you'd understand. And that she's glad she got to meet you, too."

I swallowed. "What did you two talk about?"

"Mostly? Stuff that sisters talk about. Some of it about you. But we wished each other luck, I can tell you that."

I nodded, enjoying the renewed freshness of the air, and the sudden warmth that seemed to breaking through the clouds. And then I took one last look at the dead slab of stone that by itself had nothing to do with anybody I'd ever known. Then I smiled and let Kate lead us out.

We left the checkerboard behind. And despite years of wind and rain and snow, and the potentially interfering hands of all the caretakers assigned to keep that place respectfully clean, it has remained there ever since, looking as new as the day I bought it . . . the only noticeable change from one visit to the next being the positions of the pieces, and which side seemed to be winning.

This one's for Jill

The Funeral March of the Marionettes

1.

It was in the third year of my indentured servitude that I rescued Isadora from the death-dance of the marionettes.

This happened on Vlhan, a temperate world of no strategic importance to either the Hom.Sap Confederacy or any of the great off-world republics. An unremarkable place with soft rolling hills, swampy lowlands, and seasons that came and went too gently for anybody to notice the change, it was indistinguishable from a million similar worlds throughout the known universe, and it would have been charted, abandoned, and forgotten were it not for the Vlhani themselves. They were so different from every other sentience in the universe that seven separate republics and confederacies maintained outposts there just to study them. Because the Vlhani had been declared sentient, we called our outposts embassies instead of research stations, and ourselves diplomats instead of scientists, but almost nothing we did involved matters of state; we were so removed from real power that the idea of a genuine diplomatic incident — let alone a war — seemed a universe away.

My name was then Alex Gordon. On Vlhan, I was a twenty-two-year old Exolinguist, born and raised in the wheelworld known as New Kansas; the kind of bookish young man who insists he dreams of visiting the real Kansas someday even after being told how long it's been uninhabitable. Like the three dozen other indentures who made up the rest of our delegation, I'd bartered five years of service in exchange for a lifetime of free travel throughout the Confederacy, but I'd been so captured by the mysteries of the Vlhani people that I seriously considered devoting my entire life to finding the choreographic Rosetta Stone that would finally make sense of their dance. For it was the Ballet that, once every sixteen standard lunars, made them the center of attention on a thousand worlds. It was simultaneously tragedy, art form, suicide, orgasm, biological imperative and mob insanity. The first time I saw it I was shattered; the second time I wept; the third. . . .

But this story's about the third.

The one that belonged to Isadora.

2.

It was a warm, sunny day, with almost no breeze. We'd erected a viewing stand overlooking the great natural amphitheater, and installed the usual holo and neurec remotes to record the festivities for future distribution throughout the hytex network. As was customary, we gathered on the north rim, the assembled Vlhani spectators on the south. I sat among the mingled humans and alien diplomats, along with ambassador Hai Dhiju, and my fellow indentures. Kathy Ng was there, making her usual sardonic comments about everything; as was our quartermaster Rory Metcalf, who talked gossip and politics and literature and everything but the spectacle unfolding before us; and Dhiju's sycophantic assistant Oskar Levine, who waxed maudlin on his own personal interpretation of the dance. We were all excited by the magic we were about to witness, but also bored, in the way that audiences tend to be in the last few minutes before any show; and as we murmured among ourselves, catching up on gossip and politics and the latest news from our respective worlds, few of us dwelled on the knowledge that all of the 100,000 Vlhani in the bowl itself were here to die.

Hurrr'poth did. He was my counterpart from the Riirgaan delegation: a master exolinguist among a reptilian race that prided itself on its exolinguists. He usually liked to sit among the other delegations rather than sequester himself among his own people; and this year he'd chosen to sit beside me, which had a chilling effect on my conversations with anybody else. Like all Riirgaans, he had a blank, inexpressive face, impossible to read (a probable reason why they'd had to develop such uncanny verbal communication skills), and when he said, "We are all criminals," I was uncertain just how to take it.

"Why? Because we sit back and let it happen?"

"Of course not. The Vlhani perform this ritual because they feel they have to; it would be immensely arrogant of us to stop it. We are correct in allowing their orgy of self-destruction. No, we are criminal because we enjoy it; because we find beauty in it; because we openly look forward to the day when they gather here to die. We are not innocent bystanders. We are accomplices."

I indicated the neurecs focused on the amphitheater, for the benefit of future vicarious spectators. "And pornographers."

Hurr'poth trilled, in his race's musical equivalent of laughter. "Exactly."

"If you disapprove of it so much, then why do you watch?"

He trilled again. "Because I am as great a criminal as any one of you. Because the Vlhani are masterpieces of form following function, and because I find them magnificent, and because I believe the Ballet to be one of the most beautiful sights in a universe that is already not lacking for beauty. Indeed, I believe that much of the Ballet's seductive power lies in how it indicts us, as spectators . . . and if I must be indicted for the Ballet to be a complete work, then I happily accept my guilt as one of the prices of admission. What about you? Why do you watch?"

I spoke cautiously, as lower-echelon diplomats must whenever posed sufficiently uncomfortable questions. "To understand."

"Ahhhh. And what do you want to understand? Yourself, or the Vlhani?"

"Both," I said — glibly, but accurately — and then hurriedly peered through my rangeviewers as a quick way of escaping the conversation. It wasn't that I disliked Hurrr'poth; it was that his way of cutting to the heart that had always made me uncomfortable. Riirgaans had a way of knowing the people they spoke to better than they knew themselves, which may have been one reason they were so far ahèad of us in decoding the danced language of the Vlhani. We could only ask childlike questions and understand simple answers. The Riirgaans had progressed to discussing intangibles. Even now, much of our research on the Vlhani had to be conducted with Riirgaan aid, and usually only succeeded in uncovering details they'd known for years.

This rankled those of us who liked to be first in everything; me, I just thought we'd accomplish more by cooperating. Maybe the Riirgaans just liked watching others figure things out for themselves. Who knows? If the thriving market in Vlhani Ballet recordings means anything at all, it's that sentient creatures are subject to strange, unpredictable passions. . . . and that the Vlhani are plugged into all of them.

A wind whipped up the loose dirt around the periphery of the amphitheater. The Vlhani spectators on the far rim stirred in anticipation. The 100,000 Vlhani in the amphitheater mingled about, in that seemingly random manner that we knew to be carefully choreographed. Our instruments recorded the movements of each and every Vlhani, to determine the many subtle ways in which tonight's performance differed from last year's; I merely panned my rangeviewer from one end of the amphitheater to the other, content to be awed by the numbers.

Vlhani have been compared to giant spiders, mostly by people with an earthbound vocabulary, and I suppose that's fair enough, if you want a description that completely robs the Vhani of everything that renders them unique. Personally, I much prefer to think of them as marionettes.

Imagine a shiny black sphere roughly one meter across, so smooth it looks metallic, so flawless it looks manufactured, its only concession to the messy biological requirements of ingestion, elimination, copulation and procreation a series of almost-invisible slits cut along one side. That's the Vlhani head. Now imagine anywhere between eight and twenty-four shiny black tentacles attached to various places around that head. Those are Vlhani whips, which can grow up to thirty meters long and which for both dexterity and versatility put humanity's poor opposable thumb to shame. A busy Vlhani can simultaneously a) stick one whip in the dirt, and render it rigid as a flagpole, to anchor itself while occupied with other things; b) use another four whips to carve itself a shelter out of the local raw materials; c) use another three whips to spear the underbrush for the rodentlike creatures it likes to eat; d) flail the rest of its whips in the air above its head, in the sophisticated wave-form sign language that Vlhani can use to conduct as many as six separate conversations at once. Even a single Vlhani, going about its everyday business, is a beautiful thing; one hundred thousand Vlhani, gathered together to perform the carefully-choreographed Ballet that is both their holiest rite and most revered art form, are too much spectacle for any human mind to properly absorb at one time.

And too much tragedy too. For the 100,000 Vlhani gathered in that great amphitheater would soon dance without rest, without restraint, without nourishment or sleep; they'd dance until their self-control failed, and their whips carved slices from each other's flesh; they'd dance until their hearts burst and the amphitheater was left filled with bodies. The ritual took place once each revolution of their world around their sun, and no offworlder claimed to understand it, not even the Riirgaans. But we knew it was some kind of art form, and that it possessed a tragic beauty that transcended the bounds of species.

Hurr'poth said, "They are starting late, this year. I wonder if—"

I took a single, sharp, horrified intake of breath. "Oh, God. No."

"What?"

I zoomed in, saw it again, and shouted: *"Ambassador!"*

Hai Dhiju, who was seated two rows away, whirled in astonishment; we may have been an informal group on Vlhan, but my shout was still an incredible breach of protocol. He might have taken it a little better if he weren't intoxicated from the mild hallucinogens he took every day — they left him able to function, but always a little slow. As it was, his eyes narrowed for the second it took him to remember my name. "Alex. What's wrong?"

"There's a woman down there! With the Vlhani!"

It wasn't a good idea to yell it in a crowd. Cries of "What?" and "Where?" erupted all around us. The alien reactions ranged from stunned silence, on the part of my friend Hurr'poth, to high-pitched, ear-piercing hoots, on the part of the high-strung Ialos and K'cenhowten. A few of the aliens actually got up and rushed the transparent barriers, as if inspired by one insane, suicidal terran to join the unknown woman in that bowl where soon nothing would be left alive.

Dhiju demanded, "Where?"

I handed him my rangeviewer. "It's marked."

He followed the blinking arrows on the interior screen to the flagged location. All around us, spectators slaved their own rangeviewers to the same signal. When they spotted her, their gasps were in close concert with his.

I wasn't looking through a rangeviewer at that moment; I didn't see the same thing the others saw. My own glimpse had been of a lithe and beautiful young woman in a black leotard, with short-cropped black hair and unfamiliar striped markings on both cheeks. Her eyes had burned bright with some emotion that I would have mistaken for fear, were it not for the impossibly level grace with which she walked. She couldn't have been older than her early twenties. Just about everybody who saw her the same moment the ambassador did now claims to have noticed more: an odd resonance to the way she moved her arms . . .

Maybe. Neither the ambassador, or anybody else around us, commented on it at the time. Dhiju was just shocked enough to find the core of sobriety somewhere inside him. "Oh, God. Who the hell — Alex, you saw her first, you get to man the skimmer that plucks her the hell out of there. Hurry!"

"But what if —"

"If the Ballet starts, you're to abort immediately and let the universe exact the usual fine for idiocy. Until then — run!"

I could have hesitated, even refused. Instead, I whirled, and began to fight my way through the crowd, an act that was taken by most of those watching as either a testament to my natural courage under fire, or a demonstration of Dhiju's natural ability to command. The more I look back, and remember my first glimpse of Isadora, the more I think that it might have been her that drew me.

Maybe part of me was in love with her even then.

3.

I was free of the crowd and halfway to the skimmer before I noticed Hurrr'poth running alongside me, his triple-segmented legs easily keeping up with my less-than-athletic gait. He boarded the vehicle even as I did. He anticipated the inevitable question: "You need me. Take off."

My official answer should have been that this was a human matter and that I was not authorized to take any liberties with his safety. But he was right. He had years' more experience with the Vlhani; he possessed more understanding of their language. If nothing else, he was my best chance for getting out alive myself.

So I just said, "All right," and took off, circling around the rear of the viewing platform and then coming in as low over the amphitheater as I dared. Once I was over the Vlhani I slaved the skimmer to my rangeviewer and had it home in on the woman. Thousands of shiny spherical black heads rotated to follow our progress; though a few recoiled, many more merely snapped their whips our way, as if attempting to seize us in flight. The average whip-span of a grown Marionette being what it was, they came close.

He peered over the side as we flew. "We don't have much time, Alex; they're all initiating their Primary Ascension."

I was clipping on a Riirgaani-patented whip harness. "I don't know what that means, Hurrr'poth."

"It's what we call one of the earliest parts of the dance, where they gather their energies and synchronize their movements. You would probably call it a rehearsal, or a tune-up, but it's apparently as fraught with meaning as anything that follows; unfortunately, it doesn't last very long, and it tends to be marked by sudden, unpredictable activity." After a pause, he said: "Your flyby is causing some interesting . . . I would say clumsy and perhaps even . . . desperate variations."

"Wonderful." The last thing I needed was to be known all my life as the man who disrupted the Vlhani Ballet. "Do you see her yet?"

"I've never lost sight of her," Hurrr'poth said calmly.

A few seconds later I spotted her myself. She was . . . well, the best possible word for her walk is, undulating . . . down the slope on the far side of the amphitheater, into the deepest concentrations of Vlhani. She was waving both of her long slender arms over her head, in a gesture that initially struck me as an attempt to catch my attention but almost immediately made itself clear as an attempt to duplicate the movements of the Vlhani. She moved like a woman fluent in the language, who not only knew precisely what she was saying but also had the physical equipment she needed to say it: all four limbs were so limber that they could have been Vlhani whips and not human arms and legs. One of the first things I saw her do was loop each of her arms all the way around her other one, not just once but half a dozen times, forming a double helix.

"Jesus," I said, as we descended toward her. "She's been enhanced."

"At the very least," agreed Hurrr'poth.

Her arms untangled, became jagged cartoon-lightning, then rose over her head again, waggling almost comically as little parentheses-shapes moved from wrist to shoulder in waves. As we came to a hovering stop three meters ahead of her, she scowled, an expression that made the scarlet chevrons tattooed on each cheek move closer to her dark penetrating eyes. Then she lowered her gaze and retreated.

"Leave her be," said Hurrr'poth.

I stared at him. "She'll die."

"So will all these others. It's why they're here, and why she's here. If you save her, you'll be disturbing the Ballet for no good reason, and demonstrating to the Vlhani that you consider her life more valuable than any of theirs. No: leave her be. She's a pilgrim. It's her privilege to die if she wants."

Hurrr'poth was probably right; being right was his way. But he did not know human beings, or me, anywhere near as well as he knew Vlhani, and could not understand that what he advised was unacceptable. I set the skimmer to land, and hopped out almost a full second before it was strictly safe to jump, hitting the slope ground with an impact that sent jabs of pain through both knees.

The Vlhani loomed above me on all sides: great black spheres wobbling about on liquid flailing whips. One stepped daintily over both me and the skimmer, disappearing without any visible concern into the roiling mob further down the slope; another half-dozen seemed to freeze solid at the sight of me, as if unsure what improvisations I might require of them. None seemed angry or aggressive, which didn't make me feel any better. Vlhani didn't have to be aggressive to be extraordinarily dangerous. Their whips had a tensile strength approaching steel and moved at speeds that had been known to exceed sound. And though we'd all walked among Vlhani without being harmed — we were often picked up and examined by curious ones — those had been calm, peaceful Vlhani, Vlhani at rest, Vlhani who still possessed their race's equivalent of sanity. These were driven pilgrims here to dance themselves into a frenzy until they dropped; they could slash me, the woman, Hurr'poth and the skimmer into slices without even being fully aware they were doing it . . .

Fifteen meters away, the woman twisted and arched her back and flailed arms as soft and supple as ribbons. "Go 'way!" she shouted, in an unidentifiably-accented Human-Standard. "Don't dang yeselves! Le' me alone!"

I switched on my harness, activating the pair of artificial whips that immediately rose from my shoulders and snaked above my head, undulating a continuous clumsy approximation of the Vlhani dance for *Friend.* Our delegation had borrowed the technology and much of the basic vocabulary from the Riirgaans; with its built-in vocabulary of fifty basic memes, it was sufficient to allow us clumsy four-limb humanoids to communicate with the Vlhani at the level of level of baby talk. Which by itself wouldn't be enough to get me and the girl out of the amphitheater alive . . .

. . . broadcasting *Friend* in all directions, I ran to her side, stopping only to evade a huge towering Marionette passing between us. When I got close enough to grab her, she didn't run, or fight me; she didn't even stop dancing. She just said, "Le'me go. Save yeself."

"No," I said. "I can't let you do this."

She twisted her arm in a way wholly inconsistent with human anatomy, and twisted out of my grip without any effort at all. "Ye cannae stop me," she said, flitting away in a pirouette graceful enough to hurt my eyes. I hadn't even succeeded in slowing her down. I turned around, shot a quick Why-the-Hell-Aren't-You-Helping-Me look at the impassive Hurrr'poth, then ran after her again.

I found her dancing beneath, and in perfect sync with, a Marionette five times her height; the eight whips it held aloft all undulating to the same unheard music as her own arms. It had anchored four of its whips in the ground, one on each side of her; turning itself into a enclosed set for her solo performance. The effect was sheltering, almost maternal, which didn't make me feel any safer scurrying past those whips to join her in at the center. Again, she made no attempt to evade me, merely faced straight ahead, looking past me, past the Vlhani, and past the eyes of all the sentients who'd be watching the recordings of this scene for more years than any of us would be alive . . . past everything but the movements her dance required her to make next.

The harness piped a thousand contradictory translations in my ear. *Danger. Life. Night. Cold. Hungry. Storm. Dance.* I had no idea whether it translated her or the Vlhani.

"All right," I said, lamely. "You want to play it like this, go ahead. But tell me why. Give me some idea what you think you're trying to accomplish!"

Her head rotated a perfect 360 degrees on her long and slender neck, matching a similar revolution performed by the featureless Marionette head directly above us. Her eyes remained focused on mine as long as her face remained in view; then sought me out again, the instant her features came around the other side. Her expression was serious, but unintimidated. "I tryin' to waltz Vlhani. What are ye trying to accomplish? Kill yeself bein' a Gilgamesh?"

"I'd rather not. I just want you to come with me before you get hurt."

"Ye're in a lot hotter stew than I be. Leastin' I ken the steps."

The Vlhani didn't stop dancing; they didn't slow down or speed up or in any visible way react to anything either this woman or I said. If anything, they took no visible notice of us at all. But I was there, in the middle of it, and though my understanding of Vlhani sign language was as minimal as any human's, I did . . . feel . . . something, like a great communal gasp, coming from all sides. And I found myself suddenly, instinctively, thoroughly certain that every Vlahni in the entire amphitheater was following every nuance of every word that passed between this strange young woman and I. Even if they were not close enough to see or hear us, they were still being informed by those around them, who were in turn breathlessly passing on the news from those farther up the line. We were the center of their attention, the focus of their obsessions. And they wanted me to know it.

It wasn't telepathy, which would have shown up on our instruments. Whatever it was couldn't be measured, didn't translate to the neurecs, wasn't observed by any of the delegations. I personally think I was only making an impossible cognitive leap in the stress of the moment and for just one heartbeat understanding Vlhani dance the way it's meant to be understood. Whatever the reason, I knew at once that this impasse was the single most important thing taking place in the entire valley ...

Love, my harness squeaked. *Safety. Dance. Food.*

Sad.

She'd gone pale. "What are ye plannin' to do?"

What I did was either the bravest or most insane or most perceptive thing I've ever done.

Reversing our positions, placing my life in her hands, I simply turned my back on her and walked away ... not toward Hurrr'poth, the skimmer, and safety, but farther down the slope, into the densest concentrations of Vlhani. It was impossible to see very far into that maze of flailing black whips, but I approached a particularly thick part of the mob, where I might be filleted and sectioned in the time it took to draw a breath, as quickly as I could without actually breaking into a run. It was far easier than it should have been. All I had to do was disengage my terror from the muscles that drove my legs. ...

She cried out: "Hey! *Hey!*"

Four Vlhani whips stabbed the earth half a meter in front of me. I flinched, but didn't stop walking. The Vlhani moved out of my way with another seven-league step. I stepped over the stab wounds in the earth, continued on my way ...

... and found her circling around in front of me. "Just what the crot do ye ken ye're doin'?"

My first answer was obliterated by stammering: a sign of the terror I was trying so hard not to feel. I swallowed, concentrated on forming the words and speaking them understandably, and said: "Taking a walk. It seems like a nice day for it."

"Ye keep waltzin' this direction, ye won't last two minutes."

"Then you've got yourself a moral decision," I said, with a confidence that was a million kilometers away. "You can bring me back to my skimmer and hold my hand while I pilot us both back to safety. Or you can stay here and dance, and let me die with you. But the only way to avoid putting you on my conscience is to put myself on yours."

Danger. Dance. Danger.

Hot wind fanned my back, a razor-sharp whirr following in its wake: the kind of near-miss so close that you feel the pain anyway. I stiffened, held on to my last remaining shreds of self-control, and walked past her.

She muttered a curse in some language I didn't know and wrapped her arms around my chest. I mean that literally. Each arm went serpentine and encircled me twice before joining in a handclasp at my collarbone. They felt like human flesh; they were even warm and moist from exertion. But there was something other than muscle and bone at work beneath that too-flexible skin.

Her heart beat in sync with mine.

"I ought to let ye do it," she breathed. "I ought to let ye waltz in there and get torn to gobs."

I managed to turn my head enough to see her. "That's your decision."

"And ye really think you ken what that's goin' to be, don't you? Ye think ye ken me well enough to guess how much I'm willin' to toss for some mungie catard tryin' to play martyr. You . . . think . . . you . . . ken."

Sometimes, in crisis situations, you find yourself saying things so banal they come back to haunt you. "I'm a good judge of people."

"Ye're a good judge of vacuum. Ye sit on that mungie viewing stand and ye coo at the spectacle and ye shed a brave tear for all the buggies tearin' each other to gobs for yer ball-tinglies. And ye wear those ridiculous things," indicating my artificial whips, "and ye ye write mungie treatises on how beautiful it all be and ye pretend ye're tryin' to understand it while all the while ye see nothing, you ken nothing, ye understand nothing. Ye don't even appreciate that they been goin' out of their way to avoid gobbing ye. They been concentratin' on ye instead of the show, usin' all the leeway their script gives them, steppin' a little faster here and a little slower there, just for ye, me mungie good judge of people. But if ye keep waltzin' this direction, they won't be able to watch out for ye without turning the whole show to crot, and they gob ye to spatters before yer next gasp!"

If she paused for breath at all during her speech, I didn't notice. There were no hesitations, no false starts, no fleeting *uh*s to indicate blind groping for the phrase she needed; just a swift, impassioned, angry torrent of words, exploding outward like wild animals desperate to be free. Her eyes brimmed with an anguished, pleading desperation, begging me to leave her with the death she had chosen: the look of a woman who knew that what she asked was bigger than any of us, and desperately needed me to believe that.

Danger. Dance. Birth.

I almost gave in.

Instead, I spoke softly: "I'm not interested in the moral desisions of the Vlhani. I'm interested in yours. Are you coming with me or not?"

Her grip loosened enough for me to wonder if my bluff had been called. Then she shuddered, and the beginnings of a sob caught in her throat. "Crod it. *Crod* it! How the hell did ye ken?"

At the time, I didn't know her nearly well enough to understand what she meant.

But already, it was impossible not to hate myself, a little, for defying her.

4.

The trip back to the skimmer wasn't nearly as nerve-wracking as the trip out, with her providing us a serpentine but safe path directly through the heart of the Ballet. She told me when to speed up, when to slow down, when to proceed straight ahead, and when to take the long way around a spot that inevitably, seconds later, became a sea of furiously dancing Vlhani. I followed her directions not because I considered her infallible, but because she seemed to believe she knew what she was doing, and I was completely lost.

Before we even got near the spot where I'd left the skimmer, I heard the hum of its drive burning the air directly above us: Hurrr'poth, piloting it to a landing beside us. Which was itself not the least of the day's surprises, since the skimmer was set for a human gene pattern, and Hurrr'poth had no business being able to control it at all. Even as he lowered it to boarding altitude, I called, "What the hell—"

He waved. "Hurry up and get in. I don't know how much time we have to do this."

She trembled, not with fear, but with the utter heartbreak of a woman being forced to give up that which she wanted above all else. Getting her this far had shattered her; forcing her onto the skimmer would carve wounds that might not ever heal. But at least she'd have a chance to survive them . . . something I couldn't say for her chances dancing among the Vlhani. I said, "You first."

She took Hurrr'poth's outstretched hand, and climbed aboard. I followed her, taking a seat directly beside her in case she decided to try something. Hurrr'poth took off, set the controls for the return flight, then turned around in his seat, so he could gently trill at us. "I hope you don't consider me impolite, Alex."

His manners were the very last thing on my mind. "For what?"

"For taking such liberties with your vehicle. But there were a number of very large Vlhani determined to pass through the spot where we'd landed — and I thought it best for the purposes of our safe escape that I argue with your genetic reader instead. It saw reason a lot faster than I thought it would."

"Think nothing of it."

He turned toward the girl. "My name is Viliissin Hurrr'poth. I am a third-level wave-form linguist for the Riirgaan delegation, and whatever else happens now, I must state my professional opinion that you are an astonishingly talented dancer for one of your species; you did not appear to be at all out of place, among the Vlhani. It is a grand pleasure indeed to make your acquaintance. And you are—"

"Isadora," she said, sullenly. It was a good thing he'd asked; I'd been too preoccupied by matters of survival to get around to it myself.

"Is-a-do-ra," he repeated, slowly, testing each syllable, committing it to memory. "Interesting. I do not believe I've encountered that one before. Is there an adjunct to that name? A family or clan designation?"

She looked away: the gesture of a woman who no longer had the energy or the inclination to answer questions. "No. Just Isadora."

I saw the silence coming and ached for the wit to come up with the words that would break it. I wanted to come up with a great, stirring speech about the sanctity of life and the inevitability of second chances: about the foolishness of suicide in a universe filled with millions of choices. I wanted to tell her that I was glad that she'd chosen to come with me and live, for I'd sensed something special about her — a strength of will and purity of purpose that would have rendered her special even without the enhancements that had made flexible whips of her limbs. I wanted to tell her that there were better places to apply those attributes than here, on this planet, in this amphitheater, among thousands of doomed Vlhani. I wanted to say all of that, and more, for I suddenly needed to understand her even more than I'd ever needed to understand the creatures who danced below. But Hurrr'poth was right: she'd been perfectly at home among the Vlhani, and was just a trembling, devastated young woman beside us.

Below us, the Vlhani writhed: a sea of gleaming black flesh and snapping black whips, their spherical heads all turning to watch us as we passed.

"They look like they're slowing down," noted Hurrr'poth.

I couldn't tell. To me, their Ballet looked every bit as frenetic now as it had five minutes ago. It all seemed perfectly graceful, perfectly fascinating, and perfectly alien: an ocean of fluid, undifferentiated movement, diminished not at all by the deletion of one strange young woman with chevrons on both cheeks. Why not? They'd always danced without her; they could just go ahead and dance without her again. If anything, they were probably relieved not to have her getting underfoot anymore . . .

I tried very hard to believe that, and failed. Hurrr'poth knew more about their dance than I. Not, it seemed, as much as Isadora — he wouldn't have been able to stride into the middle of the Ballet and expect to keep his skin intact — but enough to read the essence of what he saw. If he said they were slowing down, they were slowing down.

And it could only be because I'd taken away Isadora.

They were as devastated as she was.

Why?

5.

We landed the skimmer in the open field behind the viewing stand. Dhiju led a small mob of humans and aliens from their seats to meet us. They all wanted to know who Isadora was, where she'd come from, and why she was here; I don't honestly think anybody actually stayed behind to watch the Ballet. They crowded around us so densely that we didn't even attempt to leave the skimmer: an ironic, unintended parody of the dance we'd all come here to witness.

Dhiju's face was flushed and perspiring heavily — a condition owing as much to his intoxication as his concern — but he retained enough self-control to speak with me first. "Astonishing work, Alex. I'll see to it that you get some time taken off your contract for this."

"Thank you, sir."

He next directed his attention to Hurrr'poth. "And you too, sir — you didn't have to risk yourself for one of ours, but you did anyway, and I want you to express my thanks for that."

Hurrr'poth bowed slightly, a gesture that surprised me a little, since I would have expected much more than that from a sentient who so prized the sound of his own voice. Maybe he was too impatient for the part that we all knew would have to come next: Dhiju as disciplinarian. And Dhiju complied, with the fiercest, angriest, most forbidding expression he knew how to muster: "And as for you, young lady: do you have any idea just how many laws you've broken? Just what the hell was going through your mind, anyway? Did you really wake up this morning and think it would be a good day for being torn to pieces? Is that what you wanted out of your afternoon today?"

Isadora stared at him. "The buggies invited me."

"To what? Die? Are you really that blind?"

Whereupon Hurrr'poth returned to form: "Forgive me, Mr. Dhiju, but I don't believe you've thought this out adequately."

Dhiju didn't like the interruption, but protocol forced him to be polite. "Why not? What mistake am I making?"

"I daresay it should be obvious. What do we know about this young lady so far? She's obviously had herself altered to approximate Vlhani movement; she's evidently learned more about their dance than either your people or mine have ever been able to learn; she's made her way here from wherever it was she started, apparently without any of your people finding out about her; and she's snuck herself into what may be the most thoroughly studied native ritual in recorded history, without hundreds of observers from seven separate confederacies spotting her until she was in the middle of it. No, Mr. Dhiju, whatever else you might say about her wisdom in trying to join the Vlhani Ballet, I don't think you can fairly accuse her of coming here on a foolish spur-of-the-moment whim. What she's done would have required many years of conscious preparation, a fair amount of cooperation from people with the resources to give her these enhancements, and a degree of personal dedication that I can only characterize as an obsession."

Dhiju digested that for so long that for a moment I thought the hallucinogens had prevented him from understanding it at all. Then he nodded, regarded Isadora with a new expression that was closer to pity, and met my eyes. He didn't have to actually insult me by giving the orders.

Find out.

I nodded. He turned and strode off, not in the direction of the viewing stand, but toward his own skimmer, which was parked with the rest of the embassy vehicles. A half-dozen indentures, including Rory and Kathy and Oskar, scurried along behind him, knowing that they'd be required for the investigation to follow.

I looked at Isadora. "You can save us all a lot of trouble by just telling us everything we need to know now."

She glared at me insolently, the dark alien fires burning behind her eyes: still unwilling to forgive me for saving her life, or herself for saving mine. "Will it get me back to the show?"

"No. I'm sorry. I can't imagine Dhiju ever allowing that."

Her look was as clear as Dhiju's: Then go ahead. Find out what you can. But I'm not going to make things easier for you.

Fair enough. If she could learn to understand the Vlhani, then I could sure learn to understand her. I turned to Hurrr'poth: "Are you coming along?"

He considered it, then bobbed his head no. "Thank you, Alex, but no. I think I can be of better use conducting my own investigation using other avenues. I will, however, be in touch as soon as I have anything relevant to contribute."

"See you, you old criminal," I told him.

It was a personal experiment, to see how he'd react to a joke, and he made me proud: "See you soon . . . pornographer."

6.

It may have been the only time in the history of the human presence on Vlhan that the delegation was actually expected to deal with a Major Diplomatic Incident. Oh, we'd had minor crises over the years (uneventful rescue missions to pick up linguists and anthropologists who'd gotten themselves stranded in the field, tiffs and disagreements with the representatives of the other delegations), but never anything of life-and-death import; never anything designed to test us as representatives of the Confederacy, never a dozen separate mysteries all wrapped up in the form of one close-mouthed, steadfastly silent young woman.

And so we worked through the night, accomplishing absolutely nothing.

We took DNA samples, voice-prints, and retinal scans, sending them via hytex to the databases of a thousand planets; nobody admitted to having any idea who she was. We went through our library for record of human cultures with ritual facial tattooing. We found several, but none still extant that would have marked a young woman with chevrons on both cheeks. We seized on the slang phrases she'd used, hoping they'd lead us back to a world where they happened to be in current usage, and found nothing — though that meant little, since language is fluid and slang can go in and out of style at weekly intervals.

She silently cooperated with a medical examination which elaborated upon that which we already knew: that her entire skeleton, most of her musculature, and much of her skin had been replaced by enhanced substitutes. Her arms alone were a minor miracle of engineering, with over ten thousand flexible joints in just the distance between shoulder and wrist. Her nervous system was also only partially her own, which only made sense, since the human brain isn't set up to work a limb that bends in that many places; she had a complex system of micro-controllers up and down her arms, to translate the nerve impulses on their way to and from the brain. She only had to decide the moves she wanted to make; the micro-controllers let her limbs know how to go about making them. There were also special chemical filters in her lungs, to maximize the efficiency with which she processed oxygen, several major improvements made to her internal connective tissue, and uncounted other changes, only some of which made immediate sense.

There weren't many human agencies capable of this kind of work, and most of them operated at the level of governments and major corporations. We contacted just about all of those, from Transtellar Securities to the Bettelhine Munitions Corporation; they all denied any knowledge of her. Of course, they could have been lying, since some of her enhancements were illegal; but then they operated in the realm of profit, and there was no possible profit in turning a young woman into a sort of quasi-Vlhani, geared only toward her own self-destruction.

That left nonhuman agencies, some of which could be expected to harbor motives that made no human sense. But we couldn't contact many of them by hytex, and the few we could were a waste of time, since they had a relaxed attitude toward the truth anyway. Kathy Ng, who was in charge of that aspect of the investigation, got fed up enough to grouse, "How am I supposed to know who's telling the truth? None of them have ever been consistent liars!" Everybody sympathized; nobody had any better suggestions.

As for me, I spent four hours at the hytex poring through the passenger manifests of civilian vessels passing anywhere within a twenty light-year distance of Vlhan, finding nobody fitting her general description who couldn't be accounted for. Then I stole a few minutes to check on Isadora, who we'd locked up in our biological containment chamber. It was the closest thing we had to a prison facility, though we'd never expected to use it that way. Hai Dhiju sat in the observation room, glaring at the sullen-faced Isadora through the one-way screen. Oskar Levine sat beside him, alternately gaping at Isadora and feeding Dhiju's ego. When Dhiju noticed me, something flared in his bloodshot, heavy-lidded eyes: something that could have been merely the footprint of the hallucinogens still being flushed from his system, or could have been something worse, like despair. Either way, he didn't yell at me to go back to work, but instead gestured for me to sit down beside him.

I did. And for a long time neither one of us said anything, preferring to watch Isadora. She was exercising (though performing was more like it; since even though the room on her side of the shield was just four soft featureless walls, she had to know that there would be observers lurking behind one of them.) Her form of exercising involved testing the flexibility of her limbs, turning them into spirals, arcs, and jagged lightning-shapes; a thousand changes each instant. It was several different species of beautiful — from its impossible inhuman grace, to the sheer passion that informed every move.

The translation device squeaked out a word every thirty seconds or so. *Death. Vlhani. World. Sad. Dance. Food. Life. Sad.*

Human.

None of it meant anything to me. But my eyes burned, just looking at her. I wanted to look at her forever.

Dhiju took a hit of a blue liquid in a crystalline cylinder. "Anything?"

It took me several seconds to realize he'd spoken to me. "No, sir. I don't think she left a trail for us to find."

Cold.

"It makes no sense," he said, with a frustration that must have burned him to the marrow. "Everything leaves a trail. In less than one day I could find out what you had for breakfast the day you turned five, check your psych profile and find out which year if your adolescence featured the most vivid erotic dreams; get a full folio on the past fifteen generations of your family and still have time to get a full list of the dangerous recessive genes carried by the second cousins of all the children you went to school with. But everybody's drawing a blank with her. I wouldn't be surprised to find out she was some kind of mutant Vlhani."

"It would certainly make her a lot easier to deal with," said Oskar. "Just send her back to the Ballet, and let nature take its course."

I would have snapped at the bastard had Dhiju not beaten me to it. "Not an option."

"Then ship her off-planet," Oskar shrugged. "Or keep her in detention until the Ballet's over."

"I can't. It's become bigger than her." Dhiju looked at me. "In case you haven't heard, the Ballet's off."

I felt no surprise. "They stopped, then?"

"Cold. We weren't really sure until about an hour ago — it took them that long to wind down — but then they just planted their center whips in the dirt and began to wait. They've already sent a message through the Riirgaans that they need her back in order to continue. I've been fending off messages from all the other delegations saying I ought to let her, as the Vlhani have jurisdiction here."

I thought of our superiors back home, who'd no doubt want the Vlhani appeased to preserve future relations. "That kind of pressure's only going to get worse."

He emitted a sound midway between a sob and a laugh. "I don't care how bad it gets. I have a serious problem with suicide. I think anybody foolish enough to choose it as an option is by definition not competent to be trusted with the decision."

Storm. World.

I thought of all the Vlhani who made that decision every year — who came, as honored pilgrims, to the place where they were destined to dance until their hearts burst. We'd always found a terrible kind of beauty in that ritual . . . but we'd never thought of them as incompetent, or mad, or too foolish to be trusted with the choice. Was that only because we considered them nothing more than giant spiders, not worth saving?

Fire. Love. Danger.

Disturbed, I said, "I was with her, sir. She was one of the most competent people I've ever met."

Dance.

"Not on that issue. It's still suicide. And I don't believe in it and I'm not going to let her do it."

I faced the shield, and watched Isadora. She was running in circles now, so swiftly that she blurred. When she suddenly stopped, placed a palm against one wall, and hung her head, I couldn't believe it was fatigue. She wasn't sweating or breathing heavily; she'd just gotten to the point where it made Marionette sense to stop. After a moment, I said, "Has anybody actually tried talking to her directly?"

"That's all I've been doing. I had people in there asking questions until their breath gave out. It's no good. She just keeps telling us to, uh, crod ourselves.'"

World. Dance.

"With all due respect, sir, interrogating her is one thing. Talking to her is another."

Dhiju came close to reprimanding me, but thought better of it. "Might as well. You're the only one here who's ever demonstrated the slightest clue of how to deal with her. Go ahead."

So I went in.

The containment chamber was equipped with a one-way field, permeable as air from one side but hard as anything in existence on the other. It was invaluable for imprisoning anything too dangerous to be allowed out, which up until now had meant bacteria and small predators. The controls for reversing the polarity were outside the chamber, on a platform within easy reach of Oskar and Dhiju. The second I passed through the silvery sheen at the doorway, I was, effectively, as much as a prisoner as she was. But it didn't feel that way; at the moment, I didn't want to be anywhere else but with her.

She had her back to me, but she knew who I was even as I entered; I could tell that just by the special way she froze at the sound of my step. She turned, saw me, and with a resignation that made my heart break, leaned back against the opposite wall.

I did not go to her. Instead, I found a nice neutral spot on the wall and faced her from across the width of the chamber. "Hello."

Her expression would have been strictly neutral were it not for the anger behind those dark, penetrating eyes. Facing those eyes was like being opened up and examined, piece by piece. It should have been unsettling; against my will, I found I liked it.

"I've got to hand it to you," I said, conversationally. "The Vlhani are on strike, the other delegations are going crazy, nobody here has the slightest clue who you are, and I'm supposed to come in here and get the information that everybody else can't. Who you are. Where you come from, where you got those augmentations, and how you got here."

Impatience. Establishing that she'd already been through this — that she hadn't answered the questions before and wouldn't be answering them now. Wondering just what I thought I was accomplishing by throwing good effort after bad.

And then I folded my arms and said, "The thing is, I really don't care about any of that. Wherever you come from, it's just a place. How you got here, is just transportation. And as for who put in those augmentations? That's just a brand name. None of that makes any difference to me at all."

She rolled her eyes incredulously. "What does?"

"Why."

"In twenty-five words or less?"

"Counting those? Sure. You have nineteen left.""

She blinked several times. back-counting, then flashed an appreciative smile. "Only if ye ken twenty-five as two words instead of one. Ye shouldn't."

"All right. But that still brings you down to . . . uh . . ."

"Seven," she said, simply. And then: "I'm madly in love with their show."

Damned if she hadn't done it, on the dot. We grinned at each other — both of us understanding that she hadn't told me anything I couldn't have guessed already, but enjoying the little game anyway. I said: "So am I. So's everybody on Vlhan, and half the known universe. That doesn't explain how you came to understand it so well . . . and why you're so determined to risk your life dancing among them."

She waggled a finger at me. "Uh-uh, boyo. It's yer turn. Twenty-five words or less, how can ye say ye love the Show when ye don't ken it one bit?"

It didn't come off as rude, the way she asked it — it was a sincere question, expressing sincere bafflement. I measured my response very carefully, needing to both be truthful and match the precision of her answer. "I suppose . . . that if I only loved things I understood perfectly, I'd be living a pretty loveless existence. Sometimes, love is just . . . needing to understand."

"That's not love, boyo. That's just curiosity. Give ye'reself an extension and riddle me this: what do ye feel when ye watch their show? Do you ken their heart? Their creativity? Their need to do this, even at the edge of dyin'?"

"Maybe," I said. "Some of it."

"And how do ye ken ye're not croddin' the whole thing to bloody gobs? How do you ken you're not seeing tears when the buggies mean laughs? Or that it's really a big show and not a mungie prayer?"

It was hard to keep my voice level. "Is that what you're saying, Isadora? That it's not an art form?"

She shook her head sadly, and dared me with eyes like miniature starscapes. There was pain, there: entire lifetimes of pain. But there was arrogance, too: the kind that comes from being able to understand what so many others cannot. And both were tempered by the distant, but genuine hope that maybe I'd get it after all.

After a moment, I said, "All right. How about I tell you what we think we know, and you tell me how and where we're sadly mistaken?"

She shrugged. "Ye're free to toss."

"All right. The Marionette dance isn't a conventional symbolic language, like speech, but a holographic imaging system, like whalesong. The waveforms rippling up those whips aren't transmitting words or concepts, but detailed three-dimensional images. They must be tremendously sophisticated pictures, too, since the amount of information being passed back and forth is huge. And if a Marionette can paint a detailed map of the immediate environment in about ten seconds of strenuous dance, then the Ballet may have enough detail for a complete scale model of this solar system. The problem is, we haven't been able to translate more than a few simple movements — and even then we think they're talking down to us."

Isadora nodded. "Ye're right. That they be."

I had made that part up. Excited now, certain she had the key that the rest of us had missed, I leaned forward and said, "But they weren't talking down to you, were you? They respected you. They made a place for you. How is that? Who are you to them?"

"Someone who kens them."

"And how is it you understand the dance when we can't?"

"Because I ken it's a show, not a mungie code." When I reacted to that with a mere uncomprehending blink, she just shook her head tiredly, appeared to reconsider silence as an option, and said: "Peer this. There's a species out in space, known by a name I can't make me lips say. They're pitifully boring folks . . . born filing-systems, really . . . but they're totally tingled to crot by the idea of the human pun. The idea of ringin' two chimes with one phrase seems as sparkledusty to them as the buggie dance be to us. And their greatest brains been wastin' years of sweat just tryin' to ken. Ye can buy the whole libraries they've penned about it."

I seemed to recall reading or hearing about the race in question, at some point in the distant past. "So?"

"So they crod up the whole sorry mess. They don't ken humor and they don't ken that a pun's supposed to be funny. They think it's time-time instead . . . a, how-ye-put-it, ironic human commentary on the interconnectedness of all things. Once upon a time, I peered a pair of the dingheads pickin' apart a old terran comedy about professional athletes with wack names — names that were questions like Who and What and Why. It didn't seem all that laugh-time, to me, but I could ken was supposed to be silly — and they didn't. I vow to ye, Alex, it was like peering a couple of mathematicians dustin' up over an equation. Like ye folks, they peered the mechanism, and missed the context."

Damn it, she did know something. I pushed myself off the wall, and went to her. "So tell me the context. You don't have to give me all of it, if you don't want to, but something. A clue."

And she smiled at me. Smiled, with eyes that knew far more than I ever would. "Will it get me back in the show?"

Against my will, I glanced at the featureless wall that concealed the outer lab; I didn't need to be able to see through it to know what what

Ambassador Dhiju was doing on the other side. He was leaning forward in his seat, resting his chin on a cradle of locked hands, his eyes narrowing as he waited to see if I'd make any promises he couldn't allow me to keep. He was probably silently urging me to go ahead; like all career diplomats, he'd spent a lifetime sculpting the truth into the shapes that best suited the needs of the moment, and would see nothing wrong with doing the same now. But he hadn't been with her in the amphitheater, as I'd been; he hadn't bartered his life for hers, and been the beneficiary of the sacrifice she made in return; he couldn't know that it would have been unthinkable for me to even attempt to lie to her. So I came as close to being honest with her as I dared. I said nothing.

She understood, of course. It was inevitable that she would. And though she must have known the answer even before asking the question, it still hit her just as hard; she lowered her face, and looked away, unwilling to let me see what was in her eyes. "Then the deal's bloody gobbed. I don't speak one crot more 'less I get back to the show."

"But—"

"That's final."

After a moment, I understood that it was. It was all she cared about, all she had to negotiate with. Any attempt to pretend otherwise would be an insult. And so I nodded, and went to the door, waiting for Oskar to reverse the field so I could leave.

Except that I was wrong. It wasn't final, after all; there was still business between us, still something she couldn't say goodbye to me without saying.

She said: "Alex?"

I looked at her. "What?"

She didn't meet my eyes: just stared at her feet, as if peering past the floor and past the ground to face a scene now half a day in our past. "Were ye just blowin' dust, back at the show? Were ye . . . really goin' to waltz with the buggies and me . . . if I'd not ridden that skimmer out with ye?"

"Absolutely. I wasn't about to leave there without you."

She nodded to herself, as if confirming the answer to a question that nobody had bothered to ask out loud . . . then shook her head, flashed a dazzling smile, and, in perfectly proper Human-standard, said: "Then you deserve this much. The Ballet doesn't end, each year, just because the last dancer dies. Think . . . the persistence of vision."

7.

We didn't find out about it until the post-mortems, but first blood was shed on a swampy peninsula over a thousand kilometers from our embassy: a place equally inhospitable to both Vlhani and Men, with terrain soft enough to swallow wanderers of either race.

Dr. Kevin McDaniel wasn't officially attached to the embassy. In truth, he was an exobotanist, on Vlhan as part of an unrelated commercial project having something to do with a certain smelly reed native to the swamps; it may have been important work, but to the rest of us it was nowhere near as compelling as the mysteries of the Vlhani, which interested him not at all. Usually, we only remembered he was on-planet at all because he was a clumsy oaf, and one of us had to keep him company at all times, lest some absent-minded misstep leave him drowning in the ooze with nobody to pull him out. It was an annoying detail that everybody lower than Dhiju had pulled at least once. We made jokes about it.

Today, McDaniel's babysitter was a plump young kinetic pattern analyst by the name of Li-Hsin Chang, who had entered her servitude one year behind me. Li-Hsin had bitterly complained about the duty rotation that had obliged her, and not anybody else, to miss the spectacle of the Ballet in favor of a week spent trudging through muck in the company of the single most boring sentient on the planet. And the strange developments at the amphitheater only made matters worse: even as she sat in the skimmer hovering five meters up and watched McDaniel perform his usual arcane measurements among the reeds, she was deeply plugged into the hytex, eagerly absorbing all the latest bulletins about me and Isadora and the Vlhani crisis.

Under the circumstances, Li-Hsin can be forgiven for failing to spot the Vlhani until it was almost upon them.

Vlhani can weigh up to a thousand kilos, but they have a controlled way of running that amounts to keeping most of that weight in the air, and even at full speed they can make significantly less sound than a running man. It's not deliberate stealth, but tremendous inherent grace. And while even they're not quite as quiet splashing through muddy swampland as they are galloping over dry, densely packed earth, they still never stumble, never make a misstep, never release one decibel of sound that they don't absolutely have to. This one's approach was drowned out until the very last minute by the hum of the skimmer's drive and the clumsy splashing-about of Dr. McDaniel. When Li-Hsin heard a particularly violent splash, she peered over the railing, saw that McDaniel had wandered only a few meters from where he was supposed to be, then heard another, louder, splash from the north.

It was a ten-whip mature Vlhani, approaching at top speed. It ran the way Vlhani always run when they push themselves to their limits — spinning its whips like the spokes of a wheel, with the shiny black head at the center. It ran so fast that the whips blurred together in great gray streaks. It ran so fast that it seemed to be flying. And it was coming their way.

Li-Hsin can also be forgiven for not immediately realizing that it was hostile. In the first place, it wasn't wholly unheard-of for a huge adult Vlhani to be running around in the middle of the swamp. It was unusual, but they did sometimes wander far from their usual habitat. She'd seen a mating pair just the other day. In the second place, Vlhani simply weren't hostile. They may have been too dangerous to approach during their Ballet, but that was a function of the Ballet, not of the Vlhani. In their everyday existence, they were extraordinarily gentle; Li-Hsin had walked among them without protection for two years, and had even developed an easy familiarity with those she saw most frequently. She even considered one or two of them friends — at least, as much as she could when the best our harnesses could do was pipe the meme *Friend* back and forth. That was enough for her. As it was for me. And the rest of us.

So it was that even when she saw that Dr. McDaniel was directly in its path, it still didn't occur to her that it might be deliberately attacking him. She did nothing more drastic than just flip on the amps and cry out: "Mac! Get out of the way!"

McDaniel, who'd been too absorbed in his measurements to see or hear the big Vlhani's approach, glanced up at the skimmer, annoyance creasing his pale, sweaty features. He spotted the Vlhani a second later, stood there dumbfounded, wholly unwilling to believe that this was actually happening to him, then saw that he was about to be run over and leaped to one side, belly-flopping in the middle of a pool of stagnant water. He sank beneath the surface and did not come up for air. Vlhani whips sank deep into the ooze where he had been, with a force that would have pulped him. The Vlhani didn't even slow down. It was ten meters past him before Li-Hsin even had time to yell, *"Mac!"*

She grabbed the controls and swooped low over the water where McDaniel had disappeared. He came to the surface choking and spitting, but waving that he was all right. She was about to descend further to pick him up when he spotted the Vlhani, fifty meters away and circling around for another go. Unlike Li-Hsin, he was totally ignorant about the Vlhani, and therefore had no preconceptions to shed; he knew immediately that the attack was real, and that the Vlhan would be on him again long before Li-Hsin managed to pick him up. He frantically waved her off: "Go away! It's circling back!"

Li-Hsin looked up, and saw that McDaniel was right. If she still had any doubts about its intentions, the speed of its approach would have banished them: were this an accident, it would have slowed down and returned with exaggerated caution, hanging its head at the angle that we'd all come to recognize as mimed remorse. She glanced at McDaniel and shouted: *"Stay down!"*

McDaniel yelled back: *"Don't—"* But it was too late for Li-Hsin to hear him. In one smooth movement, she'd turned the skimmer around, aimed it toward the approaching Vlhani, and instructed it to accelerate. She did this without thinking, and without hesitation, seized by the kind of desperate inventiveness that takes over only when there are no other options available. A direct collision with a skimmer, moving at those speeds, would splatter even the largest Marionette; Li-Hsin had to know that such a crash would certainly kill her too. She probably hoped it would be intimidated enough to duck and run.

Except that it didn't happen. Just before the moment of collision, the Marionette leaped, and came down on top of the skimmer. Two of its whips were broken at the moment of impact: another one was cleanly amputated by the lift coils. The rest cushioned its landing. The neurec connections, which had so clearly captured all of Li-Hsin's actions and sensations up until now, now documented her helpless astonishment as she suddenly found herself surrounded by a cage of undulating whips. The Marionette's head loomed close behind her for an instant, then disappeared out of frame. A whip slashed across the frame, blurred, and then disappeared, leaving her without a right arm.

The horizon behind them spun like a dial.

Then the skimmer crash-landed into the swamp, and both Li-Hsin and the Marionette were killed instantly.

It took McDaniel four hours to dig out the hytex and call for help. By then, those of us still left alive were way too busy to hear him . . .

8.

The only question anybody really managed to answer before everything fell to pieces was the precise manner of Isadora's secret arrival on Vlhan. It was Rory Metcalf who made the connection with a supply transport that, about eight months ago, had entered Vlhan's atmosphere half a world away from its assigned landing position, come within a hair's breadth of a landing before seeming to realize that it was in the wrong place, then risen back to 50,000 meters to travel the rest of the way. This might have seemed suspicious at the time, but the bickering pilots had struck everybody as just a couple of incompetents with no real talent for the work. When Rory looked up their courier license, she found that they'd subsequently been arrested on several charges of carrying unregistered passengers. It was a mildly impressive piece of deduction, which probably solved one minor part of the mystery, but still explained absolutely nothing.

And even if we could put together the parts that mattered, we were running out of time.

We'd placed our embassy on an isolated plateau that was both higher and colder than the Vlhani found comfortable — a location we'd chosen not out of fear for our own safety, but common courtesy and respect for their privacy. After all, we could reach any place on their planet within three hours; we could walk among the Vlhani as frequently as they cared to let us, without obtrusively cluttering up any land they were already using. So, like the Riirgaans and the K'cenhowten and the Cid and all the other embassies, we'd placed our cluster of buildings far outside their normal migration patterns, and normally didn't entertain Vlhani guests more than once or twice a year. Usually, we could stand outside the collection of prefabricated buildings that made up our compound, look down upon the rolling gray hills that surrounded us, and feel completely alone, as if we were the only sentients on the entire planet.

But not today. Today, when a few of us took a break to face the Vlhani sunset, we found a landscape dotted with thousands of spiders. The ones we could see were all approaching from the west; the other embassies reported many more approaching us from every direction, but the herds in the west had been closer, and were first to show up. They didn't approach in formation, like an army, but in randomly spaced groups of one or two or three, like strangers all heading the same way by coincidence. They moved so quickly that every time they crested the top of a hill their momentum sent them flying in great coltish leaps. The sun behind them turned their elongated shadows into surrealistic tangles. The few that had reached the base of the plateau seemed content to mill about there, looking up at us, their trademark flailing whips now reminding me of nothing so much as fists shaken in anger.

Kathy Ng intoned, "The natives are restless."

She gave it the special emphasis she used whenever she lifted a quote from the archaic adventure fiction she enjoyed so much; I'd never heard it before. "Do you think we're going to have to fight them?"

"They certainly look like they're trying to give us the impression, don't they?" She bit her lower lip hard enough to turn it white. "I just hope it's just their ancestral scare-the-shit-out-of-the-bipeds dance, or something."

"Ancestral or not, it's working."

Our chief exopsychologist, Dr. Simmons, tsked paternally. "You're being ethnocentric, people. We can't say they're acting hostile just because, to our eyes, it happens to look that way. Especially since, in all the years we've been here, nobody's ever seen the Vlhani react to any conflict in an aggressive or violent fashion."

"What about the Ballet?"

"That's violent, all right . . . but it's not conflict. It's a highly stylized, intricately planned annual ritual, choreographed down to the very last step. Which means that it's about as relevant to typical Vlhani behavior as your birthday party is to the remaining four-hundred-and-ninety-nine days of the year."

"Which would make me feel a lot better," said Rory Metcalf, "if not for one thing."

"What's that?"

"Today's Ballet Day . . . and it hasn't been typical at all."

That started everybody arguing at once. I missed most of what got said because Oskar Levine chose that moment to scurry out of the main building and summon me to Dhiju's quarters. I hesitated just long enough to spare one more look at the army of marionettes gathering down below, contemplate just how long we'd be able to hold them off if we had to, and realize that if it came to that, we wouldn't even be able to slow them down. We were a peaceful embassy on a peaceful world; we didn't have anything to fight them with, beyond a few inadequate hand-weapons. We might as well start stockpiling sticks and stones . . . and if it came to that, we were all dead.

I shuddered and went to see Dhiju.

A funny thing. Desks, as practical pieces of office furniture, have been obsolete for over one thousand years. They were helpful enough when most work was done on paper, or on computer screens that needed to be supported at approximately eye-level . . . but since none of that's true anymore, desks no longer serve any function important enough to merit all the space they take up. They're still used only because they're such effective psychological tools. There's something about the distancing effect of that great smooth expanse that inherently magnifies the authority figure seated on the other side. And men like Dhiju know it. When I ran into his office, he was in position behind his, glowering as if from Olympus.

He gestured at the hytex projection floating in the air beside his desk. There were four main images fighting for supremacy there: a panoramic view of the amphitheater, where the participants in the Vlhani Ballet still stood motionless, patiently waiting for the show to go on; another view of the Vlhani gathering at the base of our plateau; the surveillance image of Isadora, serenely doing multi-jointed leg lifts in the Isolation Lab; and finally, a head shot of Hurrr'poth, looking as grave as his inexpressive Riirgaani face ever allowed him. I was unsure which image I was supposed to look at until Hurrr'poth swelled to fill my entire field of vision. The giant head turned to face me. "Alex," he said. "The pornographer."

"Hurrr'poth," I said. "The criminal."

He trilled, but it struck me as the Riirgaani equivalent of forced laughter: it went on a little too long, and failed to convey any amusement at all. "I thank you for coming, Alex. This is a very important communication, and since you were with Isadora in the Ballet, I felt that you might possess the keen perspective that your Ambassador Dhiju seems to lack. — Have I disturbed you in any way?"

I glanced at Dhiju, saw only anger, and remained mystified. "Uh . . . no. How can I help you?"

"You can listen," said Hurrr'poth. "I was telling your Ambassador, here, that I speak not only as the chosen interpreter of the Vlhani people, but as the elected representatives of all the other embassies stationed on Vlhan. The Vlhani have spent the past several hours communicating their wishes on this matter, and we are at their request lodging an official protest against your embassy's continuing interference with the indigenous culture of this planet."

Dhiju made an appalled noise. "This is like something out of Kafka."

"I am unfamiliar with that term, ambassador, but the Vlhani are trying to be fair about this. They understand that, armed with insufficient information, you and Alex acted to preserve the life of a fellow member of your species. They know that this was only natural, under the circumstances, and they bear you no ill will for doing what seemed to make sense at the time. Indeed, they respect you for it. But they also believe that they've shown you they consider the woman Isadora an integral part of this year's Ballet . . . and that, by irresponsibly prohibiting her return to the amphitheater, you are inflicting irrevocable damage upon the most sacred ritual of their entire culture. They demand that you surrender her at once, so the Ballet can continue."

"Will she die in the Ballet, like they do?"

"Of course," said Hurrr'poth.

"Then the answer's No," said Dhiju.

"You are interfering with a tradition that has lasted hundreds of generations."

"I am deeply sorry about that, Mr. Hurrr'poth. But Isadora's not a member of Vlhani tradition. She's a human being, and as such part of a tradition that abhors suicide. Nobody authorized her presence here, and I'm not about to authorize her participation in any ceremony that ends with her death. The Vlhani will just have to understand that."

Then Hurrr'poth did trill: but it was a grim, bitter species of amusement . . . one I never would have expected from a sentient I'd imagined a harmless eccentric. "Sir: you are an idiot."

Dhiju's natural impulse to show anger crashed head-on with his professional duty to be totally courteous to all the other members of every alien delegation at all times. "Pray tell. Why?"

"Her presence here is not up to you to authorize. It is up to the Vlhani. It is their law and their judgment that applies on this world, and they have clearly recognized her and welcomed her and honored her with a integral position in their Ballet. When you behave as if you are the sole arbiter of who is and who is not supposed to be here, you demonstrate that you understand even less about this species than you understand about your own — which, if you still think the young lady doesn't know what she's doing, is saying a lot. If you persist in this course of action, you will only get the Vlhani more angry at you than they already are. And everything that happens from this moment on will be on your head."

I broke protocol by interrupting: "Are you saying they'll attack?"

Hurrr'poth faced me directly. "Yes."

We had no way of knowing that the first skirmish had already taken place; neither Dhiju or I even happened to think of Kevin McDaniel or Li-Hsin Chang, who were half a world away, and well outside the usual Vlhani habitat. After a moment, Dhiju just said, "Understood. I'll be back in touch with you as soon as I confer with my people."

"You are making a terrible mistake! The Vlhani—"

Dhiju thumbed a pad beside him. The hytex projection folded up, shrank into a mote of blackness the size of a pea, then faded. Dhiju stuck out his lower lip, made a "t-t-t-t" sound from somewhere deep in his throat, and aside from that, remained in place, apparently finding volumes of meaning in the way his hands sat on the smooth desk before him. Eventually, he just said, "Susan." And a new hytex projection took the place of the one he'd taken away: this one the static image of a girl in her early teens. She was fresh-faced, but wan, and she smiled in the patently artificial way that's been common to all portraits, captured by any recording media, since the beginning of time.

"My daughter," he said.

I had no idea what to say. So I lied. "She's pretty."

"You think so? — The truth is, I barely even saw her after she turned nine. Her mother and I became just too much of a bad mistake together, and I found it easier to stay away, on one off-world assignment after another. I got letters and recordings, but saw her in person maybe for a couple of months out of every year. And then, one day, when she was fifteen, a friend at a party introduced her to the latest fashionable import from off-world: a sort of . . . vibrating jewel . . . capable of directly stimulating the pleasure centers of the brain. . . ." He shuddered. "It took six months, Alex. Six months of killing herself a little bit more every day. Six months I didn't even get to hear about until I was rotated home and got to find her gone."

He sat there, thinking about that a while, letting Susan's enlarged, joylessly smiling face accuse him at length.

And then he said: "Every once in a while, some poor bastard gets saddled with the kind of impossible decision that destroys his career and makes his name a curse for the next hundred years. — Go tell the others we're evacuating. Deadline one hour. After that we're taking the little gatecrasher with us and leaving everything we haven't packed behind. Then we'll take the transports into orbit and wait there until we can summon a ride home."

My heart pounding past the threshold of pain, I stepped toward him, faced his gray, deceptively watery eyes, and choked out what he already knew: "They'll never let us back. You'll be throwing away all our relations with the Vlhani, and everybody at home will blame you. You know that."

"Yes. I do." He looked past me, past the hytex projection, past the wall, and past the entire worsening crisis, and said: "But at least this time I'll be here to save her."

9.

The Vlhani were a black horde, covering the hills like flies; and though there were far, far more of them than anybody had ever documented in one place before, it was still impossible to look at them without sensing deliberate choreography at work. Even when threatening war, everything they did was still a dance, albeit a different kind of dance, with nothing graceful or balletic about it. This time, it was more like a march of death, their normally fluid gait reduced to something joyless and rigid, that seemed as forced and unnatural coming from them as a goose-step coming from Man. They were packed most densely in the rocky terrain at the foot of our plateau, more crowded by far than anything I'd seen in the amphitheater, but never advancing beyond the rocks, even when the competition for space flattened them like creatures being crushed against an invisible wall. If that wall crumbled, the wave of Vlhani swarming up the slope would be upon us in seconds.

There weren't many people visible; everybody was too busy performing the frantic business of a last-minute evacuation. That mostly meant clearing out the food stores, the infirmary, the records, and the tool lab; but everybody was human enough to spend a few precious seconds in their own quarters sweeping them clear of items so personal we couldn't bear to leave them behind. There wasn't much of that, though; indentured diplomats don't get much space for clutter. All I had was a pocket hytex and a length of severed Vlhani whip I'd salvaged from the amphitheater after last year's Ballet; I irradiated it regularly to discourage decomposition, but time had taken its toll anyway and the chitin that had once been harder than steel was now soft and spongy and cracked at the edges. Only a few days ago, an unworthy part of me had looked forward to the mass carnage at the Ballet so I could later search the amphitheater for a new coil to seal in permaglass. I remembered that, shuddered, and left the old one untouched on the shelf beside my bed. It was Vlhani, and if we were truly leaving, it belonged to Vlhan.

With twenty minutes to go, it fell to me, as the closest thing we had to an expert on the Isadora problem, to figure out a way to safely get her onto a transport. After all, her enhancements made her physically more than a match for any of us; if she decided to resist, she could easily be as formidable as any Vlhani. Drugs were out, since so much of her was artificial that nobody had any idea how to even begin to figure out what dosages would be safe or even effective on those portions of her anatomy that remained; and the embassy didn't stock anything that could restrain her or be legitimately used as a weapon.

In the end, I snagged Oskar Levine — who, as I've said, I'd never liked much, but happened to be the only person not doing anything — and armed him with two tanks of compressed cryofoam from the infirmary, one hose strapped to each arm. We kept the stuff on our skimmers in case of injuries in the field; we hadn't used any at the embassy itself since last year, when Cecilia Lansky came down with a rare form of cancer we couldn't cure on-site and had to be stored on ice until we could send her home for treatment. There was enough in those two tanks to wrap up a single full-grown Vlhani. If Isadora tried to break, Oskar would foam her.

He tried to talk me out of going in. "Use the intercom. Turn off the field, tell her to come out, I'll get her in the doorway. It'll be fast and easy."

"I know. But I still think I can turn this thing around. I want to talk to her first."

He gave me the kind of look most people reserve for unredeemable idiots. "If you walk out together, and I see no reason to trust her, I'll foam both of you."

"That's reasonable enough. Long as you get me on a transport."

"Fine," he said. "Give me more work to do."

"Oskar. . .!"

"It's a joke, jerkoff. Don't worry about it, I'll take care of you either way."

She'd pulled out the folding cot built into the rear wall of the chamber, and curled up to sleep there; a reasonable enough thing to do, given the circumstances, but still one that surprised me no end, as it was the first genuinely human gesture I'd ever seen from her. Somehow, without me ever realizing it, I had come to think of her as far beyond such considerations as any other perfectly designed machine. But she didn't look like a machine now: she didn't even look adult. With her eyes closed, and her knees hugging her belly, and her hands tightly clasped beside her chin, she resembled nothing so much as a little girl dreaming of the magic kingdoms that existed only inside her head. The tattoos on her cheeks could have been make-believe war paint, from a game played by a child . . .

Something stirred in me. A connection, with something. But whatever it was, was too unformed for me to make any sense of it yet.

I knelt down beside her and said: "Isadora."

The illusion of normalcy was broken as both her arms and legs uncoiled, like liquid things that had never been restricted by bones. When her eyes opened they were already focused on me: wholly unsurprised by my presence, wholly unintimidated by anything I might have to say. The shadow of a smile played about her lips, revealing a warmth that surprised me. She did not get up: merely faced me from that position, and said. "Alex."

"I thought you'd like a progress report."

She refused to blink. "That's fuzzy-pink of ye."

"The Vlhani have surrounded us. Dhiju's practically thrown away his career by giving the order to evacuate. We're packing up, getting out, and taking you with us."

She hugged her coiled arms a little closer to her chest. "I don't want to go."

"Like hell," I said softly. "Whatever else you are, Isadora, you're far from stupid. You knew we were watching the Ballet, you knew we would spot you, you knew we'd be honor-bound to try to stop you, and you knew how the Vlhani would react if we succeeded. You could have avoided this whole crisis by explaining everything in advance, or by enhancing yourself so much we couldn't distinguish you from a Vlhani. Instead, you just made a surprise appearance — and got exactly the response you expected."

Her eyes closed. "I didn't ken what ye could do to get me out. Had no idea I'd waltz into a boyo gallant enough to hold himself hostage for me."

Her tone put the word gallant in little quotes, defanging it, making it a joke . . . but not a bitter one. Encouraged, I pushed on: "And that's the real reason you're withholding the explanations, isn't it? Even why you're using that ridiculous dialect of yours, when you've already proven you can abandon it when you want to. Not because you're trying to negotiate your way back to the dance. But because you're trying to put off going back. You don't really want to die. You're looking for a way out. Any way out."

"There is no way out."

"Just refuse to participate!"

"I can't do that. It will ruin the show."

"So one year's Ballet gets ruined, and the Vlhani are traumatized. But there's another Ballet next year. So what? What's really at stake here, Isadora? Why are they so determined to get you back?"

"Ye wouldn't ken."

"I . . . ken . . . enough to know when they're angry, and when they're afraid, and when they're so desperate they don't know what to do . . . but most importantly, enough to know when they're holding back. They could have over-run us a couple of hours ago, and they haven't. Because they don't want to hurt us. They don't want to hurt anybody . . . but they're still ready to march all over us to get you back. Why is that, Isadora? What's so special about you that they can't just replace you with one of their own? And what's so special about them that you can't say no?"

In the silence that followed, I could almost hear Oskar fidgeting, outside the door . . . maybe even Dhiju himself checking his timetables and demanding to know just where the hell I was . . . but it was worth it. Her eyes glistened, and she faced her delicately tooled fingers. "Alex . . . have you ever dreamed of something so much, for so long, that you had to have it . . . even though you still weren't certain it was what you wanted?"

I just waited.

She still didn't look at me. "If I tell you, will it get me back to the Ballet?"

"Maybe yes and maybe no . . . but either way it might stop a whole lot of good people from getting hurt."

She sat up then — a wholly unremarkable act rendered remarkable by the graceful precision with which she performed it. When a normal person rises from a prone position, their center of gravity shifts. Their muscles come into play, and there's a subliminal moment of danger when they're momentarily off-balance. It's not something you notice in the way normal people move . . . unless you've seen Isadora, simply gliding from one position to the other. She rubbed the bridge of her nose, smiled ruefully, and once again spoke in a voice free of the thick accent she'd used to define herself for me. "Have to hand it to you, Alex . . . you know what strings to pull."

I rose from my kneeling position and sat down beside her. "I better. We're on a planet of marionettes."

She snorted. "Should I go for twenty-five words or less?"

"Let's not limit ourselves."

"When I was eight years old, I was living in my Uncle's house, as his provisional ward pending . . . well, where I came from, there was a whole legal lexicon for such things, and I don't really have to go into it. The Steinhoff recordings of the '57 Ballet had just come out; I had myself plugged into the neurec, with the feed down low so I could still pay attention to everybody else in the house . . . not full gain, because I always had this need to know everything that's going on around me. And my Uncle and his husband were plugged in too, also low because they were the kind of people who couldn't ever stop talking about everything they saw, and my Uncle recited something straight off the hytex about how dark and mysterious the Vlhani were, and how their minds were so dark and alien that no human would ever understand them.

"It was the sort of platitude-laden gibberish that people learn to repeat so they can imagine themselves clever without ever bothering to think an original thought themselves. And I was eight years old. . . . mesmerized by what I was watching . . . and I knew that what my uncle was saying was gibberish. Because it was the third recording I'd seen, over the past few months . . . and I was beginning to have some idea what the Vlhani were getting at."

I swallowed. "How?"

"Crod it, I don't know. Maybe it's just some quirk in me that visualizes things differently, something in my perceptions that's a little more Vlhani than human being . . . and maybe I was just young and impressionable enough to let the message seep through. Maybe it's even a question of talent . . . something that transcended species and gave me the ability to understand when you and Dhiju and my Uncle just saw dancing buggies. But put that aside. What matters is that I saw one tiny aspect of the Ballet *clearer* than the Vlhani. I saw a critical flaw in their performance, something they didn't even see themselves . . . something that made their Ballet a lie, and that only I knew how to correct." She groped for my hand, found it, and gave me a tight squeeze. "I can't describe what it was like, Alex. It was like . . . hearing a single discordant note in the greatest symphony ever written . . . and knowing that only I knew how to correct it. And that night I slipped out the window and ran away from home, determined to make it to Vlhan."

I squeezed her hand right back. It felt human enough: nothing at all like the intricate arrangement of circuitry and plastics I knew it to be. "You were eight years old. How far could you get?"

"As far as I had to. You don't understand: I wasn't really eight years old anymore. The part of me that had been a child was dead. In its place was just this hungry, needful thing, with . . . with a responsibility . . ." She sighed. "I don't want to tell you all the risks I took, all the laws I broke, all the ways I . . . indentured myself . . . to get where I needed to go . . . but I had a primitive version of these enhancements within two years . . . and I was on Vlhan, communicating with the spiders, within four. They saw I was right, and let me know that when the time came for them to incorporate my ideas, I would have to be the one to dance them. As I always knew."

"But you're not a Vlhani. You can't move like a Vlhani, no matter what crazy modifications you've made to yourself."

Her nose wrinkled. "Maybe so. But don't you see? That doesn't matter. Art isn't just technique, in any culture . . . it's also Content. It's understanding not just How, but also What, to express. And while I may not know everything the Vlhani do . . . the Vlhani still saw that I had something to offer them. Something they hadn't even known they needed. And I've spent all the years since then preparing for that."

"For Death."

"You think I don't have doubts? That I genuinely, honestly want to die? I want to have a life. I want to have all the things other people have. But I have no choice. It's my responsibility. I have to do this."

"No you don't! What if I said that the Vlhani have no right to ask this of you? What if I said that you matter more than the Ballet? What if I said that the Vlhani will just have to muddle along without you, and try again next time?"

"You'd be demonstrating that you understand nothing," she said. "Remember the Persistence of Vision—"

And maybe it the sheer madness of everything that had happened between us, and maybe it was the memory of that one moment in the amphitheater when I sensed some small part of how much the marionettes counted on her, and maybe it was a single moment of perfect telepathy . . . but all of a sudden the bottom dropped out of the universe, and I understood exactly what she'd been getting at. She saw the light dawn, and the most tragic thing happened to her eyes: they filled up with fresh hope she did not necessarily want.

Her hand squeezed mine again, this time with enough pressure to cross the threshold of pain. I didn't particularly mind.

I said, "Maybe—"

And that was really all I had a chance to say.

10.

She could have told us we were running out of time. She could have let us know that the Vlhani have a calendar, of sorts — not a written one, since they have no writing, but one they continually calculate themselves, using the passing of the seasons and the movement of the stars across the sky. She could have let us know that they placed an almost astrological importance on such things, especially where the Ballet is concerned; and that while, by their lights, it's all right to put off the Ballet for maybe one or two of their days, everything was lost if they permitted us to delay the festivities much more than that. I'm certain she knew all that: she understood more about the Vlhani than any human being who had ever lived.

Some of the people who later arrived to pick up the pieces said that Isadora as good as murdered everybody who died. They're wrong. Because Isadora also understood about us, and she knew that we wouldn't have listened, any more than we'd listened to Hurrr'poth, who'd advised me to leave her alone in the first place. And I think that even she never expected the attack to come as soon as it did. If she had, she might have tried to warn us harder . . .

In any event, we didn't need to see outside to know that something very bad was happening. The walls and floor shook hard enough to make me think of charging cavalry, trying but failing to keep out the sounds of the invasion in progress outside: shouting, skimmers flying low overhead, wounds being ripped in buildings, and the thunderous drumbeat of thousands upon thousands of heavy metallic whips pounding holes in the ground. I shouted out the stupidest question imaginable: "Oskar! What's going on out there?"

The voice that emerged from the intercom was sweaty and driven by panic. "I don't know — I'm hearing —"

I found the wherewithal to ask the question properly. "Oskar! Are the spiders attacking?"

A siren wailed. Our emergency warning system. Installed as a matter of policy, not because anybody had ever expected it to be used. Against that, Oskar's voice was tinny and distant: "Yeah. Yeah, Alex, I think they are."

"Shit," I said, with feeling.

Isadora said, "We have to let them know I'm going back to the Ballet."

"To hell with that," I said. I patched in to Oskar again: "All right, stay close. Let us out in two minutes. And keep your hose ready; you might have to use the foam."

Somewhere not very far away, something metallic — a skimmer, probably — smashed into an infinite number of pieces with enough force to drown out every other sound in the universe. The silence that followed was one of those completely soundless intervals that happen randomly even in the midst of totally uncontrolled destruction — that don't signal the end of the destruction, but merely serve to punctuate it, putting everything that follows in parentheses. By the time Oskar spoke again, the pounding had resumed, and I had to strain to make out his voice. He said: "Take your time. I'm sure as hell not going out there alone."

I turned to Isadora. "You guided us past the Vlhani before. You're going to have to do it again."

She was stunned. "It's two completely different situations, Alex. The Ballet was choreographed. I knew every move, I could predict where the Vlhani were going to be. This is chaos: a thousand individuals rioting in panic. I'm not going to have much more of a clue out there than you do. If I don't let them know you're taking me back to the Ballet—"

"Lie to them."

"Their language can't be lied in. It's . . . like you said, a holographic imaging system, painting a perception of the world. To lie, I'd have to—"

"Then at least get them to back off while we make our way past them."

"I don't know they'll all listen. Some of them have got to be half-insane with grief. Some of them are going to want to drag me back to the Ballet by force, others are going to hate me so much that they'll fall all over themselves trying to kill me. I don't know if—"

I grabbed her by the upper arm. "Isadora. Enough of Can'ts. Can you at least get us to a skimmer and into the air?"

She stared at me, stunned. "Just us?"

"And Oskar. And anybody else we can save. Can you do that?"

For one horrible second there, I thought she was going to offer the condition that I allow her to return to the Ballet. I thought that she truly wouldn't care about all our lives, or for anything beyond going back to this destiny she'd selected for herself; that she would seize upon the opportunity to blackmail us into giving her what she wanted. I expected it. I waited for it.

Her eyes narrowed. And she said: "Yeah. I can try."

I had Oskar reverse the field, and ran for it.

11.

Neither Oskar or I had the time to find and don a whip harness, but by the time we got outside, we saw that they would have been superfluous anyway.

The compound had been overrun by Vlhani.

A dozen had attacked the dormitory building. Four were on the roof, punching holes in the building with repeated blows from their long flailing whips. The rest had staked out the windows, and were busily using their whips to probe inside. One gave a sharp tug, and pulled something scarlet and ragged and human out the window.

One of the spiders towered over Foster Simmons and Kathy Ng, rotating in' place so quickly that its whips strobed, becoming a transparent gray blur, behind which Foster and Kathy knelt bloody and imprisoned and screaming. The spider didn't seem particularly inclined to tighten its grip and slice them to ribbons — but they must have tried to get past it, because Foster's severed hand lay by itself only a few feet away. His whip harness whined *Hurt Help Hurt Help*, to no avail. I couldn't see enough to tell if Kathy was hurt too.

Rory Metcalf and a bunch of others had gotten to one of the skimmers. They'd managed to take off, but a group of three Vlhani anchored to the ground had reached up and wrapped their whips around the housing. The skimmer strained in mid-air, veering from one side to the other in a vain attempt to break free. Rory pounded at one of the whips with her bare hands. As I watched, the skimmer lurched in a random direction and was promptly reined back in, but not before a burly figure I recognized as Wesley Harris flipped over the side and hit the ground hard.

Ambassador Dhiju staggered through the midst of the carnage, clearly moved by it without ever being touched by it; beyond the fresh bruise on his forehead and a shallow cut on his upper arm, he wasn't hurt at all. He walked blindly, without making any special attempt to avoid the marionettes striding back and forth across the compound; and though they made no special attempt to avoid him either, their long sinuous whips stabbed the ground to the right and the left and the rear of him without once hitting him. When I got close enough to grab him by the hand I took a close look at his eyes and recognized his secret as the luck of the intoxicated: in trying to dull the pain of what had to be the greatest defeat of his life, he'd pumped himself up with so many recreationals that he simply didn't see anything unusual about the chaos around him. I had to shout his name three times before he recognized it and followed us.

A ten-whip Marionette slashed at me. A cold wave knocked me back; I hit the ground with patches of cryofoam stealing pieces of sensation from my upper arms. The Marionette lay on the ground, four of its whips paralyzed, the others still flailing. Oskar stared, unwilling to believe that he was the one who'd brought it down. I caught a momentary glimpse of the dormitory building collapsing in on itself, saw Isadora frantically signing something in the air above her head, then spotted the silver glint of parked skimmers behind the commissary. There were several Vlhani blocking the way between us and that holy grail, but it was as good a direction as any. I yanked the mumbling Dhiju out of the nearest marionette's reach, and yelled "There!" We made a run for it.

On our way there, the Marionette tethering Rory's skimmer succeeded in upending it and tossing her out. Half a dozen indentures, some already wounded, fell too far to the ground. I turned, and caught a glimpse of Rory getting batted to one side by a flailing whip. She got up limping and with one hand clutched to her side. The three Vlhani released the now unoccupied skimmer, (which rocketed over the edge of the plateau and plowed at full speed into a fresh assault wave of Vlhani), then converged upon her. I heard her shout as three of the newer indentures, who'd somehow avoided getting hurt or killed or trapped so far, overcame their panic enough to dart in her direction. One went down. I didn't get to see what happened to Rory or the others, because that's when the big bull Vlhani got me.

It wasn't the first time I'd been lifted into the air by a Marionette. They were peaceful, playful people, most of the time, and some of them liked to hoist humans in their whips as a way of saying hello. They'd always indicated their intentions before doing so, and always shown both gentility and a keen understanding of the fragility of human flesh. Not so now. This one looped its whip around me from behind and yanked me into the air with a force that realigned my vertebrae. I didn't know I'd been grabbed until I was already off the ground, being spun around and around with a speed that reduced the compound and the people and the rampaging Marionettes into undifferentiated streaks of color. As its whip tightened around my belly, the air whuffed from my open mouth, and I realized that this was the moment I was going to die.

And then the world stopped spinning and about thirty seconds later my head stopped spinning with it and I stared dazed and confused at a sky dominated by the sun, which abruptly up-ended and was replaced by the ground as the whip holding me circled around and showed me the reason I wasn't dead.

Isadora.

Face flushed, eyes desperate.

Forehead covered with a sheen of fear.

Arms in the air, twisting into impossible wrought-iron loops and curves, circling around each other in ways that hurt the mind to imagine.

The Marionette lowered me gently to the ground, placing me in a standing position, though I was so dizzy that I almost immediately tumbled to my knees. Then it not only stood guard over us, as Oskar and Isadora helped me to my feet; but also silently escorted us, as they helped Dhiju and I stumble drunkenly toward the skimmers.

There were five of the vehicles parked behind the commissary. None were intact. The Vlhani had pounded three into unrecognizable masses of twisted metal and plastic; torn out the hytex and propulsion systems of the fourth; turned the fifth into a collection of dents and broken instrumentation that may have looked like hell, but seemed capable of wobbly flight. The seats had been ripped out, leaving only the metal housings. We got in anyway. The Vlhani protecting us merely looked down at us impassively, flailing its whips in a manner that could have meant anything at all.

I managed to ask Isadora one question, as Oskar lifted off: "Did you tell it you were going back to the Ballet?"

She refused to look at me. "I told you: it's next to impossible to lie to them. I don't know enough of the future to promise that."

"Then . . . what did you tell it?"

"That you were my friend. And that, whatever happened, I wouldn't dance if you died."

Oskar flew low over the embattled compound, looking for other people to save. Everybody we saw was either dead or too tightly surrounded by Vlhani to go after. I saw several indentures running zigzags through the wreckage, clumsily dodging the whips that herded them from one near miss to the next. I saw a few others who through exhaustion or despair had simply given up running; they knelt in the middle of the carnage, hostages to the mercy of the spiders. About half the people I saw were wearing whip harnesses, their little windup cables seeming a pathetic joke in light of all the real whips raining destruction all around them.

The one time Oskar saw an opportunity to save somebody, and tried to go in, about twenty marionettes went after us, with great springing leaps that drove them thirty meters straight up. We hadn't expected that at all; none of us, with the possible exception of Isadora, even had any idea they could jump. One collided with the skimmer so hard we almost flipped, then grabbed at us in a clumsy attempt to seize hold before falling back down. Oskar took us a hundred meters higher up, circled away from the plateau to put us even further out of their reach, then wiped fresh blood from a gash in his forehead and said: "So? Is there even any place to go?"

Dhiju murmured something incomprehensible. Isadora and I glanced at each other. We held the look a little longer than we had to, exchanging recriminations, apologies, thanks, regrets . . . and more. Neither one of us wanted to break the silence.

In the end, I spared her that much, at least.

I said, "The amphitheater."

12.

We were damaged too badly to make top speed, but the wind-bubble did curl over us when we asked it to, so we were able to go supersonic. At that, it would take us three hours instead of the usual forty minutes to reach the amphitheater . . . which simultaneously seemed too long and not long enough.

I called the Riirgaans. They patched me through to Hurrr'poth, who was — unsurprisingly — already in the air taking a rescue squad to our plateau. He'd started prepping the mission when I pulled Isadora from the Ballet. He'd suspected what was coming, too; had even tried to warn me, more than once. Even so, I had trouble seeing his help as magnanimous. When he jokingly called me pornographer, I disconnected him.

Less than two hours passed before Oskar and I used up our store of conversation, and Isadora crawled off into the rear screen to stare wordlessly at the landscape racing by down below. Under the circumstances, I was almost grateful when awareness limped back into Dhiju's eyes. He croaked: "Y-you're not taking her back . . ."

I spoke in a tightly controlled whisper, because I didn't want Isadora to hear. "I'm sorry, sir. But yes, we are."

He tried to muster up enough strength to be indignant. "I . . . specifically ordered . . ."

"I know. And I'm still hoping to work out a way where it doesn't have to happen. But we have to do this. We have no choice."

"They're killers," he said, almost petulantly. "We owe them nothing.

Now that they've murdered everybody, they don't even have anything left to threaten us with. We don't have to throw good blood after bad. We can still get her off-world. We can still save her. We can still . . ."

"The persistence of vision," I murmured, hearing not my own voice, but hers.

"What?"

"The persistence of vision." When Dhiju showed no signs of comprehension, I shook my head, as if sheer denial could erase everything I knew. Oskar must have sensed something wrong, just about then, because he left the controls and took a seat between us, looking haggard and grim and desperate to understand. I didn't acknowledge him, or even Dhiju; at the moment, I was too lost in the size of it, too unable to fit other people into a universe which had suddenly changed all shape and form. "You can't even blame them," I said, distantly. "They thought they were going to lose everything. They had to go mad."

"You're not making any sense," crabbed Dhiju.

Isadora didn't turn around even then; but then she didn't have to. I knew she was listening. I shook my head to fight off the shock, and spoke as earnestly as I could, in words meant for all of us. "It's not something I'm comfortable knowing, sir. But with all the things she's said, and all the things that have happened, I've begun to understand, a little. And I've learned . . . that we never had the slightest idea how big this was, for them. We knew their language was holographic. We knew they were drawing pictures for each other. We knew that whatever they were making with the Ballet was more important to them than their lives. And we were right about all that. But we also thought that a new Ballet began and ended every year . . . and in that we were wrong. The picture they paint, sir . . . it's just a single frame. And it blends together, in their minds, with the picture they painted last year . . . and the one they're going to paint one year from now. All arranged in sequence, and merged by the persistence of vision . . ."

"A motion picture," Oskar said hoarsely.

Dhiju's eyes flickered in his direction, then bored in on mine. "So?"

"So that's why she can't quit. For the same reason she surrendered when I threatened my own life. Because she's driven by responsibility. And she knows that if she quit it wouldn't just ruin one Ballet — which would traumatize the whole species but still leave them room to rebuild. No. It would shatter a single evolving work of art that they've been creating for the better part of their history. It would destroy everything they've ever been, everything they've ever dreamed about, and everything they've ever tried to accomplish. It would leave them with nothing to live for. And that's why she can't quit. Because it's either her life . . . or the lives of every Vlhani that ever lived."

Oskar breathed, "Holy," utterly forgetting to specify a Holy What.

Dhiju remained silent. He just looked at me, and then at Oskar, and then at Isadora, who still sat staring out the screen, giving no indication that she heard any one of us. And then he turned back to me, and said, "I'm sorry, Alex. But even if this theory bears any relation to reality, which I doubt, it changes nothing. I'm still ordering you to stop her."

Damn it, he had to understand. "Like I said, sir . . . I intend to try. I don't want her to die any more than you do. But the Vlhani—"

He drowned me out. "The Vlhani are not my problem! It's not my fault they've dedicated theirselves to this thing! Their insanity is not my responsibility — and hers is! I won't let her kill herself! And I'm ordering you to turn this crate around and demand asylum at one of the other embassies!"

"I can't. I have to leave our options open . . . in case there's no other way."

Dhiju stared, unwilling to believe that a third-year indenture would risk everything by daring to defy him. He wrested control of his voice, and spoke with the kind of controlled quiet that can be overheard in the middle of an explosion. "Alex. If you don't do what I say within the next five seconds, I'll consider it a gross act of insubordination and extend your contract fifty years."

Oskar said: "Then you'll have to extend mine too."

I glanced at Oskar, astonished. I hadn't expected him to join in my mutiny; I'd been counting on Isadora to help me overcome the two of them. But he faced Dhiju with the stoic intractability of a brick wall, and he gathered up the cryofoam harness, and he held it in his hand, to demonstrate what awaited if Dhiju tried to interfere in any way. It was funny. I'd never liked him, not even the slightest bit; he'd never been anything more to me than just somebody I had to deal with in order to do my job. But right now, I found myself hard-pressed to remember exactly why that was.

As for Dhiju, he nodded, unsurprised, all the strength going out of him all at once. And he reached into the pocket of his tunic and took out one of his vials of blue liquid and swallowed it down in one gulp. He closed his eyes before we got to see them go fuzzy and dilated again, and murmured, "You're both throwing away the rest of your lives."

I began to protest, but Oskar rode me out. "No, Alex . . . that's fair. Get out of the way and I'll foam him, so he doesn't have to watch."

After a moment, I complied. Why not? Had I been in Dhiju's position, I wouldn't have wanted to be conscious either. And the ambient temperature in the skimmer dropped thirty degrees as the liquid bubbling sound filled the air around us.

13.

I sat beside Isadora for much of the hour that remained of our flight, not speaking, just making my presence known. Not that she spent all of that remaining hour or so just looking out the screen. All it showed was a nondescript series of hills and valleys and plains and lakes, none of which were by themselves particularly different from the those that puckered the landscape of ten million other worlds. Sometimes we passed over small herds of Vlhani, who were visible only as black dots against brown fields; if they heard the hum of our drive and looked up, to catch a glimpse of the vehicle bearing this year's most honored dancer, it wasn't what she needed to see. And so she spent most of that last hour just quietly sitting with me, not speaking much, not remaining entirely quiet either: just sharing the space, and the wait, for that place which we both knew we'd reach all too soon.

Near the end of that hour, I asked her about the markings on her cheeks, already suspecting what she'd tell me. And I was right: they were merely desperate affectations left over from her first few days on her own — the legacy of an eight-year-old girl struggling to re-invent herself as she finagled her way from one world to another. Both they, and her made-up slang, were remnants of a past she'd created for herself — the kind of past that only could have been created by a frightened child forced to become adult before her time. I thought about the long hours Rory had spent searching her databases for a society that used those ritual markings, and those idioms . . . and wondered whether she'd still be alive to laugh about it when I told her.

Not long after that, I began to spot landmarks — the otherwise nondescript rock formations and dried riverbeds that my previous journeys to this place had taught me to recognize as the vicinity of the amphitheater. When Oskar pointed out a cratered plain pockmarked by the tracks of the one hundred thousand Vlhani dancers who had passed this way on their journey to the place where they were scheduled to die, my stomach seized up. And when we saw the Ballet. . . .

. . . it had always been a magnificent sight. It still was. But today was the first time it filled me with dread.

Seen from a distance, with or without rangeviewers: a sliver cut into the face of the planet, filled with a gleaming black sea that swelled and surged like an intelligent amoeba. With the reflective Vlhani skin glowing red in the light of the rising sun; it looked like a lake of fire. An unworthy part of me wished for plasma cannons so I could make it one.

As we drew closer, we saw that not all of the Vlhani were in the amphitheater itself — there were several hundred gathered above the northern rim, arranged in two semicircular mobs with single wide pathway between them. The pathway led straight to the heart of the

Ballet. An invitation, set out for Isadora.

As for the viewing stand on the opposite rim: it was packed again. Not quite to capacity — since this time, there were no humans and only a few Riirgaans in the seats — but close enough to let me know that all of the alien delegations had returned to their places, eager to see the Ballet resume as scheduled. From this side of the amphitheater, it was easy to hate them, for their eagerness to see that which I would given anything to stop. Would any of them mourn the Vlhani who died? Would any mourn Isadora?

Oskar told the skimmer to hover, then came over and knelt beside us. His eyes were tearing. "I was . . . going over this in my head. About what we're doing . . . what we're about to let her do. I kept . . . thinking . . . that there had to be some other way. And I think I have one."

Isadora's smile was grateful, but without much hope. "Oh?"

"Participate via hytex."

It hit me like an electric current wired right into the spine. "What?"

"You heard me," said Oskar. He turned to her. "You can dance your part somewhere safe; we'll rig up a micro-remote to hover over the amphitheater and broadcast your image wherever you have to be. You can do everything you have to do without being anywhere near the Vlhani when they start losing muscle control."

My heart pounded in my chest. "Isadora! Would that work?"

She shook her head sadly. "If the Vlhani were human, maybe. But they don't see on the same wavelengths."

"We can recalibrate! Project something they can see! Even sound, if we need to! Damn it, Isadora, we know so much more than you think! Give us a couple of hours to arrange it, and you'll live!"

"But don't you see what an insult that would be? All those Vlhani dying, and their most honored guest staying alive by remote control? Showing herself above them, by continuing to walk and breathe while everybody who waited for her dies? I can't mock them that way. I won't."

"The spiders killed a lot of good people today," Oskar pleaded. "They can use a little mockery."

"I'm sorry," she said, and leaned forward to kiss him. "But, please. I have to do this. If that means anything to you, please land so I can get it over with."

He lowered his head, shuddered, and went off to the controls.

For me, it was not like we were sinking. It was like the ground was rising to meet us; like the entire planet was a single predator, and the horizons were razor-studded jaws inexorably closing shut. It was hard to remember that neither Oscar nor Dhiju nor I were in the same danger Isadora was: if we just stayed in the skimmer, let her disembark and then took off, the only person being swallowed whole tòday was the strange, beautiful, terrified, but unwavering woman who knelt beside me. It didn't make me feel any safer. If she died, it would still be too much like dying myself.

We were still some distance from the ground when I said: "Isadora."

She abandoned the view and looked at me. "Alex."

"Was everything you told the Vlhani true? Back at the compound?"

She smiled sadly. "I told you. It's impossible to lie to them."

"Then please. Listen. You don't have to do this. There are alternatives. You can make them understand—"

She hugged me. "Thank you. But no. I have to do this."

. . . and then she jumped tightened her arms on the edge of the Skimmer and lightly jumped to the ground.

We were still about twenty meters up, so both Oskar and I yelped, instinctively certain that she'd just suicidally leaped to her death. But no: when I leaned over the edge I saw her lightly touch ground, wave at me, and start running toward the amphitheater. She was as fast as one of them; before I even had time to react she had disappeared among the Vlhani.

I wasn't enhanced. There was no way I'd ever be able to catch her. But catching her was not part of the plan. I'd always known that she had to do what she had to do.

Now it was my turn.

I shouted at Oskar. "For Christ's sake! Land this thing! I have to go out there and talk to them!"

"Talk to—" Oskar started. "Are you out of your mind?"

"Just do it! Now!"

He aimed for a spot fifty meters from the Vlhani spectators. As we landed, I said, "Don't wait for me, I'll be okay! Just get back to the embassy and see if you can help any of the others!"

"B-but . . . what are you talking about, you can't—"

I leaped over the side and hit the ground running.

All my instincts rebelled against the idea of charging creatures who I'd so recently seen on the rampage. But the part of my mind still capable of remaining rational knew that I'd be in no danger from them at all; they no longer had any need to hurt me. They already had Isadora. If I had any fear at all it was that they would be able to recognize me as the one who'd rescued her once before; that for fear of me doing it again they'd bar my way and refuse to allow me into the amphitheater.

They didn't. The ones on the rim just stood passively by as I ran among them, using the same path they'd cleared for Isadora. Their heads did swivel to watch me as I passed; expressionless globes that could have been registering annoyance, or disgust, or pity, or nothing at all. I like to think that they recognized compulsion when they saw it: that they didn't stop me because they knew stopping me would do no good.

Maybe, in that, I reminded them of Isadora.

I made it over the edge of the bowl and began to half-run, half-fall, down the slope. It was not a gentle grade, like the place where I'd found her the first time, but a dirt slide that with a few more degrees of pitch would have begun to qualify as a cliff. I couldn't remain upright and stay out of the way of the dancing Vlhani at the same time; I allowed myself to fall on my rear end and slide. I caught a glimpse of the viewing stand on the southern rim and wondered if anybody there could see me; if any of them were feeling little twinges of horror at the thought of the great spectacle being delayed yet again. Not that I cared; all I cared about, all I worried about, was Isadora. And she was nowhere in sight.

I came to rest in a sea of slashing whips. There was blood in my mouth and on the backs of my hands. The Vlhani around me were so densely packed that I couldn't see more than twenty yards in any direction. Their whips, waving in the air above their heads, spun so passionately that the whirrs of their passage drowned out everything, even the ragged rasp of my breath.

Isadora wasn't around to lead me out, this time.

That didn't matter. What mattered was being here.

Because though I didn't understand Vlhani dance (and didn't even have the harness that would have physically equipped me to dance it), the language barrier has always been a poor excuse for not making the attempt to communicate.

And as Isadora herself had said: *Art isn't just technique, in any culture . . . it's also Content. It's understanding not just How, but also What, to express.*

So I stood up, and took a deep breath, and appealed to them in the only way I knew how. With words. I spoke to them in sounds they couldn't possibly understand, hoping that the feelings would come through. I painted a word-picture that not only apologized for never truly understanding them before, but also mourned and celebrated the differences between us. It was a picture that flashed upon my friends lying dead or wounded at the embassy, and of just how many light-years they'd traveled to meet such an end; it was a picture that talked about how they'd deserved more, then came back to Isadora and how she deserved more too. It was a picture of a young woman who'd already given up everything – her home, her childhood, her normalcy, and now, probably, her life – for the Vlhani. I let them know that, however they measured such things, it was a sacrifice: and that it was a sacrifice only they were empowered to stop. And finally, I let them know how beautiful she was: as beautiful, in her own way, as their Ballet, and how much it mattered to me that she still be alive when the last dancing Vlhani fell to the trampled earth.

I never spoke at such length, or with such eloquence, in my entire life.

Had they understood the language, I would have broken their hearts.

But even as I poured everything I had into my words, I knew that I was nothing to them but a yapping little creature making noise. They surrounded me without reacting to me, their great spherical heads bobbing like toys.

And when I finally ran down, exhausted, unable to plead any more, unable to think of anything else that I hadn't already said a dozen times, a Vlhani moved toward me, so gracefully that its whips barely seemed to brush the ground. One of its whips came down, gently curled around my waist, and lifted me up to the head. I had the distinct impression of eyes studying me, even though Vlhani don't have eyes; the head merely rotated first one way, then the other, in no way conveying any expression at all. Out of reflex I reached out and placed a palm against its cool, polished surface, thinking of the alien brain that sat pulsing beneath. What did it think of me? Did it think me strange? Ungraceful? Ugly or beautiful?

It passed me to another Vlhani further up the slope. Which passed me to another one, and then to another one after that; until I was handed over to the ones standing up on the northern rim, who gently put me down and encircled me to ensure I wouldn't dash into the amphitheater again.

They needn't have bothered. I was done.

There was nothing left.

14.

Many hours later, the Riirgaan air cruiser flew in from the south, circled above me, and came to a rest on packed dirt a short distance away. The Vlhani who'd come to watch the Ballet milled about all around us, taking special care not to step on me or inconvenience the aircraft in any way. Rory and Oskar were both aboard, looking tearful and exhausted. They gave me weak little waves as Hurrr'poth hopped over the side, approached me, and then, folding his limbs in a manner that must have been painfully uncomfortable for a Riirgaan, knelt by my side. His face was as expressionless as always, but there was a tentative, concerned, uncharacteristically deferential manner to the way he regarded me. I mistook it for simple respect for my grief, and said nothing.

At length he said, "Alex."

I asked him: "How many dead?"

"Vlhani or humans?"

I was in no mood to care about Vlhani. "You know I meant humans!"

"Seventeen. About half your delegation. Foster Simmons, Li-Hsin Chang, Kathy Ng . . ." When he saw how every name made me wince, he trailed off. "It could have been much worse. Almost half your number survived."

"And Isadora? Did she?"

He placed a reptilian hand on my shoulder. "No."

So I hadn't pulled off the impossible miracle after all. For all these hours, I'd dared to persuade myself that I might have. I thought of her eyes, and the way she moved, and how I'd been the one to deliver her to the moment of her death, and I just knelt there, my shoulders shaking and my mind spinning between the rustle of the wind and the beating of my triphammer heart.

And then, once again, Hurrr'poth said, "Alex."

I refused to look at him. "What."

"I do not know if this will make a difference to you . . . but everybody among the spectators saw what you tried to do for her. What you did do for her. Everybody witnessed it: all the delegations. . . . and, soon, thanks to the holos and neurecs, all their worlds."

I closed my eyes more tightly. Yes, that was all I needed. To have the single greatest failure of my life played endlessly throughout the universe. "And?"

"And," he said, "it was not just Isadora and the Vlhani who danced magnificently today."

Whereupon he stood, and returned to the air cruiser, leaving me alone with that.

Neither Hurrr'poth nor Rory nor Oskar came out to hurry me.

Eventually, I got off my knees, and went to them. Not because I'd accepted what he'd had to say. But because the show was done, and it was time for all the performers to go home.

15.

The Riirgaans offered Oskar and I citizenship and diplomatic immunity. Oskar took the deal, I didn't. Oskar went home, legally nonhuman; I was court-martialed, got twenty years added to my contract, and went to the rancid, half-molten hellhole known as New Pylthothus, where I would be rotting still had I not smuggled myself AWOL two years later. Since then, I've been officially a fugitive. I have no intention of telling you where I am, how I changed my appearance, or what name I use now. I found a world acceptable for spending the rest of my life in hiding; I changed my face and my name and found a life for myself. I have friends, family. It's happiness, of a sort. I'm not complaining.

The Confederacy attempted to suppress the holos and neurecs of that year's Ballet, but when the anger over the violence against our people faded, the recordings still became the biggest thing to hit popular entertainment in centuries. They succeeded in making the long-time interest in the Vlhani an obsession for trillions; even the vast majority who still didn't understand just what the marionettes were getting at had to agree that, in some indefinable way easier felt than understood, Isadora had just brought their Ballet to an entirely new level. There was some half-hearted talk of reprisals and the "permanent" withdrawal of the installation — but within five standard years the triple-threat combination of a new administration, humanity's notoriously short memory, and the ravenous demand for the new recordings still being made by the other embassies and distributed to human space on the black market, got a new embassy established on the ruins of the old. This one, I understand, is considerably better armed than ours was, though the indentures there haven't yet been forced to prove it.

People love to speculate on who Isadora was, and where she came from; a hundred separate worlds have laid claim to being the place where she was born. Most of them don't put forth very persuasive cases for themselves. All I know for sure is that if I ever did find out the name of the place she came from, I wouldn't feel any pressing need to go there. It has nothing to do with her.

Close to three thousand young people have tried to do what Isadora had done. The vast majority of those never made it off their own home-worlds; they were dreamers, yearning to be special and willing to do anything to emulate somebody who was. They either destroyed themselves or found somebody else to imitate. Of those that remained, a few actually succeeded in picking up enhancements somewhere: usually, pale imitations of Isadora's, that took away their humanity without giving nearly enough in return. A very small number — four women and two men — made it to Vlhan and into the Ballet, where they died. They'd understood little pieces of the show, too. But their names faded. Nobody remembers them, the way they remember her.

I don't know. Whatever the Vlhani are relating with this great fatal Ballet of theirs, I'm told it's beautiful and profound and meaningful and worth dying for. But the other side of the story is that it's not worth seeing the people you care about die . . . and I've personally lost all desire to decode that message for myself.

As a result, I have never seen Isadora's Ballet. I refused to watch it on Vlhan, and I've refused to view the holos or neurecs. I would not be able to stand obsessively watching and re-watching either my own famously doomed appeal or the equally famous, inspirational moment when she fell.

Instead, I live with my memory of that moment at the compound, when she danced to save my life. Unlike the Ballet, which has been picked to pieces by experts all over the known universe, that performance was not recorded. There are no holos, no neurecs, no hytex analysis breaking it down into the tiniest millisecond fragments. Oskar was half-blind from the blood in his eyes; Dhiju, who lay on his back dazzled and open-jawed, was so much under the influence that no amount of artificial memory enhancement would ever succeed in separating the real from that which his mind created. As for me, I caught only the last ten seconds.

But I understood it all. Every single nuance.

When she later spoke to me in human words, she did not tell me the full truth about everything that dance had meant.

And what she really told the Vlhani keeps me warm, in a universe that would otherwise now seem dark and empty and cold.

Afterword

*W*ildside is doing two of these collections; one vaguely focused on dark sf/fantasy, and one vaguely focused on horror/fantasy. "Vaguely" is a very deliberately chosen word. To the extent that my writing career can be said to have a plan, it was to avoid any easily recognizable plan. Good or bad, my stuff isn't always easy to categorize; it ranges all over the map from vaudeville absurdity to unrelieved grimness, from tales of finely tuned character to over-the top gorefests designed to garner the response "You're Sick!" It's better than standing in place long enough to say That's a "Typical" ATC story — even if I do occasionally run into diehard horror fans who've missed all my science fiction and therefore think my last fiction publication was "Clearance to Land" in *Pulphouse Hardcover #5*, circa 1988.

*A*nyway, this is the dark sf/fantasy volume, and these are the story notes, presented for those scholars among you. Please note that I recommend these notes as afterwords, not introductions; they will include some serious spoilers.

*T*he Last Robot": Three writers were responsible for making me a voracious reader. One of them was Isaac Asimov. Back in the days before I was flush enough to buy new books compulsively, I re-read his works compulsively, dog-earing the paperbacks until I practically every page by heart.

Many years later, I was driving to work when the WINS newsradio reported his death. I almost went off the road. I got control of the car, then about two blocks later, without really trying, spontaneously came up with the phrase, "The Last Robot." The entire plot, and the Robot's final eulogy ("The same thing you built. A monument.") hit me fully-formed ten seconds later. I almost went off the road again, but survived to complete the story in two frenzied days.

I will confess being of two minds about this story. On the one hand, it's certainly heartfelt; it came out as easily as it did because multiple re-readings of Asimov's "The Last Question" did so much to absorb the rhythms of his classic tale into my psyche. (I sometimes find it hard to give myself credit for writing this one; grandiose as it sounds, it honestly felt more like channeling). On the other, it feels ghoulish to have pounced on the idea so quickly. Poor Kris Rusch, then-editor of *F&SF*, received it a week after Asimov's death and seemed dumbfounded. All I can say is that, like many stories, it just didn't give me a choice. I needed to write it.

Scott Edelman bought it, and eventually used it as the first story in the first issue of *Science Fiction Age*.

*B*aby Girl Diamond": My parents and sister don't read the majority of the stuff I write; this one was a major exception. Before publication, it probably achieved more circulation among relatives and acquaintances in photocopied form than it eventually did in its anthology appearance. I wasn't handling the distribution, you understand. The nuclear family was, with very little encouragement from me.

It helps, of course, that this was a fairly down-to-earth story, easily accessible by non-genre folks. More to the point is the fact that the story of the Diamond children, as summarized in the first few paragraphs, is almost exactly the story of the Castro children . . . although my sister Jill and I didn't learn about our departed older sister until we were both well on the way to adulthood. The result was a story that the folks were bound to take personally.

The story was eventually nominated for a Bram Stoker Award (losing to Stephen King's "Lunch at the Gotham Cafe"), but that wasn't the best thing that ever happened to it. You see, when I first gave Jill a copy, I did not tell her what it was about . . . only that it was important for her to read it.

That night, she called me at my apartment, incoherent from sobbing.

People: I may not be a famous or best-selling writer, or any real-world sense, but I have enjoyed some egoboo over the past few years. Not a tremendous amount, but enough to stoke the self-confidence, you understand? I have had occasional con attendees stammer in my presence in the dumbfounding belief that I was some kind of celebrity . . . I have received magnificent compliments from writers I've admired since childhood . . . I have been nominated for awards and I have been asked for autographs and I have been sent fan mail. But that phone call, and the knowledge that I'd utterly destroyed my little sister's composure with something I'd written, was the emotional highlight of my writing career. Nothing has happened since to match it. Go figure.

"Cerile and the Journeyer": this is one of the two high fantasies I've written; alas, I don't own the rights to the other. I will note only that it was used illegally by a bunch of internet folks who changed the woman's name to "Titania" and distributed it far and wide without so much as asking me. Most had the courtesy to apologize; one guy editorialized at length about how writers should not care about money and should just want to be widely-read. If you ever see a version of this story where the woman is named "Titania," it was not used with my permission; feel free to tell the culprits to cease and desist.

"The Batman and Robin Murder Mystery — Solved": This is one of several pop-culture theories of mine. One posits that Moe and Larry, from the Three Stooges, were serial killers . . . an idea that shows up in another story here. Another posits that *Gilligan's Island* makes perfect sense if you take the famous inconsistencies of the show and treat them as cleverly-planted clues to a criminal conspiracy of monstrous dimensions. Clearly, I watched too much TV as a kid.

"Fuel": This one appeared in *Whitley Streiber's Aliens*, an anthology prefaced with an apparently seriously-meant speculation that its contributors may have been sublimating UFO abduction experiences. Uh . . . ok. (I will note that I didn't realize until I'd finished writing this one that it works, on some level, as a homage, however tin-eared, to Harlan Ellison's work. Some people think I did it deliberately. Nope. But reading a lot of one author will sometimes do that to you.)

"Neither Rain Nor Sleet": This one owes a lot to Barry Malzberg, I think.

"The Guy Who Could Make These, Like, Really Amazing Armpit Noises, Etc": Never could find a home for this one, alas. I left it up to

Alan Rodgers whether I should be permitted to run it here; blame him.

*"E*go to Go": Robert Sheckley influence, mixed with a little blatant self-analysis. You can thank Kris Rusch for taking the skeleton it was and forcing me, via several revision requests, to a much better final draft. My first *F&SF* story, the realization of what was at that point a lifelong dream.

*"M*s. Found Paper-Clipped to a Box of Jujubes": This one got one of the best rejection letters I ever received, from one of the field's leading editors. He wrote, "I really badly want to publish this one, but if I did I'd have to change my definition of a good story first." No further explanation; I scratched my head for hours over that one. (It also appears for the first time here).

*"W*oo-Woo Vengeance": Okay, this is the story that merits the Spoiler Warning. Don't read any further here if you haven't read it yet, okay?
    Okay.
    Last Chance?
    I like the Three Stooges, in small doses; I think Jerome Howard (better known as Curly), who died way too young in part because a venal studio intent on overworking their cash cow ignored years of warnings that the man needed serious medical attention, was a genuine comic genius. Certainly, his talent significantly overshadowed his brothers Moe and Shemp, his colleague Larry Fine, and his notably-inferior replacements Joe Besser and Curly Joe De Rita. (See? I told you I've watched too much television).
    This is a spoiler mostly because you're not supposed to realize that the story is a contemplation of the Three Stooges until you're more than halfway through it.
    Do I see any cognitive dissonance between my appreciation of the Stooges and the message of the story? No. Read enough of my fiction and you'll know I don't shy away from depicting violence. But the concerns raised by the story are always in my mind.

*"T*he Funeral March of the Marionettes": As the guy on *Saturday Night Live* used to say, this one been barry barry gude to me. It was the cover

story on *Fantasy and Science Fiction*, a Nebula nominee, and a Hugo Nominee (coming in second place). Only a few random facts need concern us here: first, that the same dedicated gadfly who believed "Locusts" a rewrite of "I Have No Mouth and I Must Scream" considered this a rip-off of Roger Zelazny's "A Rose for Ecclesiastes" (a story I pointedly haven't read; what can I tell you, some people have too much time on their hands). Second, that I'm not finished with the Vlhani; this tale leaves a lot of questions unanswered, and some of the answers are prominent in the pipeline. Thirdly, that I'm sure glad I didn't go with my original angle on the story, a comic contemplation of alien borscht-belt comedy. You don't want to know . . .